I0525986

PRAISE FOR *CHRISTMAS IN CATALONIA*

Determined to walk the Way of Saint James, the spiritual walk that her grandparents and her parents had intended to do but never completed, Gwen, a photojournalist, takes a trip to Spain. Arthur Pendred is the CEO of a publishing empire and Gwen's brand new fiancé. Gwen's spiritual walk starts as soon as she boards the plane when she recalls her childhood and adulthood. She even begins to question if what she feels for Art is love . . . or what? She feels safe with him. But shouldn't she feel more, she wonders? Once in Spain, she joins a few other pilgrims and begins to follow quiet country lane, footpaths through cattle country, and some of Spain's oldest Benedictine monasteries. In other words, the twists and turns begin.

I have read other books by Karen Hulene Bartell, and she didn't disappoint this time. Her characters jump off the pages. Her descriptions put you right there in the scene with her characters. And the twists and turns . . . well, you get the gist. I absolutely loved *Christmas in Catalonia* and I highly recommend it.

— ICA IOVA, AWARD-WINNING AUTHOR OF THE RESILIENCY SERIES

If you like history, symbology, travel or relationship stories, this is the book for you. Karen starts this story with a bit of romance and it becomes one of surprises, mystery and history with more romance along the way. What a wonderful pilgrimage the reader takes with the characters as Gwen tries to find answers that will help her decide her future! And just when you think you have it figured out, Karen brings in another little twist. Don't miss this enjoyable, uplifting story!

— DIANNE MUELLER, MSLIS

This book gave me plenty to think about as I almost immediately felt that Gwen and I were almost identical. The insights in myself helped me resolve some of my own family difficulties as well as my overall personal relationships. The author's use of literary classics such as The Wizard of Oz and Canterbury Tales gave more insight to the various characters as well as myself. The use of visions makes the story more exciting. The discussions on faith also gives a better understanding of my own as well. I also always enjoy reading about the settings of Karen's books as they help me feel that I really know the place especially since I have been to an area near the setting for two books so I know the local has been researched.

I read the book in less than a day probably in less than six hours as it drew me so much that I did not want to put the book down. This is just another of her great novels.

– Mary Jo Carman

Christmas
IN *Catalonia*

OTHER BOOKS BY KAREN HULENE BARTELL:

Belize Navidad
Sovereignty of the Dragons

THE SACRED JOURNEY SERIES:
Sacred Gift
Sacred Choices

COMING SOON . . .
Peshtigo: River of the Wild Goose
Christmas at the Alamo
Holy Water: Rule of Capture

CHRISTMAS
IN *Catalonia*

BY KAREN HULENE BARTELL

P
Pen-L Publishing
Fayetteville, AR
Pen-L.com

Copyright © 2015 by Karen Hulene Bartell

All rights reserved. No part of this book may be used or reproduced in any
manner, including electronic storage and retrieval systems, except by explicit
written permission from the publisher. Brief passages excerpted for
review purposes are excepted.

All characters appearing in this work are fictitious. Any resemblance to real persons,
living or dead, is purely coincidental.

ISBN: 978-1-942428-58-9

First Edition
Printed in the USA

Cover and interior design by Kelsey Rice

*With love to Peter Bartell, for keeping
the Christmas spirit in my heart all year long*

For all spiritual pilgrims

Contents

CHAPTER 1:

Of Cabbages and Kings

" . . . more things in heaven and earth . . . than are dreamt of . . ."
— William Shakespeare, *Hamlet*

Gwen Alton clenched her knees together, an involuntary reflex to the butterflies in the pit of her stomach as the 767 lifted off Kennedy's runway. Then she took a deep breath. As the altitude increased, her spirits soared.

Eight hours to Barcelona, an overnight flight. If I can sleep, I'll wake up in Spain.

But try as she might, she couldn't rest. Too many thoughts crowded her mind. She lifted the window shade, hoping to see the last of Manhattan's lights, but already their flight was over the Atlantic. All she saw through the port window was her reflection.

Mirror, mirror . . .

Shoulder-length blond hair framing her face, hazel eyes stared back. She smiled her signature half smile, cynical, suspicious. Even in the dim light, her left eyebrow rose quizzically in a perpetual look of skepticism. She laughed at herself.

Story of my life. Take nothing at face value. Maybe that's why I went into photojournalism. Through a camera's lens, the focal point's clear. I can see what's real.

As she closed the shade, her engagement ring flashed in the dim light. Its glimmering twinkle captured her attention. She turned her hand this way and that, staring, mesmerized by its sparkle, by its significance.

Art. She took a deep breath, recalling. *Was that only two hours ago?*

"You really didn't have to drive me to the airport." Gwen watched him maneuver through rush-hour traffic. "I know you're busy with that conference call tonight."

"Glad to do it."

She tried once more. "I could've taken a cab."

Art took his eyes off the traffic long enough to give her a benevolent smile.

"You're going to be gone ten days. I wanted to see you off."

"You could've said goodbye after the two o'clock—"

"Privately." Again, he glanced at her, an amused glint in his eye. "Not in front of the publications team."

She snickered as she glanced out the window. Grand Central Parkway was at a crawl.

"Traffic's heavy. For a change."

"Why don't we stop for dinner, wait until it subsides?"

"At this rate, we'll probably get to the airport at the same time." Gwen gave him a nod. "Good idea."

A half hour later, they were seated in front of a roaring fireplace at a table for two.

"Since you're going to Spain, why not begin your journey right here with a Spanish sparkling wine?"

"Sounds great."

He turned toward the waiter. "We'll start with Cava." Then he turned back to her, gentle eyes glowing warmly in the firelight.

She loved it when he gave her his full attention. No one else ever had. She studied his face. Light-brown eyes, thick eyebrows, cropped dark hair, pointed ears, as if he was always alert, always listening to her. Always watching out for her.

She took a deep breath. *I feel safe with him.*

"So you're determined to make this pilgrimage?" he said.

"I am."

"Even in late October?"

"It's the only way to combine the Christmas in Barcelona with the *Camino de Compostela* stories. And don't worry about the weather. It's not like I'm crossing the Pyrenees. Besides, I'll be staying in posadas, not sleeping in albergues or hostels." She held up her cell. "Plus, I'll be in touch daily."

"We could've let another photojournalist take this assignment."

"This fit in perfectly with my schedule." Smiling, she shook her head. "Actually, it's something I feel compelled to do. What's ironic is how things fell into place."

He watched her, a hint of a smile playing at his lips. "Isn't it, though?"

His tone perked her ears. "What do you mean?"

"Your Cava, sir," said the waiter, bringing a chilled bottle in an ice bucket. He opened it with a flourish, presented the cork, and poured a taste.

"Perfect." Art took the bottle from him. "Thanks, I'll pour."

"Are you ready to order yet?"

"Give us a few minutes, would you?"

As the waiter left, Art filled their glasses.

"What did you mean about the schedule?" She stared pointedly at him.

The hint of a smile morphed into a sheepish grin. "Since you were set on taking this pilgrimage, I talked the editorial department into making it a paid assignment. We'll incorporate your Camino story in one of the spring issues and your Christmas story in next year's December issue."

Gwen sat back in her chair, scrutinizing him. "I should've known things dovetailed too smoothly." She pursed her lips, pretending to be annoyed, but found herself grinning with him. "So you arranged it?"

He shrugged and then held up his glass. "To dual purposes converging."

She raised her eyebrow and nodded. "I like that." Clinking her glass against his, she toasted.

As she tipped her glass, she noticed movement in her peripheral vision. He slowly slid something across the table toward her. She set down her glass and stared at the purple, velvet box. Then narrowing her eyes, she examined him.

"What's this?"

He shrugged his shoulders. "Look."

She crinkled her forehead as she mentally debated. Slowly, she reached for the box and opened its lid. Nestled in velvet was the largest diamond she had ever seen.

"What do you think you're doing?" She peered up at him through long lashes.

"What do you think?"

"Will you stop with the questions and give me a straight answer?"

"Will you?"

Gwen shook her head as she dipped her chin, chuckling at his forensics. She fingered the box, thinking.

He's a good guy. I like him, respect him, even admire him . . . but love him?

As he took her hand in his, he drew her back to the moment, forcing her to concentrate.

"We've been dating nearly a year now, exclusively for the past few months. Don't you think it's time we took it to the next level?"

She swallowed, recalling how her cube mate, Suzanne, had summed him up.

"He's only the CEO of a publishing empire, not to mention editor in chief of Trails n' Treks Publications." Suzanne had given her a sly wink. "You could do worse than Arthur Pendred."

Then Art stared at her with his full intensity, his expressive, light-brown eyes homing in on hers, engaging her. "You know how I feel about you."

Deep into unfamiliar territory, she smiled uncertainly. Flattered, her reservations began slipping away, like bad dreams in the morning light.

He smiled back, his eyes crinkling into his characteristic smile lines.

He's so appealing when he looks at me that way. Cocking her head to the side, she did a double take. *And he reminds me of someone. Who?*

"I think we can make a go of it." With his other hand, Art took the ring from its case and slid it on her finger. "I want you to know I'm here for you." He kissed her fingertips. "Wear this until you come back, until we make . . . a more permanent commitment."

Normally not shy about speaking her mind, Gwen remained silent. She blinked back unexpected tears, gripped by dueling emotions. For twelve years, she had struggled to prove she could make a success of herself. On her own, no family, no husband to help. It had been lonely, daunting.

Now realizing what she meant to Art, she was equally beguiled and baffled. She loved him, but as a friend.

Is that enough? He understands me, accepts me for who I am, but shouldn't I feel more?

Was that only two hours ago?

She pulled the plane's blanket around herself and, fluffing the tiny pillow, turned away from the window. She found herself nose-to-nose with a snoring woman, leaning into her space. With a gasp, Gwen sat up straight, now wide awake. After switching on the overhead light, she reached in her bag for her iPad.

Might as well get a head start on the article, jot down my thoughts, since I can't sleep.

Instead of the iPad, her hand connected with the brochure. Even before she pulled it into the light, she knew it by its shiny texture and dog-eared corners.

I ought to recognize it. I've handled it enough these past two weeks.

She reread the Peregrino Paths brochure for the hundredth time since she had discovered it in her father's lockbox.

Dad . . .

She recalled her father visiting her in Manhattan two weeks after her mother had passed away. He had told her about renewing an acquaintance with an old friend, that he was flying to Florida to visit her.

"You're eighteen now. I won't interfere in your life, so don't interfere in mine."

She had been dumbstruck. Still reeling from her mother's unexpected death, she suddenly found herself a virtual orphan in Manhattan.

She remembered two weeks later, a month after her mother's death, when he had invited her to his wedding in New Jersey. From the start of his second marriage, Gwen had been *persona non grata*.

Barely civil at the ceremony, his new wife, Milly, hung up if Gwen called and banned her from visiting his house, the home where she had grown up. Even when her father had phoned her, the calls were stilted, with Milly breathing heavily into the extension.

This had continued for two years, until one night her father called her, inviting her to Thanksgiving dinner. Although surprised, Gwen had accepted, hoping relationships were finally beginning to warm.

Then, the night before Thanksgiving, he had called, stammering, his breathing jagged. "The plans have changed. I . . . uhm . . . instead of your coming to New Jersey for dinner, why don't I stop by your apartment for a late supper Thursday night?"

Her jaw dropped. Blinking, she tried to wrap her mind around what her father was saying.

"You're calling the night before Thanksgiving to uninvite me?"

"No . . . uhm . . . I . . . uh . . ." His speech stiff, he stuttered.

"Milly's listening in, isn't she? I can tell by your voice." Gwen scoffed. "You're afraid to call me, let alone invite me to your house. You don't let me visit you, and Milly hangs up if I call you. You make me feel like the 'other woman.' This isn't a family. It's a farce."

She listened to him slam the receiver. Her chest heaving, Gwen stood there, phone in hand, vowing never to speak to him again.

Ten years passed. Then her aunt Irene had called.

"Your father's been diagnosed with cancer and wants to see you."

Though dreading the reunion, she drove to New Jersey that same morning. Walking into the house that had been her home for the first eighteen years of her life was like seeing an old friend. One she had missed for the past twelve years. The memories of her mother, of her childhood, overwhelmed her. Then she saw her father's second wife, glaring at her from the sofa.

No welcome, no hello. Instead, cigarette in hand, Milly thumbed her nose at her.

Silently fuming, Gwen strode past her toward her father's bedroom.

"Not there!" Milly gestured to what had been her bedroom. "There."

The door was open. Tapping on its frame, Gwen tentatively entered the small room. Intended to hold a single bed, it was cluttered with oversized furniture.

What a cramped life Milly's allowed him. She looked at her father, grayer, more grizzled than she remembered. He needed a shave, but his hazel eyes still had their twinkle.

"Hi."

He looked up. "Glad you could come. Sorry I can't get up."

Her jaw fell open. *Is he that ill?* She swallowed, trying to regain her composure.

"Don't worry, stay where you are. I'll come around where you can see me better." She stepped sideways, squeezing between the chest of drawers and double bed.

"Pull up a seat."

She looked around. The only chair was half tucked under the desk, the space too cramped to pull it out and turn it toward the bed.

"That's all right. I'll just stand." She struggled for something to say. "How do you feel?"

"Considering the doctor diagnosed it as lung cancer—"

Voices arguing in the next room drowned out his words.

"I'm sorry. What did you say?"

Shoes tapping on the linoleum, a toddler ran into the room and climbed on the bed. Gwen saw Milly's gray head peek around the door.

"This is Alice, Milly's granddaughter," he said.

Gwen grimaced. *Not even a moment's privacy. What else can Milly steal?*

Speaking loudly for Milly's benefit, she purposely turned her head toward the door. "I couldn't hear what you said. So how are you feeling?"

When she turned back, she saw her father was reaching for his characteristic cigarettes and lighter.

He gave her a sheepish smile. "I was trying to quit." He shrugged as he lit up. "But what's the point of stopping now?"

The fumes of his lighter and cigarette brought back unwelcome memories. She suddenly felt nauseous.

"How old are you?"

She cocked her head as she studied him. *How could he forget the age of his only child?*

"I'll be thirty, two weeks from today, on Father's day."

Grunting in bewilderment, he shook his head. Then his eyes fixed on the toddler. "Seems like only yesterday you were her age."

From the other room came the sound of a vacuum cleaner starting up. The decibel level rose as it approached and then entered the tiny bedroom.

"Don't mind me," a woman shouted over its roar. "I can work around you."

As the woman pushed the vacuum closer to her, Gwen had no alternative but to sit on the bed and lift her feet. There was no room to move, nowhere to go.

"Are you still living in Manhattan?" he shouted over the vacuum's drone.

She nodded. "Same eastside apartment for the past ten years."

"Come again?"

Repeating, Gwen shouted her words.

Finally, the woman worked her way out of the room. Still the vacuum roared in the background.

"Maybe you'd like to see my apartment? I'd be happy to pick you up, if you like."

With the vacuum droning in the next room, a sharp rap at the door caught their attention. Gwen recognized her father's half brother Ed, from another of her paternal grandmother's marriages.

"Clark, how ya' doing?" Then he fixed a stern eye on her. "Who do we have here? Gwen? Is that you? High time you visited your dad!"

"It's the first time I've been inv—"

"Who's this?" asked Ed's wife, squeezing past him. Then she looked from Gwen to the toddler and back again. "Is this your little girl? Did you have a baby?"

"No, that's my granddaughter," said Milly from the doorway. "Who's hungry? I've got sloppy joes in the kitchen."

Bantering with Milly, Ed and his wife filed out. Gwen sighed. *Maybe now we can talk.*

The toddler picked up the lighter and began clicking its top, trying to light it. "Alice, no." Clark took it from her.

"Clark, you ready for lunch?" called Milly from the door.

"Well . . ." He looked sheepishly at Gwen. "I . . . uh . . . uhm . . ."

She recognized the labored breathing. He was afraid to speak in front of his wife.

Milly gave him a stern look. "I'll bring your sloppy joe."

As his wife left the doorway, he sucked hard at his cigarette.

The woman who had vacuumed brought in a paper plate. "Alice, here's your lunch. Don't spill it on the covers." She stood by the bed, arms crossed, eyes narrowed, scrutinizing their every gesture, openly listening to their every word.

Gwen leveled her eyes at her father. "Nothing's changed, has it?"

"You see how it is," he said quietly.

Handing him her card, she stood up. "Maybe we could talk another time?"

"Yes." He nodded enthusiastically. "Yeah, that would be better. Much better. I'll call you."

Milly pushed past Gwen and slapped a paper plate into Clark's hands. "Here's your sloppy joe. Eat it while it's hot." She gave Gwen a pointed look as she stood between them, arms crossed. "Don't let your lunch get cold."

When the phone rang a few days later, Gwen knew it was her father, even without waiting for Caller ID.

"Gwen?"

She tried to keep all emotion out of her voice. "Yeah." It had been a long drive back to Manhattan, and she had had time to do a lot of thinking. "Doesn't it bother you that your second wife won't let us talk?"

"She thinks you're trying to change my will."

"What?" Disgusted, she counted to five. "Is that the same reason she's hung up on me every time I've called?"

"No, she . . . she said you hung up on her every time she answered."

She shook her head at the lack of logic. *Why try? Reason isn't possible.* Gwen took a deep breath. "Why did you call?"

"You left so early, I wanted to talk to you."

"Left?" Closing her eyes, she exhaled, trying to blow off steam. "You mean your wife drove me out."

"Things got hectic when Ed and his wife appeared."

She heard the click of his lighter as he lit a cigarette and then closed the lighter against his thigh, as she'd seen him do a thousand times. She listened to him inhale.

Enervating. That's the word. He drains me emotionally.

Again, she counted to five. "When I was eighteen, two weeks after Mom died, you made it clear. You wouldn't interfere in my life, and you didn't want me interfering in yours."

"You see how it is."

"This is the life you chose. *You* chose, no input from me for the past twelve years." She took a deep breath. "Our visit was a sad joke. We were constantly interrupted, watched, never allowed to talk."

"Well, it's too late to change the way things are."

"You seem to think that's acceptable. It's not. The way we communicate isn't normal. I can't visit or even call you."

"We're talking now."

"Only because you called me."

"What difference does it make who called who? The fact is, we're talking." His tone brightening, he wheedled. "You don't mind, do you?"

She recognized that tone of voice, and it irked her. It was really a statement, not a question, as if her feelings were irrelevant. She breathed shallowly, remembering all the band competitions and photo exhibitions he had missed, even her high school graduation, and always with the same words. "You don't mind, do you?" He had always had something more important to attend. Something had always taken precedence over her.

"Yes, I do mind. In fact, I don't like it one bit."

"Remember who you're talking to. I'm your father!"

She remembered that tone, too. He had always used that authoritarian voice to command her attention. *Father.* Though biologically true, the term was ludicrous. It curdled her blood.

"You don't act like a father. You don't treat me like a daughter. I feel like the red-haired bastard at the family picnic." She pressed her fingers to her temples, trying to stave off the sudden headache. "I wish you well. I truly hope you recover and live a long life, but after twelve years of this farce, I don't see the point in perpetuating the myth that we're family."

Two weeks later, on Father's Day, her thirtieth birthday, her aunt Irene called again.

"Florida Floozy just called. Your father's in the ICU."

Gwen froze. Of course, she'd known the day would come. Since her mother's passing twelve years before, she had lived in dread of the moment the other shoe would fall. Especially since his second marriage, after they had become estranged, she had shrunk from the thought.

Two weeks ago, his death had not seemed imminent. He had aged, but he had not looked like a man with two weeks to live.

Wounded pride. She took a deep breath. At the time, it had seemed more important to stand up for herself, but now? Now that the time had arrived, it was hard to accept.

"Did you hear me?"

"Yes, I . . . I . . . did she say how he's doing?"

"Remember who we're talking about? Mil-*dread*, the Florida Floozy."

Mil-*dread*, the Florida Floozy, her aunt's nickname for her father's second wife. Gwen's nostrils pinched as she inhaled sharply.

"Did she have anything else to say?"

"Just that he's on life support, 'if anyone cares.'" Irene blew a derisive snort. "Trailer trash to the end."

Gwen immediately called Art. "An emergency's come up. My father's in the hospital, and I have to leave work."

"Do you want me to go with you?"

The concern in his voice broke through her shell of regrets and resentments. *He's here for me.* As his words resonated with her, she took a deep breath, feeling reenergized.

"No, this is something I have to do alone," adding in a shy whisper, "but I really appreciate your asking."

In that instant, a thousand thoughts had jumbled through her mind. The only two men in her life, Art had never met her father. She'd only recently started dating Art seriously, and she had not seen or spoken with her father in twelve years, other than the awkward visit and his follow-up phone call two weeks prior. Art's place in her life suddenly took on deeper significance.

The plane's turbulence jolted Gwen back to the present. Roused from her thoughts, she stretched and yawned. Then her eyes fell on the brochure in her hands. Remembering the first time she had seen it, she smiled, recalling happier times in third grade, coin collecting.

CHAPTER 2:

Pennies from Heaven

"Pennies do not come from heaven; they have to be earned here on earth."
— Margaret Thatcher

What had started as a Campfire Girl project became a family hobby. Every night, her father had emptied his pockets on the kitchen table. Then they would finger through the pennies for a 1959-D or an elusive 1943 copper cent.

One penny coin folder soon expanded to three. A piggy bank gave way to penny filled coffee cans lining her dresser.

"Why not start a savings account with these pennies?" suggested her mother, eyeing the dusty canisters.

"What for?" Eight years old, Gwen could not imagine needing anything but hordes of pennies to see her through life.

"How about a vacation fund?" Her father's eyes twinkled.

Visions of Mickey Mouse swept through her head. "For Disneyland?"

"What about Spain?" Her mother's eyes had sparkled as she turned to Gwen. "Your grandfather came here from Barcelona when he was your age. Your grandmother came from Compostela. They always dreamt of returning to Spain one day and walking the Camino de Santiago."

Gwen cocked her head, vaguely recalling a story her grandmother had once told her.

"Walking the *what*

"The Way of Saint James," said her mother. "It's a pilgrimage, a spiritual walk my parents always meant to take."

Gwen squinted, trying to remember.

"Like many, they believed Saint James, one of Christ's disciples, is buried in the Cathedral of Santiago de Compostela."

"Why would anyone go all the way to Spain for a walk?"

Her mother had smiled patiently. "It's a way to soul-search. People go on pilgrimages to find themselves, search for their purpose in life." Her eyes took on a wistful glow. "Even to find God."

Gwen peered up at her mother's necklace, still trying to recall its story. "Didn't that walk have something to do with your crucifix?"

Clasping it, her mother looked off into space. "It's something my parents had wanted to do, something I always promised myself I'd do. Someday."

"Then let's make the Camino de Santiago our goal," said her father. "By the time we save enough money, Gwen will be old enough to walk the Way with us."

They spent the evening gathered around the kitchen table, wrapping pennies in rolls of fifty. The following day, her father took her to the bank to open her first account with a grand total of eight dollars and ninety-three cents.

Their next stop was at a travel agency, where the agent handed them a Peregrino Paths brochure about the Camino de Santiago.

This brochure. The drone of the plane's engines hacked into Gwen's thoughts, and she roused herself. Recalling the daddy of her childhood was more painful than remembering the estranged father of her adulthood. She swallowed. *Him, I loved.* Then she opened the brochure. Seeing it reminded her of the lockbox.

A week after her mother's death, she and her father had rented a safe deposit box. They carefully placed four things in it: her mother's crucifix; a tattered, yellow letter; the Camino de Santiago brochure; and the vacation-fund pass book noting ten years of savings—two hundred forty-eight dollars and ninety-three cents.

"We can add to it, take that trip your mother always wanted." He fought tears as he turned the key in the lock.

Doubting it would ever happen Gwen struggled to be polite. She had not been close to her father for a decade. Soon after the coin-collecting phase ended, so had their relationship. Sharing nothing but space, they had lived together in the same house as tenants, not family. Still, she commiserated with the grieving man before her.

"Mom and her parents never made it to the Camino de Santiago, but maybe we'll make the pilgrimage for them." She shrugged, still not believing it. "Someday."

It was a week later that he had met her in Manhattan and told her about visiting Milly. His parting words still haunted her.

"I won't interfere in your life . . . so don't interfere in mine."

After twelve years, she had all but forgotten about the safe deposit box. Then, two weeks before, FedEx had delivered the proceeds of her father's estate: a key and a will. The will declared everything other than the key belonged to his beloved widow, Mildred.

Engraved only with the number twenty-four, the key contained no logo, no name. Nor did any paperwork or explanation accompany it, but Gwen approached it as a challenge since it was all she had of her parents.

The key could belong anywhere. The possibilities were endless: a long-defunct luggage storage bin at a bus station, a gym locker. *It's like looking for a needle in a haystack*. Yet a mousy thought nibbled at the back of her mind. *Could it belong to that lockbox from so long ago?*

Shaking her head, convinced she was wasting her time on a wild goose chase, she laughed at herself as she drove along Route 3 to New Jersey.

Even if it belongs to a bank, it could be any one of a thousand institutions. And even if it's the bank I remember, there's a good chance it's moved or closed its doors.

But the building was still on Washington Avenue. Her world may have turned topsy-turvy in twelve years, but the bank had not budged.

Now to see if they have a safe deposit box that fits it.

She felt foolish showing the teller the key. "I'm not sure—"

He asked for identification and checked her name against the database. "This way, please," he said as he led her to the vault. He inserted his key into the lock. She inserted hers and gave it a twist.

14

A small gasp escaped her lips as the door sprang open.

"Let me know when you're finished."

Alone with the box, Gwen paused, recalling the only other time she had seen it. It had been just after her mother's death. Now it was following her father's.

Though I was grieving the first time for my mother, how do I feel now? She inhaled as she gathered her thoughts. *Bitter.*

Holding that thought, she opened the narrow box's elongated lid. Her mother's antique gold crucifix glinted in the low light. She smiled, remembering the many times she'd seen her mother wear it. Then she scanned her earliest memories and vaguely recalled her mother's mother wearing it. She picked it up, inspecting its front and back, touching the tiny scallop shells at each of the crucifix's four points.

Odd, I don't recall noticing the shell motif before.

On impulse, she fastened the crucifix around her neck. Then clasping it between her fingers, it occurred to her: *This is all I have of my mother's.*

Next, she opened the brochure and skimmed its contents. She smiled at the memory, recalling when her parents and she had first gotten the idea to walk the Camino de Santiago more than twenty years before. *We were a family then, before everything changed. At some point, when I was eight, my father stopped talking to me, other than to lecture or criticize me.* She shook her head, asking herself for the hundredth time, *What happened?*

She stared at the next item, a smudged, yellowed envelope she had seen once before but had never read. She gently opened its brittle note, but it had been unfolded and refolded so many times, it tore apart in her hands. Reading from its dog-eared halves, Gwen saw the date. February 28, 1938.

Clark,

You can't understand now, but please try to forgive me someday.

Love,

Mother

A letter from her grandmother to her father in 1938. *He'd been eight years old. What had his mother done to him to ask forgiveness? And why had he kept this letter hidden all these years?*

She tried to recall stories of his childhood, but nothing came to mind. He had never talked about his early life, but his sister Irene had mentioned something once. *What was it?* She wrecked her brain, but nothing came to mind. *It'll come to me.*

Then, setting aside the letter, she picked up the last item in the lockbox. The vacation-fund pass book, the account they had started for their Camino de Santiago goal. She opened it, expecting to see no entries after her mother's death. But page after page was filled with dates of tiny deposits. Five dollars one month, ten another. The last entry had been dated two months earlier. She looked at the balance: three thousand, eight dollars, and ninety-three cents. *What was he thinking?*

She reviewed the items, one-by-one. The letter made no sense. It fit into no category, but as she stared at the other three items, she saw a common thread. Her maternal grandmother's crucifix with its tiny scallop shells, the brochure, and the bank book were all linked to the Camino de Santiago.

Was he planning on walking the Way of Saint James?

CHAPTER 3:

Pilgrims on a Journey

"We are pilgrims on a journey
We are travelers on the road
We are here to help each other
Walk the mile and bear the load."
— *Servant Song*, Richard Gillard

The next thing Gwen heard was the pilot instructing them to fasten their seatbelts and prepare for landing. She lifted the shade, and the sun poured in. Below them lay Spain.

"Let me get that for you." As they debarked, the man on the aisle closed his book and lifted her carry-on from the overhead bin.

"Thanks."

Thirty-something, he smiled slowly as his violet-blue eyes, hidden behind glasses, caught hers. "De nada."

Again, they bumped into each other at the shuttle bus.

"After you." With a slight nod, he stepped aside, pushed up his glasses, and waved her aboard. Tall, lanky, he towered over her.

"Chivalry's not dead." This time she took a second look, noticing the slight cleft in his chin and his thick, dark hair.

He grinned as he let another woman board after her.

Gwen took a window seat, and the woman sat beside her. He sat across the aisle. She noticed he traveled light, only a backpack. *Could he be going on a pilgrimage, too?* She snickered. *Of course not. It's just a coincidence.* When the bus stopped at her hotel, she half expected him to look up and wave, but he was too engrossed in his book.

After unpacking, she grabbed her camera and began a walking tour of Barcelona. *It's the only chance I'll have.* She hiked the half mile to the Mirador de Colom and read its inscription. *So this is where Columbus landed when he returned from America. Maybe I can squeeze a third article out of this trip next Columbus Day.*

She took the elevator to the viewing gallery two hundred feet above the city. Snapping a series of photos, she looked out the east side, over the harbor on the Mediterranean.

"Is this how you view life . . . from behind a camera?"

Recognizing the truth, she turned to see her critic's face. She sneered more than smiled when she identified him as the man from the plane and shuttle.

"Is it different from experiencing life vicariously from behind a book?"

"Touché."

Raising her eyebrow, she gave her challenger a curt nod and side stepped through the narrow gallery to the west cityscape side, photographing the cathedral's bell towers and the bustling La Rambla below.

The next morning, she boarded the train to León.

"Shutterbug," said a familiar voice. "We meet again."

She turned toward the voice, her eyes narrowing. "You again, Bookworm? Are you following me?"

He showed her his ticket. "León. Where are you headed?"

Karma. She snickered, appraising him as she held up her ticket. "What takes you there?"

"Pilgrimage."

Her jaw dropped. "Me, too."

"Since we're headed the same way, mind if I join you? You'll probably never notice me. Your eyes will be glued to your viewfinder."

Pursing her lips, she chuckled. "Suit yourself since you'll probably never notice me. Your nose will be stuck in a book the whole time."

He placed his backpack in the overhead bin and sat beside her. "Could've taken the overnight train and skipped the hotel," he gestured to the passing scenery, "but I wanted to see the countryside as we travel through it."

She nodded. "My thoughts exactly. After the taste of Barcelona yesterday, I hoped to glimpse more."

"Aren't you planning to spend time in Barcelona after the pilgrimage?"

"Just enough time to catch my flight back home. Got to get back to work." She turned toward him. "Why? Do you plan to spend time there?"

"Oh, yeah." He nodded. "Quite a bit of time at Montserrat and then Christmas in Barcelona." He smiled. "I live there."

"Montserrat." She squinted as she searched her memory. "I've heard of it, but I can't recall how or where. What's the attraction?"

"From what perspective?"

She hunched her shoulders. "Surprise me."

"From a religious perspective, it's a Benedictine abbey that's stood there for over a thousand years. From a geological viewpoint, it's a serrated range of mountains, honeycombed with caves. From a mythological angle, it's permeated with legends and traditions."

"Really?" She snickered. "Like what?"

"Have you seen *Raiders of the Lost Ark*?"

"Yeah."

"Supposedly, the movie was based on local folklore, as well as Himmler's and Hitler's beliefs that the Ark of the Covenant is hidden in one of the Montserrat caves."

"Interesting, anything else?"

"There've been reports of electromagnetic disturbances, mysterious lights, even extraterrestrial activity in the mountains."

"So which is your perspective?"

His violet-blue eyes glinted merrily behind his glasses. "None of them."

"Then what's the attraction?"

Hesitating, he took a deep breath, as if debating whether or not to share it.

"Look, if it's personal, forget it. I was just making conversation."

"No, it's all right." He pushed up his glasses. "I've got a theory. Actually, I'm trying to authenticate the legend that Perceval hid the Holy Grail in these mountains."

"Perceval?" She swallowed a grin. "You're not talking about one of the fabled Knights of the Round Table, are you?"

He nodded. "A lot of compelling evidence points to Montserrat as the hiding place of the Holy Grail."

"Like what?"

"Folklore and ancient writings, even current media suggest it. *Indiana Jones and the Last Crusade* and *The Fisher King* are two recent movies based on the folktales surrounding the Holy Grail."

"Looks like you're out of luck, Bookworm." She gave a wry chuckle. "It seems Spielberg's already cornered the Montserrat market."

Eyes twinkling, he grinned. "Let's just say some literary resources are more consistent with fact than others."

"Do you have any evidence more substantial than movies?"

"According to legend, the Holy Grail was kept at the castle of Munsalvaesche—"

She lifted an eyebrow. "Legend, again—"

"Which Benedictine monks have identified as Montserrat."

Squinting, she studied him, debating if he were delusional or just irrational.

"Why do you take such an interest in these fairy tales?"

"*Folk tales*. I'm writing a book about the Holy Grail."

"Ah," she grinned, "an author."

"Actually, I'm an English Literature professor trying to publish a hypothesis."

"What's your theory?"

"I believe the story of the Holy Grail combines Western Christian traditions with Gothic legends and ancient Celtic myths."

"What do you mean?"

"A thirteenth-century poem first mentioned the Holy Grail in a story about a knight named Perceval. Then de Troyes wrote *The Story of the Grail* about Perceval, Sir Galahad, and several other knights. Some think the story's based on German, French, Welsh, and Irish literature. Others associate it with folk tales involving magical bowls and mystical cauldrons."

"Bowls and cauldrons? Sounds like witchcraft."

"Originally, they described the Holy Grail as the bowl or goblet Jesus used at the Last Supper. Like a cornucopia, the legendary serving bowl produced a never-ending supply of food. Sometimes it contained healing properties or could raise the dead."

"Like in *Indiana Jones and the Last Crusade*, where Indy's dying father drank from the goblet and survived."

"Good example. Still other times, it was a device to reveal the next king."

"Like Arthur and Excalibur?"

"Exactly."

She scratched her head, scanning her memory. "Wasn't the Holy Grail some-how connected with Christ's blood?"

He nodded. "In later writings, it was associated with Joseph of Arimathea. Then medieval scholars confused the Old French 'san grial,' Holy Grail, with 'sang rial,' royal blood. Building on those motifs, recent authors wrote that Joseph had used the goblet to catch Jesus' blood during the crucifixion."

"And doesn't Mary Magdalene figure into this somehow?"

His eyes crinkled in a private smile. "Yes. Lately, another theory's emerged, naming her the 'vessel' carrying Christ's bloodline. Using synecdoche, her womb was the 'chalice' containing Christ's baby."

"Christ's blood, Christ's bloodline, I see what you mean." She nodded thoughtfully.

"Some think the Holy Grail's a code name for the Ark of the Covenant. Yet others believe it's just symbolic, not real, not tangible."

Fingers pressed to her chin, Gwen nodded. "And you believe it's buried at Montserrat?"

"So the traditions say. Who knows?" He shrugged. "But it's a recurring theme. Wagner revived the legend in his opera *Parsifal*. That not only revitalized the Grail's fascination in twentieth-century pop culture, but it directly influenced Himmler to search Montserrat for it."

"Why would an opera compel the head of the Nazi SS to investigate an abbey?"

"Wagner's *Parsifal* was based on local legends and the German epic poem about the Grail. The opera's first authorized performance was at the Gran Teatre del Liceu in Barcelona, fewer than twenty-five miles from Montserrat."

"So?" Arms folded, she shrugged.

"It confirmed Himmler's belief that Montserrat was the setting for the opera, as well as the Grail's hiding place."

"I still don't understand."

Spreading his hands, he turned to look at her. "The opera takes place at the castle of the Grail and its knights . . . near Monsalvat . . ."

In that instant, his quest made sense. "Duh." She knocked the heel of her hand against her forehead. Then, caught up in his enthusiasm, she leaned toward him. "Monsalvat, which sounds like—"

"Montserrat," he smiled, his eyes opening wide. "Exactly. You get it, don't you? It's so rare anybody really grasps what I mean." Admiration shining in his eyes, he stared at her a beat too long.

She found herself staring back, intrigued, wondering what thoughts lay behind his eyes.

Then Art's engagement ring flashed in the sunlight, reminding her, making her feel awkward. Sitting up straight, she blinked and glanced left and right for an excuse to change the subject. The passing scenery caught her eye.

"Just look at that view, will you?"

His eyes tracked hers. He glanced at her ring and then quickly peered out the window as she fumbled for her camera.

"Those fields on the mountainside look like a patchwork quilt of green, gold, and orange."

"Let me capture that digitally."

Turning away from him, she raised the viewfinder to her eye and began clicking.

❄

Two hours later, he looked up from his book, glimpsed the scenery, and then checked his watch. "Doesn't this train have a dining car?"

She raised the corner of her mouth in a half grin. "That's why they call it a luxury train."

"How would you like to go on a quest to find the dining car?"

"Sure." She capped the camera's lens, placed the camera in its bag, and slung it over her shoulder. "Left or right?"

"Let's start with left and see if it leads us to the dining car."

"If it's not there, we turn around and head in the other direction." Stretching as she stood, she grinned. "Something like life, isn't it? If you're not successful on one path, you try the other."

❄

Seated at the small table, Gwen glanced at the dining car's oblong shape. Despite the car's narrow appearance, the porters managed to seat diners three across. Intimate tables for two on the left, tables seated groups of four on the right. A picture window filled each table's view, so they could watch the changing scenery as they sped through Spain's countryside.

With a pleasantly surprised smile, she noted the linen tablecloth, fine silverware, and china place settings. She unfolded her linen napkin and glanced at her dinner partner.

"I don't believe we've introduced ourselves."

"You mean Shutterbug and Bookworm won't do?" He gave her a good-natured grin.

She snickered as she held out her hand. "I'm Gwen Alton."

"Percy Gowan," he said, reaching across the table. "What brings you on this pilgrimage?"

She vacillated between telling him about her job or her family's three-generation quest to travel to Compostela. She chose the professional angle. *Safer, less personal.*

"I'm a photojournalist, writing a story for *Trails n' Treks Magazine.*"

"So this pilgrimage isn't a religious experience for you?"

She hunched her shoulders, squinting, thinking. *Good question. Is it?* She thought of her mother's dream of walking the Way. She recalled the family story of her grandfather's pledge to her grandmother. It would have been a religious experience for them.

When she didn't answer, he added, "Or is it?"

"Is it what?" Startled, she turned toward him, realizing she had been daydreaming.

He chuckled. "A religious experience for you."

She disliked personal questions and turned steely eyes toward him. "It's complicated." Then, penitent for being cranky, she asked, "Are you here for religious reasons?"

His eyes twinkling mischievously, he let his words hang in the air. "More of a quest . . ."

Grinning at his laidback humor, she finished his sentence. ". . . for the Holy Grail."

As she leaned forward to pick up her menu, her crucifix reflected the dappled sunlight.

He squinted, peering at her necklace. "Are those scallop shells at the four ends of the cross?" His focus changed to her eyes. "Did you get this crucifix for the pilgrimage?"

"This was my mother's, and before that her mother's." Her hand unconsciously fondled it.

"I'll bet there's an interesting story behind it." An arm hooked over his plush chair, he leaned back, as if waiting to hear it.

Tensing, she peered at him through narrowed eyes. "Why do you ask?"

"Handed down to the third generation, it's too beautiful an heirloom not to have a family legend associated with it."

Why should I share anything with him? She moved her jaw, debating as she studied his body language. Again, his easygoing manner calmed her. Looking into his violet-blue eyes, she felt herself relax.

"I heard this tale so long ago, I'm not sure if I'm remembering it or just imagining it, but here goes." Still clasping her cross, she gathered her thoughts as she stared into space. Then she took a deep breath. "My grandmother told me my grandfather gave her this the day he proposed. Instead of an engagement ring, he gave her a symbol of their marriage."

Blinking, he smiled gently. "What was that?"

"He promised their marriage would be a journey. He said they were two pilgrims, who'd walk hand in hand along their journey of life. He also pledged that one day they'd walk the Camino de Compostela together."

"He sounds like a romantic."

"I guess he was." She shrugged. "I never met him. He died before I was born, before he could keep his promise to my grandmother."

His eyes opened wide in recognition. "So you're fulfilling a family dream?"

She cringed at being found out, annoyed she had divulged enough personal information for him to guess. Chest heaving silently, she stared down at her crucifix. Discussion over, she raised her eyes.

"No, nothing like that." Opening her menu, she hid her face behind it. "Let's order."

They discussed only the scenery and food through lunch. Then, back in their seats, she promptly pulled out her iPad and began typing. Percy opened his book, and neither spoke until the conductor called, "León."

"See you later," she called over her shoulder, hoping not to see him again. She strapped on her backpack and rushed off.

❋

From the moment Gwen left the train, she saw the cathedral's dual towers rising above the cityscape. Their steeples seemed to wave, beckon, as if calling her to them.

She remembered something her Art History professor had once said. "Gothic architecture raises your eyes to heaven. Your eyes are drawn up to God above. It's like hands praying, but carved in stone, all pointing toward God."

His words had always stayed with her, but not until she saw the towers in the distance did she begin to comprehend. As she toured the cathedral's interior, she finally understood.

Nearly twenty thousand square feet of stained glass windows glimmered like gems. When the afternoon sun lit them, the cathedral sparkled like a kaleidoscope. Gwen slowly walked from one window to the next, gazing up in wonder. *It's like I'm inside a jewelry box.*

As she strolled through the three portals, she saw a woman kneeling at one of the pews beneath the rose window, her head bent in prayer. Pausing, Gwen noticed a knapsack beside her and wondered if she was also a pilgrim. Then she hurried on, not wanting to disturb the woman.

She visited the cathedral museum, noting the sacred art that dated from prehistoric time to the eighteenth century. She stopped in front of Antonio Canova's sculpture, *Psyche Revived by Cupid's Kiss.* Gazing at her engagement ring, she thought of Art. Though she kept in constant contact with him through emails and IMs and had Skyped with him the night before, she had trouble relating to him in any romantic capacity. Cocking her head, she tried looking at the sculpture from another angle.

"Don't you love Neoclassicism?" asked the woman who had been at prayer.

Gwen turned toward her, noticing her chin-length, dark hair and dark, sparkling eyes. "The figures are lifelike, but," Gwen paused, making a face, "this is a sculptor's idealized portrayal of love. It isn't real life."

The woman raised her eyebrow and smiled. "Love can have its moments." She held out her hand. "Hi, I'm Ruth Spinoza."

"Gwen Alton," she said, shaking hands. "I see you're carrying a knapsack. Are you a pilgrim?"

"Starting today, I am. Every journey begins with the first step."

When she smiled, it was infectious. Gwen found herself grinning along with her. "Same here. I'm going through the Peregrino Paths."

"Me, too!"

"Then I guess we'll be seeing a lot of each other during the next hundred and fifty kilometers."

Nodding, Ruth spoke under her breath. "Nine days."

Gwen cocked her head, trying to hear. "What was that?"

"Sorry, I'm thinking aloud." She gave a self-conscious smile. "I said we'll be seeing a lot of each other during the next nine days. I'm doing a novena."

Pursing her lips, Gwen squinted. "I've heard that word before, but I'm not sure what it means."

"Basically, a novena is a prayer for a special intention said for nine consecutive days."

With an understanding smile, Gwen nodded. "And since our pilgrimage is nine days long, you're saying it for our journey."

"Exactly. It's an ancient prayer for the Camino de Santiago. ending at the Pilgrims' Mass." Reaching for her backpack, Ruth added, "Do you want a copy? I've got an extra."

A prayer wouldn't be the worst thing. After all, I'm on a pilgrimage. Gwen shrugged. "Sure."

As Ruth handed her a hand-printed prayer, Gwen read silently.

> Oh God, who brought your servant Abraham out of the land of the Chaldeans, protecting him in his wanderings, who guided the Hebrew people across the desert, we ask that you watch over us, your servants, as we walk in the love of your name to Santiago de Compostela, so that with your guidance we may arrive safe and sound at the end of the road, and enriched with grace and virtue, we return safely to our homes filled with joy.
> In the name of Jesus Christ our Lord, Amen. Apostle Santiago, pray for us.

Gwen looked up from the paper and smiled. "I like that. Thank you."

"I hear the Camino can have a deep effect on pilgrims. With all the time we'll have to think, a daily prayer can't hurt."

Gwen gave a thoughtful nod.

"Have you been to the Basilica de San Isidoro yet?"

"Not yet." Gwen shook her head. "Why?"

Ruth pulled out a folded brochure from her pocket. "It's one of León's highlights. Supposedly, it holds the Holy Grail, the Chalice of Doña Urraca, the actual cup Jesus used during the Last Supper."

Gwen thought of Percy. "By any chance, are you on this pilgrimage because of the Holy Grail?"

"No." Ruth's dark eyes widened as she looked up and shook her head. "Why?"

Gwen gave her a half smile. "You sounded like someone else I met recently."

Shrugging, Ruth read from her brochure. "According to this, it's the only chalice that could be considered Christ's."

"You think it's *the* real one?" Gwen watched her response.

"Who knows?" She sighed. "Several hundred cups, bowls, and chalices contend for that title across Europe."

"Wow, I had no idea."

Ruth laughed. "And that's just in Europe. Supposedly, *the* Holy Grail also resides in Jerusalem, Nova Scotia, Maryland, and Kentucky."

"What?"

"There are too many theories to mention, each one more improbable than the last." Ruth lowered her voice to confidential tones. "This one's causing so much publicity, the museum staff at the basilica might remove the chalice from display. They're looking for an exhibition space large enough to handle the crowds."

"Oy vey."

Tilting her head, Ruth smiled as she studied her. "Are you Jewish?"

Gwen shook her head. "No, but I've lived in Manhattan the last twelve years. Yiddish is my second language." She chuckled. "Are you?"

Ruth grinned. "By culture, yes, but not by religion."

Wrinkling her brow, Gwen struggled to understand. "What do you mean?"

"I'm a Messianic Jew."

"Really?" Gwen studied her. "So you believe in Christ?"

Ruth nodded. "Don't you?"

"Yeah." Gwen shrugged.

"But?"

"But I have trouble with the whole patriarchal, bearded, God-the-Father, big-daddy image."

"Wow." Ruth breathed out sharply. "I detect just a smidgeon of cynicism."

Gwen sighed. "Sorry." She finger combed her hair. "Early exposure to chauvinism and misogyny, I guess."

Ruth spoke in a quiet voice. "We were talking about God, not men."

"Yeah." Gwen nodded. "Apologies for the whole father/Father metaphor," she added sheepishly. "Sometimes, the anger boils over into my conversation."

Ruth shrugged as she folded the brochure. "Holding on to anger's like holding a hot coal to throw at someone else; you're the one who gets burned."

Ouch. Blinking, unsure how to answer, Gwen looked at her new companion, appraising her.

"I'm going to the basilica next, if you'd like to join me," said Ruth.

"Sure." They walked in thoughtful silence a few minutes before Gwen turned toward her. "Why are you making the pilgrimage?"

Ruth looked off into space before speaking. "I'd reached a point where I needed to reassess, decide what to do with my life." She turned toward Gwen. "A friend suggested I walk the Camino."

Gwen turned toward her. "Was it a difficult decision?"

"I searched my mind, asked myself questions. 'Am I a religious fanatic? A fitness freak? An idiot?'" Ruth smiled. "None of those, at least I hope not, but I'm looking for something to *confirm* my faith."

"Anything specific?"

Nodding, Ruth rubbed her chin. "Two things. I'm hoping to find the spiritual in the ordinary and . . ." Again, she looked off into space, as if collecting her thoughts.

"And?"

"After Compostela, I'm going to Montserrat."

"Montserrat?" Gwen did a double take. "That's the second time today I've heard that place mentioned. Why? What's there?" She held up her index finger. "No, wait, don't tell me. Let me guess. We're on our way to Basilica de San Isidoro, and you'd mentioned how the Holy Grail may be there. You want to go to Montserrat because of the legend of the Holy Grail, don't you?"

"Nope." Ruth shook her head. "There's another legend that the Ark of the Covenant's buried in Montserrat's mountains."

"Really? Why does that appeal to you?"

"The Ark's important to both Jews and Christians. It reflects my Jewish heritage, as well as my Christian beliefs. It contained the tablets of the Ten Commandments and was the symbol of God's very presence." Ruth smiled gently. "As I mentioned, I'm looking for something to reinforce my faith." She held up her palms. "What better symbol than the Ark?"

"But why do you think the Ark's hidden at Montserrat?" Gwen rolled her eyes. "I mean, how would the Ark get from Jerusalem to Spain?"

"Legend has it, a secret Essene brotherhood took it to Catalonia, Spain. They created a tunnel among Montserrat's many caves and hid the Ark. Some say they hid the Grail, as well."

"The Grail?" Gwen narrowed her eyes. "Intriguing stories, but do you really believe any of them?"

"Where there's rumor, I believe there's a speck of truth."

"Where there's smoke, there's fire?"

"Something like that." She met Gwen's eyes. "At any rate, I want to see Montserrat, experience it."

As they approached a large, cobblestoned square, Gwen recognized a man sitting at the outdoor café. He raised his glass in greeting.

"Hi." Percy held out his hand, gesturing toward two chairs. "Join me in a glass of wine?"

"You two know each other?" asked Ruth, looking from one to the other. At their nods, she added, "He who knows others is wise; he who knows himself is enlightened."

Gwen gave a dry laugh. "We keep bumping into each other wherever we go."

"We were on the same flight from New York, later ran into each other in Barcelona, and then this morning ended up on the same train here." He stood up. "I'm Percy Gowan."

"Ruth," she said, shaking hands. "Ruth Spinoza."

He motioned to the waiter. "Two more glasses, please." Turning back to the women, he pulled out two chairs. "Have a seat. This table's got a great view of the Basilica de San Isidoro."

As the waiter poured their wine, Gwen chuckled at the irony. "With your interest in the Holy Grail, I had a sneaking suspicion you'd be here." She indicated Ruth with a nod of her head. "Ruth shares a similar interest in the Ark of the Covenant."

"Really?"

"After Compostela, I'm visiting Montserrat."

He pushed his glasses up the bridge of his nose. "What a coincidence. So am I."

Ruth shook her head. "There are no coincidences, my friend. Everything happens for a reason."

"Including meeting here over a glass of wine?" Raising her glass in a toast, Gwen gave them a sly smile. "To coincidences, flukes, twists of fate, and divine intervention."

As they clinked glasses, Gwen looked at her two new companions and felt strangely comfortable. She felt herself relaxing, enjoying the moment. *Maybe it's just the romance of the open road.*

"You mean, the right path."

Choking, Gwen almost spilled her wine. She had heard the words clearly, but both her companions were swallowing, not speaking.

"Is either of you a ventriloquist?" She looked from one to the other, hoping for a logical explanation for what she had heard.

"I'm not." Percy caught Ruth's eye.

"Me, neither. Why?"

Gwen scratched her head. "Thought I heard something." She glanced at the outdoor café's patrons and sighed. "Probably just overheard someone at another table."

"To overheard conversations," said Ruth, clinking glasses.

With a shrug, Gwen joined the toast.

"Did you know," said Ruth, reading from her brochure. "The Basilica de San Isidoro was built over the temple ruins of the Roman god Mercury? Its architecture's mostly Romanesque."

Gwen nodded. "It's beautiful, but I miss the uplifting Gothic lines of the cathedral." She motioned with her hand. "The columns looked like humans stretching up their arms to heaven. As they drew my eyes upward, I could not only see, I could *understand* how Gothic architecture raises our spirits."

"Understand," repeated Ruth, nodding slowly. "Understanding's the second gift of the Holy Spirit."

"What?" Squinting, Gwen turned toward her.

"It's one of the seven gifts of the Holy Spirit: Wisdom, Understanding, Counsel, Fortitude, Knowledge, Piety, and Fear of the Lord. *Understanding* lets us see our relationship with God, our role in the world. By understanding these things, we see our life in the larger context of the eternal."

Gwen blinked as she digested that.

Then, returning to the brochure, Ruth paraphrased. "Although the other areas are Romanesque, you'll be happy to hear the San Isidoro Chapel is Gothic."

"To Gothic," said Gwen, raising her glass. They clinked glasses in a toast.

"Did you know," asked Percy, "Saint Isidore was mentioned in Dante's *Paradise?*"

Gwen gave him a blank stare. "How would you know something that obscure?"

"What do you expect?" Percy's grin was shy. "I'm an English Lit professor. Obscure, that's me."

"To obscure," said Ruth, raising her glass.

They chuckled as they clinked glasses.

"Okay, I hear things," said Gwen, "and Percy's obscure. You know our flaws. Do you have any imperfections?"

Ruth thought for moment. "Proverbs are potted wisdom."

"That's your imperfection: proverbs?" Gwen eyed her skeptically.

She nodded. "If you haven't noticed already, I like to spout one-liners. In this case, 'Proverbs are potted wisdom.'" Grinning, she shrugged. "It's a gift."

"To Ruth's pithy quips," said Percy, raising his glass.

They clinked glasses, this time draining the contents, and set off together.

As they approached the basilica, Gwen saw a figure she recognized in the crowd. Then someone stepped in her way, blocking her view. She craned her neck to see around him.

Dad?

She blinked, thinking she was seeing things. Then, keeping her eyes on her target, she strained for a better look. *Hearing things. Seeing things. What's next?* Just as she caught a glimpse of the man's face, she tripped over a large stone, twisting her ankle.

"What the?" She looked down and saw a silvery, glassy stone. "What is that?" she asked, picking it up. "Mica?"

"Looks like muscovite." Percy examined the stone, breaking off a thin, nearly transparent flake. "It's pretty common in León. I believe it's mined locally."

Gwen recalled how, as a child, she and her father had found a piece of mica while hiking through the park.

"People used mica for windows over a hundred years ago," he had said. "They called it isinglass and used to mine it in New Jersey."

She fingered the mineral in her hand, recalling the stone of her childhood. *Wonder what happened to it?* Then, it came to her. *Like everything else, Mil-dread must have it.* Irritated at the thought, she started to toss the stone away.

"Keep it," said Ruth.

"Why?"

"We'll be stopping at Foncebadón."

"So? What's there?"

"The Iron Cross." Ruth grinned. "You'll find a use for it there."

Gwen shrugged but tucked the sliver of stone in her pocket. Then, keeping her eyes open for the person who reminded her of her father, she toured the basilica. She captured its architectural features with her camera, including several shots of the agate, gold, and onyx chalice believed to be the Holy Grail.

Afterwards, they walked to the Peregrino Paths' meeting place, where their guide led them to a bus.

Gwen's brow puckered as she boarded. "I thought we were walking the Camino."

"For the final one hundred and fifty-six kilometers you are." Their guide, Jaime, seemed to suppress a smile, his eyes twinkling.

"Then why are we taking a bus?" *I'm cheating or being cheated of the hiking experience.*

"It's one hundred and fifty-eight kilometers from León to O Cebreiro, slightly more than the entire distance you'll walk this week." He shrugged. "An hour-and-a-half ride versus eight more days of walking."

Gwen thought of her time schedule and gave a begrudging nod. *But it's still cheating.*

"Do the best you can," she heard

She flinched as the hair rose on the back of her neck. She looked left. She looked right. Everyone was getting settled on the bus. No one was near or paying any attention to her, let alone talking to her. *Okay, this is getting weird. Who said that?*

Again, she checked left and right. She listened, half expecting to hear a response, but no one, nothing answered her thoughts. Finally, she stowed her backpack and took a seat.

"Get any good shots at the basilica?" asked Percy, sitting across the aisle from her.

Relieved at hearing a voice she recognized, she turned toward him with a friendly smile. "I did. Got a couple good ones of the chalice, too."

"Speaking of chalices," said Ruth, taking the seat next to her. "A fourteenth-century Eucharistic miracle occurred at our next stop, O Cebreiro's church of Santa María la Real." She shrugged. "Or so I've read."

"Why? What happened?" Gwen looked at her.

"As a priest consecrated the bread and wine during Mass, the substances were literally transformed into living flesh and blood." Ruth tapped her guidebook. "The church still has the original chalice and paten on display."

"It's called the Galician Grail," said Percy.

"I'll photograph that one, too, maybe start a whole series of Camino chalices."

Gwen chuckled at the idea. Then, nodding to herself, she said, "Actually, it's not a bad angle. It might be a way to personalize the journey."

"Besides getting your pilgrim's passport stamped in each town, you can collect photos of chalices at each church," said Ruth.

"Do you have your pilgrim's passport yet?" Percy looked from one to the other.

Gwen nodded. "Oh, yeah!"

Forty-five minutes later, their bus stopped by a mound of stones. In the center rose a wooden pole, topped with a cross.

"This, my friends, is la Cruz de Ferro, the Iron Cross," said Jaime. "It's a replica of the original iron cross. Over the years, this mound has grown one stone at a time. Legend says the pilgrims were asked to contribute a stone for the construction of the Cathedral of Santiago de Compostela. Now it's customary to leave a stone here, symbolizing what you want to leave behind as you prepare for rebirth on the Camino."

Gwen looked at Ruth and shared a grin. Fingering the piece of muscovite in her pocket, she thought of the circumstances surrounding the stone. *I literally stumbled over it when I saw my . . . someone who reminded me of my father.* She mentally replayed Jaime's words: "leave a stone here, symbolizing what you want to leave behind as you prepare for rebirth on the Camino."

Is my father what I want to leave behind? Or is it the bitterness I want to forget?

Taking the stone from her pocket, she fought bitter memories as she began climbing the hill. A prayer came to mind. *Our Father, Who art in heaven . . .* She froze. *I haven't said that prayer since . . . since that day my father basically said goodbye.* She mentally replayed his words.

"I won't interfere in your life, so don't interfere in mine."

Starting over, she forced herself to take another step forward. *Our Father, Who art in heaven, hallowed be Thy name.*

She flinched as a thought occurred. *My father and my Father. The day he left is about when I stopped going to church. Could there be a connection?*

She drew a deep breath. *Thy Kingdom come, Thy will be done on earth as it is in heaven.*

Suddenly, the words took on significance, but they became a riddle. *Thy will be done on earth as it is in heaven. What does that mean? Am I supposed to do something?* She looked at the rock in her hand. *Okay, maybe this is it.*

Shaking her head to clear it, she willed herself to climb to the top. *Give us this day our daily bread. And forgive us our trespasses as we forgive those who trespass against us.*

As her chest tightened, she strugg ed to breathe. *Forgive us our trespasses as we forgive those who trespass against us. How can I forgive my father?* She swallowed. *How can I forgive myself?*

Tossing her stone on the ground, she watched it land between a rock painted with a red heart and a piece of pink granite. *And lead us not into temptation, but deliver us from evil.*

She closed her eyes, drained. *Deliver me from resenting my father, from feeling guilty about my father. Amen.*

Gwen walked back to the bus and sat alone, thinking, until the others boarded a few minutes later. When the bus pulled away, she watched the countryside morph from hilly terrain with broad vistas and narrow ravines to rolling knolls and valleys.

Then steep peaks emerged from the rocky outcrops. She heard the bus shift gears as it began its mountain ascent. Gwen glanced out the window and saw ice. In the distance, she saw white-covered hilltops.

"Is that snow?"

Ruth read from her book. "At an altitude of over forty-two hundred feet, O Cebreiro sits on top of a mountain pass."

As the bus continued to climb the two-lane road, Gwen mentally groaned. *I'm glad we're not hiking this section, after all.*

Then she spotted a building with a round, thatched roof. Its overhanging edges nearly touched the ground. "Look at that." Gwen pointed out the window, chuckling. "It looks like a hobbit's hut or a stone igloo."

"That's a palloza, a traditional round stone house." Ruth compared it to a picture. "People lived in them until the sixties."

Percy cocked his head. "Reminds me of Ireland."

"Why?"

"The thatched, stone buildings, the greenery, the hills and mist—it looks like Ireland."

When they arrived, they walked across a cobblestoned entry and checked into the hotel. As she dropped off her knapsack, Gwen glanced around her room. Stone walled, the room's ceiling was made of varnished wooden planks and log beams. The bed's wrought-iron headboard was curlicued, and when she sat on the down featherbed, she sank into it with a sigh. *Old-world charming.*

A moment later, she heard Ruth knocking at her door. "Gwen, are you in there?"

"What?" Gwen struggled to wake from a deep sleep. *I must have dozed off.*

"We're leaving for the Pilgrims' Mass."

"Just a minute," she called, disentangling reality from her dream.

Though the dream's memories were vanishing quickly, she tried to recall snippets as she gathered her purse and keys.

"Everyone's waiting downstairs in the lobby," said Ruth.

"What time is it?" In answer to her question, she checked her watch. *A half hour!* She tried to laugh it off. "Trust me, the beds are comfortable." Gwen was quiet during the short walk to Santa María la Real, still unraveling reality from her dream.

She had been walking near the Iron Cross, its rocky hill surrounded by mist. Then the hill transformed into the park of her childhood, and her father was walking beside her. She had stooped to pick up the piece of mica, but when she looked back at her father, he was gone. In his place was her fiancé, Art. *How bizarre.*

Their guide, Jaime, broke into her thoughts. "Santa María la Real, or Royal St. Mary's, is possibly the oldest church on the French Road of the Camino de Santiago. Built in 836, its sunken floors protected it from wintry storms."

"Where's the chalice?" asked Ruth, looking around the spacious church.

"Just to the right of the main altar, the twelfth-century golden chalice and reliquary are kept in the chapel. It was here the host and wine physically turned into Christ's body and blood."

Then, pointing toward an alcove, he added, "The clerk at that desk will stamp your pilgrim's credentials for you. Then please gather back here for the Pilgrims' Mass. Afterwards, we'll have dinner."

Following Mass, they walked through the drizzle to a nearby pub. As soon as the sun set, the temperature dropped substantially. The rain's icy droplets stung Gwen's face and hands. Although the walk took only five minutes, she was glad to get into the smoky warmth of the ancient pub.

Jaime said, "Try the Galician specialty, Caldo Galego. It's a local soup, traditionally made from leftover stock after the Sunday meal. Nothing fancy, it's hearty peasant fare—cabbage, turnips, white beans, chorizo, and ham—but it's comfort food on a blustery night."

Gwen found a table with Ruth and Percy. As the waiter brought freshly-made bread and they ordered wine, a fourth pilgrim approached them.

"Mind if I join you?" asked an aging hippy, a red bandanna tied around his head, his graying blond hair peeking out the sides like straw.

"Have a seat," said Percy, gesturing toward the empty chair.

"I'm Crow," he said with an engaging smile, sitting between Gwen and Percy, across from Ruth.

"I'm Gwen. Got to admit, I've never met anyone with the name Crow before." Raising her eyebrow quizzically, she grinned. "How did you come by it?"

"It's short for Jimmy Black Crow. Back in the sixties, I became blood brothers with a Lakota Medicine Man. After doing peyote on the 'wheel,' he gave me this name."

"What had it been before that?" she asked.

Sitting up straight, his facial expression and demeanor changed entirely. His loose jawline tightened. His unfocused eyes suddenly peered hard into hers. Despite his bandanna and jeans, he looked the part of a prosperous business man. Using a deep, professional tone, he said, "James Rutherford the Third."

"Wow, that's quite a transformation." She chuckled. "Pleased to meet you, Crow. This is Ruth, and to your right is Percy."

"What brings you on this pilgrimage?" asked Percy.

"Besides the fact that Santiago de Compostela's the most popular pilgrimage in Spain?"

"Yeah."

"Religion, man," said Crow, reverting to his aging-hippy persona. "I've been on a religious quest all my adult life. From peyote to LSD to ayahuasca, from saunas to sweat lodges to temazcals, I've been searching for God."

"Have you found Him?" Ruth asked.

"Not yet."

"Maybe you've been looking in the wrong places," Ruth said quietly.

"Could be." Crow winked. "He hasn't been anywhere I've looked." Then glancing from one to the other, he added, "After Compostela, I'm going to Montserrat. Maybe I'll find him there."

"You're kidding." Gwen stared at him. *Montserrat, again.* The three exchanged glances. "Percy and Gwen are going there after Compostela, too."

"Really? What a coincidence," said Crow.

"There's no such thing as coincidence." Ruth wore a wry smile. "It's God's way of being anonymous."

"So meeting you here, tonight, at this table, means I'm on God's path?"

Her wry smile becoming a smirk, Ruth nodded. "Yup. Everything happens according to God's plan."

Crow sat back in his chair. "Who'd a'thunk?"

Percy and Ruth shared their reasons for going to Montserrat.

"The Holy Grail and the Arc of the Covenant." Crow slowly shook his head. "Amazing."

"Why are you visiting Montserrat?" asked Gwen.

"Telluric energy."

"What's that?"

"Telluric energy is Mother Nature's power source. It's the life force of earth. It's the key that unlocks the secrets." Slightly cross-eyed, his eyes tracked individually.

"What secrets?" Gwen gazed from his left eye to his right eye, unsure which was looking at her.

"All secrets, any secret." Adding to his wild appearance, his hair bristled out from under his bandanna. "Telluric energies radiate through an electromagnetic grid of energy flow called ley lines. Ley lines crisscross the earth in complex patterns." Talking with his hands, his fingers met in a cross. "The places where they intersect are called Vortex Energy Points or VEP. Montserrat is a well-known VEP."

The other three looked at each other. "Vortex?" repeated Gwen, lifting her eyebrow skeptically.

Crow nodded thoughtfully. "The very fact that Percy's searching there for the Holy Grail and Ruth is searching for the Ark proves it. VEPs produce powerful outflows of energy. These areas are designated as sacred sites, with temples and monasteries built over them. But in reality, these key points act like portals to other dimensions of reality. They're vortexes, centers of energy. UFOs use ley lines to navigate."

"So you're looking for spaceships, aliens, and space portals?" Gwen tried to suppress her smirk.

"There's documented evidence of UFO activity at Montserrat."

The waiter brought wine and glasses. Percy poured and held up his glass in a toast. "To quests."

They toasted, and Gwen held up her glass. "To insights and answers."

"To finding your way," said Ruth.

"To Dorothy," said Crow.

Glasses poised midair, everyone stared at Crow.

"Who's Dorothy?" asked Gwen.

"You know, like in *The Wizard of Oz*."

Gwen raised her left eyebrow. "I don't see a connection."

"On this pilgrimage, it's like we're all on our way to see the Wizard, like we're all characters in *The Wiz*." He looked from one face to the next. "Okay, I'll go first. After all the LSD I've dropped, all the brain cells I've killed, I'm looking for a brain. I see myself as the Scarecrow." Laughing at himself, he ruffled his hair, the coarse gray-blond strands looking more straw-like than before. Turning to Percy, he asked, "Which character are you?"

Percy thought for a moment. "The Lion."

"Why the Lion?"

He scratched his head. "As a published English professor, you could say I'm a literary lion." He pushed his glasses to the bridge of his nose. "I also hide behind these spectacles or hide behind a book." Though grinning, he looked pointedly at Gwen. "Or so I've been told, in which case, you could call me the Cowardly Lion."

She met his gaze. "So what would you ask of the Wizard?"

He affected a Brooklyn accent. "'Da noive.'"

They laughed.

"Who's next?" Crow looked from one woman to the other.

"I'll go," said Ruth wistfully, almost as if she were thinking aloud. "I must be the Tin Man because I'm searching for a heart—the sacred heart, the message, the covenant that God gave us. I'd ask for an open heart."

"That's deep, man." Crow nodded thoughtfully before turning toward Gwen. "Then you must be Dorothy. Do you have an Aunty Em?"

"No." She gathered her thoughts. "But I am searching for my way back home."

She surprised herself by talking so freely to these three strangers. *Why?* She had to laugh at herself. *Probably because I'll never see them again.*

"What's home for you?" Ruth's dark eyes peered into hers.

Two words came to mind as she gestured toward the sky above. "Father and father."

"As in Heavenly Father and dad?" Ruth asked.

Gwen nodded. "You might say I lost them both twelve years ago. I don't really have any place to call 'home.'"

"Then you're an orphan spirit."

"Just another lost soul on the pilgrimage of life."

"You mean, another lost soul who's off to see the Wizard." Crow's eyes focused on her.

"Taking this from a literary perspective," said Percy. "If we're the characters in *The Wizard of Oz*, who's the Wiz?"

"God." Ruth clasped her hands toward her chest, as if she was warming them or praying.

"Then taking this metaphor another step," asked Percy. "Where's Oz?"

"Compostela?" asked Gwen, searching his violet-blue eyes.

"Monserrat," said Crow.

Ruth shook her head. "Heaven."

After dinner, Gwen called Art and told him about their dinner discussion.

"You sound enthusiastic about your pilgrimage," he said. "Are you finding what you're searching for?"

"I've stumbled into this motley group, but you know what? I find myself opening up with them." She paused, thinking back to their conversation. "No, I should simply have said, I find myself opening up. Whatever the reason, I'm beginning to sort out my thoughts, unravel a few knots."

CHAPTER 4:

The Canterbury Tales

"Then folk long to go on pilgrimages . . .
Of far off saints, hallowed in sundry lands . . ."
— Geoffrey Chaucer translated by Nevill Coghill

The next morning, the four of them met for breakfast.

As Gwen ordered coffee, she saw what looked like scalloped potatoes on Percy's plate.

"What's that?"

"Catalonian Tortilla."

"Tortilla?" She chuckled. "That sure doesn't look like any Tex-Mex tortilla I've ever seen."

"It isn't. It's a classic Catalonian breakfast: a sautéed potato and onion omelet."

"Looks delicious." Pointing to the omelet, Gwen turned to the waitress. "I'll have what he's having."

"I've been thinking," said Percy. "Instead of *The Wizard of Oz*, we're characters in Chaucer's *The Canterbury Tales*."

"Not familiar with it." Crow shook his head.

"You know, the stories pilgrims told as they walked to Saint Thomas Becket's shrine at the Canterbury Cathedral."

"Weren't they just passing the time in a storytelling contest?" Gwen squinted, trying to remember her one semester of Chaucer. "I only recall the fable about the rooster, Chanticleer."

"From the 'Nun's Priest's Tale.'" Percy nodded. "Tell it."

Gathering her thoughts, she sipped her coffee. "Chanticleer dreamed a fox would eat him, but his favorite hen convinced him dreams don't mean a thing. The next morning, now overconfident, he crowed at the top of his lungs. The waiting fox complimented him on his fine singing voice and begged him to crow again. Flattered, Chanticleer did his best, closing his eyes to better concentrate."

"So the sly fox caught him," said Crow.

Gwen nodded as she continued. "All the animals chased after them but couldn't catch them. Then Chanticleer turned the tables. He told the fox, 'You're so fast, so smart. They'll never catch up with you. Flaunt it!' Puffed up with pride, the fox stopped and jeered at the barnyard animals. As soon as he opened his mouth, Chanticleer jumped from his jaws, escaping into a tree. Chanticleer had learned his lesson."

"What's the lesson?" Crow smirked. "Never trust a brown-nose?"

"Something like that." Gwen grinned back.

"Flatterers look like friends, as wolves look like dogs." Wagging a finger, Ruth laughed. "I warned you I like to spout one-liners."

Crow chuckled and then turned toward Percy. "Since you brought up the idea, why don't you tell the next story?" Crossing his arms, Crow sat back in his chair.

"Ah, a challenge." Percy's violet-blue eyes danced mischievously as he began, tongue in cheek. "Because I'm on a quest for the Holy Grail, it's only right I tell 'The Knight's Tale.'"

The women groaned, as Crow threw his napkin at him.

"The Duke of Athens threw two knights in jail, Arcite and Palamon. They'd sworn to help each other escape, but when they saw the duke's sister-in-law, Emily, they both fell in love with her."

"So all bets were off." Crow snickered as the waitress brought their tortillas and more coffee.

Percy nodded. "Friends bailed Arcite from jail and arranged for him to be near Emily. Jealous, Palamon escaped, and the two knights fought over her. To keep order, the duke proposed a tournament, with Emily the prize. Arcite defeated Palamon but was thrown from his horse and killed. Though Palamon lost the battle, he actually won since he survived to marry her."

"So what's the moral?" asked Gwen. "Love conquers all?"

"He lost the battle, but won the war," said Ruth.

Crow snickered. "He who laughs last, laughs best."

"It shows what happens when two political opinions clash," said Percy. "In this case, chivalry and courtly love." Though they'd sworn to protect each another, both loved the same woman. From a chivalrous point of view, knights always kept their word. Period, amen. From a courtly love viewpoint, knights put love above everything else, even friendship or oaths."

"I see a pattern, a cosmic order." Crow's eyes lit up.

"A *heavenly* order," corrected Ruth.

"So, in this story," said Gwen, "the duke's the Wizard."

"Back to the Wiz, again." Groaning, Percy banged his palm against his head, pretending exasperation. "I start with Chaucer, and we end up with *The Wizard of Oz,* again."

"I'll drink to that." Gwen chuckled as she clinked her coffee cup against Ruth's, Crow's, and his.

"To the Wiz," he said, toasting.

❄

"Today, our destination's Triacastela, Three Castles," said Jaime. "We'll follow quiet country lanes and footpaths through cattle country, dotted with small villages. Then, this evening, we'll tour Samos, one of Spain's oldest Benedictine monasteries." He winked. "That is, if you feel up to it after walking twelve and a half miles."

Twelve and a half miles? Gwen swallowed as the reality of the adventure set in. Living in the city, she walked every day, but nowhere near twelve and a half miles.

Jaime caught her eye and grinned. "Don't worry. The mountains are behind us. Rolling hills will be our highest climb, and we'll go at a slow, steady pace."

"Slow but steady wins the race," said Ruth, quoting, grinning.

Gwen forced a smile, but she began to wonder if she could keep up with the tour. *Am I nuts? What was I thinking?*

Jaime took the lead, motioning them to follow. "This way. Buen Camino!"

"Every journey begins with the first step," said Ruth.

Gwen took a deep breath and ceremoniously set down her foot. *There, I've begun the pilgrimage. The rest should be easy, right?* Rolling her eyes, she said a quick prayer. *Help me.*

With that, she felt a sudden lifting of weight. Her feet felt as light as if they were in slippers instead of hiking boots. She felt refreshed as she took another deep breath, inhaling the crisp country air. With a firm nod of her head, she affirmed, *I can do this.*

The town limits ended abruptly. No suburbs, no strip malls, one minute they were in town, and the next, they were walking along a country lane. Rustic fencing lined the crushed-gravel road. Green pastures swept out like wings from both sides of the road, tipping up into rolling hills. As the morning mist rose, it unveiled the last orange-red colors of autumn.

"These are chestnut trees," Jaime said, pointing. "You're here at the perfect time: harvest. From about November first, All Saints' Day, to the eleventh, Saint Martin's Day, Galicia and Catalonia hold Magosto, the Chestnut Festival."

Chestnuts. Gwen chuckled to herself, recalling the first time she had tasted them. Her father had taken her to Radio City Music Hall to see the Christmas show. Afterwards, they'd bought roasted chestnuts, still steaming, from a street vendor. The memory was so vivid, she could almost taste their nutty flavor. It was one of her favorite Christmas recollections.

Gwen caught up with Jaime. "Besides the chestnuts being ripe, is there any other reason for starting the festival on All Saints' Day?"

He explained as they walked. "Originally, this was a Celtic festival, related to fertility. When they roasted the chestnuts in the fire, the flames represented the sun or the fertility god. Later, as the festival became Christianized, it was associated with remembering the dead."

"How so?"

"On All Saints' night, people would ring bells to celebrate the dead until the early morning of All Souls' Day. Friends and relatives would take turns ringing, and it became a party with wine, sausages, and of course, chestnuts while the family said prayers for the deceased." He lowered his voice. "Some say chestnuts were eaten in a kind of communion with the souls of the recently departed."

"Really?"

Jaime nodded and then turned his attention as another pilgrim asked him a question.

Lost in thought, Gwen fell a step behind. She replayed Jaime's words mentally: *a kind of communion with the souls of the recently departed.* She thought of her father, wondering at the significance of chestnuts, and did not see the low-hanging tree branch. Too late, she felt it brush against her head.

"Ugh!" She finger combed her hair, brushing out the leaves and twigs. Then she looked at the ground. Peeking from a bristly shuck was a shiny chestnut. She picked it up, turning it in her fingers, feeling its textures, recalling the first time she had touched a chestnut. With a half smile, she tucked it in her pocket and hurried to catch up.

Late that afternoon, as the sun was beginning to set, they arrived in Triacastela.

Gwen breathed in deeply, faintly recognizing the scent. "What is that?"

"Chestnuts," said Percy, pointing to a street vendor.

As they got closer, Gwen saw he was roasting chestnuts on what looked like a converted wash tub covered with a grill.

"Would you like some chestnuts?"

"Oh, yeah." Starving after their hike, she reached into her pocket for coins.

The vendor wore a grin as he wrapped the chestnuts, blackened by the flames' soot, in newspaper.

Gwen's fingers felt stiff in the chilly air as she handed him the euros and took the bundle from him. Immediately, the heat from the nuts transferred to her hands. As her fingers thawed, the heat radiated throughout her body, warming her with fond memories of her father. She smiled to herself as she stepped away, peeled a chestnut, and popped it into her mouth.

"Just like the ones after the Radio City Christmas show."

"What?" Swallowing hard, she looked around, but no one was near. *I didn't imagine that. Who said that?*

She looked back at the group gathered around the street vendor. The afternoon light was becoming dusky. As she peered through the deepening shadows, she thought she recognized someone who did not belong to their tour. *No, it can't be.* She froze.

Her father's image nodded at her and smiled.

She blinked and blinked again. The apparition remained until after the third blink. Then it vanished.

The next morning, Gwen woke up tired. Her feet ached before she stepped out of bed. Standing up straight was another challenge. For the first few steps, she hobbled, but eventually the muscles uncramped, and she could walk naturally. She read through her novena, praying for the physical strength to complete the pilgrimage.

After a breakfast of local sausages, tortillas, and fresh mushrooms, Jaime gathered them together.

"Are you ready for our third day's trek?"

Only our second day of walking. Gwen groaned.

"Today we're walking to Sarria, a Roman settlement. The trail's a bit hillier than yesterday." Again, Gwen groaned. "But it's country back roads, and you'll be rewarded with stunning scenery, fresh seafood, and Galician wine. Buen Camino!"

Triacastela quickly faded from view. Tree-lined paths gave way to hilly vistas. Farther along, an ancient stone fence lined the dusty trail, and they greeted a farmer herding cattle. Every so often, they passed Camino markers: a fountain that resembled a large shell and another made of stone and mortar that contained Galicia's coats of arms and the Camino symbol.

Trying to forget her aching feet, Gwen concentrated on the scenery and experiences. When they came to a village for lunch, she found she was famished. Sharing a tapa sampler with Ruth, Crow, and Percy, they ate oysters, crabs, shrimp, prawns, lobster, and Pulpo a la Gallega, the local octopus specialty. This they washed down with a loaf of handmade bread that resembled a large donut, fresh tomatoes, and rosé wine.

"How's everyone's feet doing?" asked Crow.

After a moment of silence, they all burst out laughing and groaning.

"Sore." Gwen winced.

"Here's a tip my friend gave me. Wear a pair of knee-high stockings under two pairs of socks." Ruth grinned. "Your feet will thank you."

After lunch, Gwen tried calling Art, but the signal was too weak.

"Wait 'til we get to a higher point. You'll get better reception," said Jaime. "We still have several hills to tackle."

Gwen grumbled. "I thought the mountains were behind us."

"They are." With a chuckle, he called their group together. "This afternoon, as we cross the Lugo Plateau, we'll view hórreos, or traditional, raised grain silos. We'll pass through farmland, grazing pastures, and woodlands dotted with several hamlets."

As they reached the top of a hill, they saw their first hórreo. Propped on narrow stone pillars was a small stone building. It reminded Gwen of the raised graves in New Orleans, a coffin on stilts.

Jaime pointed to its pillars. "The farmers store their cattle feed off the ground, so they lose less grain to rats, insects, and mold."

When the others moved on, Gwen lingered behind the small structure for privacy, testing her cell's reception. She wanted to hear Art's voice. *Wish we'd had more time together after he proposed.* She held out her phone, hoping for a better signal. Three bars. Four bars. *Yes!* She speed-dialed, anxious to connect with him.

But as she listened to the hollow echo of his phone ringing three thousand miles away, the distance became tangible. Loneliness seeped into her like the cold through her shoes, and she began to shiver. *What am I doing here?*

She sagged against the hórreo as she thought of her father. Their separation had lasted ten years while he lived. Now it was permanent. Art was the only man alive she had ever trusted, and she could not connect with him. She snorted at the irony. *Face it.* Regardless of cell reception, she was incapable of connecting with anyone. Separated by death or three thousand miles, or even in the same room, she was always isolated. Always alone.

"Gwen, are you okay?"

The voice jolted her from her musings. She gathered her persona about her like a jacket and zippered it, neatly covering her vulnerability. Putting on a bland smile, she stepped out from behind the hórreo.

"What's up?"

"Oh, there you are." Percy gave her a warm smile. "Just wondered where you were. Didn't want you to get separated from the group."

Separated. Her ears perked. Suddenly self-conscious, she scrutinized him, searching his face for any sign of sarcasm. Primed to do verbal battle, she held her tongue only long enough to mentally replay his words for any hint of criticism.

But all she saw was a friendly face that appeared genuinely concerned. She felt flustered, unsure now of her instincts. Then she reevaluated him. *No, not scorn, chauvinism.*

Her eyes narrowed. "I'm perfectly capable of taking care of myself, thank you." With that, she strode past him and caught up with the tour.

The following evening, their foursome shared a pitcher of sangría after dinner. Gwen listened to the conversation with one ear, her thoughts elsewhere. She had texted Art and tried to call him again before dinner, even leaving a voice mail. She needed to connect with him.

"It's my fatherland," said Percy.

At the word 'father,' Gwen tuned in to the discussion.

"Catalonia's part of Spain, man." Crow's tone was argumentative. "A state, like one of the United States."

Percy shook his head. "Catalonia's autonomous, a community of Spain. Its Statute of Autonomy designated it a 'nationality' within the Spanish parliamentary monarchy."

"Catalonia's where?" Politics did not interest Gwen, but any talk of fathers, even fatherlands, did.

"Catalonia's made up of four Spanish provinces," said Percy, turning toward her. "Barcelona, Girona, Lleida, and Tarragona. Some definitions include Andorra and the Balearic Islands."

"Hey, man," said Crow, shrugging, his palms upturned. "It flies the Spanish flag."

"Catalonia's a country within the larger Spanish nation. It's separate from Spanish mainstream culture."

"But it's *not* independent." Crow was insistent. He picked up the pitcher of sangría and swirled its contents, trying to separate the last of the wine from the ice. Other than a few watery drops that trickled into his glass, all that was left was ice. Raising the pitcher in the air, he called the waiter. "Another pitcher, por favor."

Despite the distraction, Percy stayed focused. "Under the Spanish constitution, Catalonia has political, cultural, and linguistic autonomy."

"That's my point, man," said Crow. "It's under the Spanish constitution. It belongs to Spain."

"It does have a cultural separateness, a culinary history," said Ruth. "It has its own style of cooking."

The waiter returned with a new pitcher and refilled their glasses.

"It has more than that. Catalonia's autonomous," said Percy. "The Second Spanish Republic granted it autonomy in 1932."

Gwen tuned out again. Politics held little interest for her. Bored but lonely, she sat, chin on hand. Although she did not hear it ring over the chatter, she felt her cell phone vibrate. Caller ID indicated it was Art. Excusing herself, she hurried toward the door, away from the noise.

"Art, I'm so glad to hear your voice." So relieved to connect, she sighed.

"I've missed you, babe."

Babe. That's what my father used to call me. She felt a shy smile tug at the corners of her mouth. Holding the phone to her ear, she hugged herself and, by extension, hugged Art. Again, she sighed.

"Maybe it's true. Distance does make the heart grow fonder." She chuckled at herself, waxing so romantic.

"Are you having a good time?" His voice sounded concerned. He was listening for her answer. *Something my father never did.* She shook her head to clear her thoughts. *What made me think about him?*

Distracted, she answered a beat late. "Yes . . . No, not really." She scratched her forehead. "Parts of it I'm enjoying—the scenery, the food, sometimes the company—but I feel so lonely most of the time." It suddenly occurred to her why. "I miss you."

"You needn't sound so surprised about it." Art chuckled. "I've missed you since I kissed you goodbye at the airport."

"Really?" She found it hard to believe he missed her, hard to believe he cared. *No one ever had. Well, not in a long time.* She had always felt so detached from everyone that it took a minute to register. Suddenly, she could not wait until the pilgrimage was over and she was together with Art. "It's only a few days 'til I get back."

"Your tour ends in Santiago de Compostela. How'd you like it if I met you there?"

"Compostela?" Her mind wasn't computing. "What do you mean?"

"I was invited to speak in Paris, which is only a short flight from there. I checked. How 'bout I meet you? We can celebrate your completion of the pilgrimage, and you can fly to Paris with me. When are you scheduled to arrive in Compostela?"

"This is day four." She counted on her fingers. "So five nights from tonight." She grinned. "Really? This is wonderful." She told him their hotel's name. "And we usually arrive in time for dinner."

"Then a dinner date it'll be."

"Art, I can't wait." She swallowed, shy now about speaking the words that tumbled to her lips. "I . . . I miss you."

"You can show me when I see you, but I gotta jump on a conference call in two, make that one minute." The warmth came through his voice. "Love you, babe."

She caught her breath. *It's the first time he's said those words.* "You, too," she whispered and clicked off the phone.

CHAPTER 5:
Follow the Yellow Brick Road

"You've always had the power, my dear; you just had to learn it for yourself."
— Glinda, *The Wizard of Oz*

Already, it was becoming a familiar routine. After breakfast, Jaime gathered them outside the hotel. Then he outlined their day's itinerary as he led them along the road.

"Tonight we'll stay in Portomarín but it isn't the ancient city pilgrims knew. That one sleeps with the fish beneath a reservoir built in the sixties, but you'll still be able to see part of it. The town disassembled and reassembled the twelfth-century church, stone by stone, moving it to higher ground. Are you ready?"

Their group nodded and groaned.

"Then Buen Camino!"

They turned off the road onto a dirt path that rambled beside ancient stone fences, overgrown with vines. They passed plowed fields, climbed rolling hills, and viewed the Magdalena Monastery. Then they followed the path down a steep hill to a quaint bridge that crossed the Río Celeiro.

"This must be the Ponte de Aspera," said Ruth, reading from her guidebook. "It means 'the rough bridge,' referring to its dry-stacked stone."

Gwen ran her fingertips over the age-darkened stonework. "Nothing like connecting with twelfth-century history, touching something that people handled a hundred, a thousand years ago." She turned toward Ruth. "It's like reaching across time. I love connecting with the past. Don't you?"

Ruth turned toward her as they walked, her dark eyes wide. "I do. I've felt what you're describing when I've visited ancient basilicas and abbeys, only for me it's more like reaching across space. There's something palpable, tangible, within their walls. When you touch the stonework, you can feel the presence of the divine."

"Yes, that's different yet similar to what I mean." Gwen nodded as they kept pace with the group. "Inside ancient cathedrals, it's somehow easier to believe in miracles, even believe in God."

"Anything's possible," Ruth looked at her, "with God."

Gwen shrugged. "Maybe. It's just been so long since . . ." Now that she had stumbled into personal territory, she felt vulnerable.

"Since what?"

Gwen took a deep breath. "Since I've believed in God the Father. Since I've believed in God *or* my father."

"What do you mean?"

"Long story short, my mother always called me a 'daddy's girl.' I was even born on Father's Day, for heaven's sake." She snickered. "Until I was eight, I was very close to my father, but then something happened."

"What?"

"I don't know. We just became more and more distant until we never spoke, barely connected, even though we lived in the same house. After my mother passed away, he . . ." Catching herself before she divulged too much personal knowledge, she took a deep breath. "We became estranged. At about the same time, I stopped going to church. Not sure if there's a connection, but since then I've felt alienated from God, too."

Ruth nodded, as if taking it all in, but she seemed deep in thought. For a few steps, the only sound was their feet crunching the crushed gravel of the path.

"Maybe you need to make peace with both," said Ruth, "your father and your Father."

As they trudged along, Gwen nodded without looking at her. "Yeah, I'm coming to that conclusion myself."

"Miracles do happen."

"Yeah, right." Gwen gave a cynical laugh.

"They do. In fact, let me tell you a Eucharistic miracle about a father and daughter that happened at Montserrat."

Gwen snickered and nodded toward Percy. "Like a Canterbury tale, to pass the time? Sure, why not tell me a story? We're on a pilgrimage, after all."

"In the sixteen hundreds, a widow and her young daughter went to Montserrat. The little girl begged the abbot to celebrate three Masses in memory of her dead father. She was absolutely convinced the Masses would free her father's soul from purgatory."

Gwen raised her eyebrow skeptically but kept silent.

"The abbot finally agreed. The next day, he began celebrating the first Mass with the little girl and her mother in the congregation. During the consecration, the girl shouted. She saw her father kneeling on the steps of the main altar, surrounded by flames."

"Flames?" Gwen rolled her eyes.

Ruth grinned. "You're not the only one who was suspicious. So was the priest since only the girl could see her father and the fire. As the tradition goes, the priest asked her to toss a tissue close to the flames to prove whether or not she was seeing things. She did, and the tissue burst into flames."

Pursing her lips, Gwen heaved a silent sigh.

"At the second Mass, the girl saw her father dressed in a colorful outfit, standing next to the deacon."

"Any more flames?"

"The story doesn't say, but during the third Mass, the girl saw her father dressed in snow-white clothes. She pointed toward the ceiling, saying, 'There he is! My father's rising to heaven!'"

"And you believe that?"

"Why not? The bishop and many others verified the girl's actions."

Gwen accepted none of it, but rather than offend Ruth she simply said, "Interesting."

"The point was," said Ruth, peering hard into her eyes, "the girl made peace with her father *after* he'd died. So could you. The souls in purgatory need your prayers."

She bobbed her head in a nod. *Prayer. If only it was that simple.* Now it was Gwen's turn to be silent as she thought over Ruth's words. *Pray for him. Have Masses said for him. I haven't prayed in years. For anything, let alone for him.*

They hiked through the Galician countryside, crossed another stream, and climbed uphill to the town of Barbacelo. From there, the dirt track wound through tree-flanked fields, passing through the villages of Leimán, Peruscallo, and Brea.

"This is the one-hundred-kilometer mark," said Jaime, gathering them around a graffitied, cement pillar. "It's the minimum point from which you can walk to earn your Compostela certificate."

Gwen reached out to touch the raised Camino-shell motif, wanting to connect, wanting to feel. Her engagement ring flashed in the autumn sunlight. As it caught her attention, she gave a silent sigh. *First time I've thought of Art today.* She twisted her hand this way and that, looking at the ring. *Why did I accept it? We're friends. I respect him. I enjoy his company. Last night, I told him I love him, and I do. But in that way? Do I want to be his wife?*

At Penas, their path became a downhill, stone track through the towns of Moimentos, Mercadoiro, Parrocha, and Vilachá. Finally, after a steep descent, they arrived in Portomarín.

Setting down their backpacks, the four of them flopped on outdoor café chairs.

"I'm exhausted." Gwen sat back in her chair. "How far did we walk today?"

"Twenty-two kilometers," said Crow, taking a bag of tobacco out of his pocket.

"How many miles is that?"

"Almost fourteen." Crow opened a tiny pack of papers as Gwen looked on.

"What do you call those thin sheets of paper?"

"Rollies, skins," he said. At Gwen's blank stare, he added, "Rolling papers."

"I haven't seen those in years. My father used to roll his own cigarettes. Could I see those?"

"Help yourself." Crow handed her the small packet.

As she pulled off a paper-thin tissue, she recalled her father making his own cigarettes from these tiny tissues and loose tobacco. She smiled at the once-familiar memory, forgotten for so long. Folding the thin paper, she tucked it in the small pocket of her jeans and handed the packet back to Crow.

Crow pulled off a paper, poured loose tobacco on it, evened it out, expertly licked its long edge, and pressed it all together, creating a cigarette in seconds. He held it out for all to see.

"Voilà!"

Watching Crow's antics, she noticed movement out of the corner of her eye. Turning to focus past Crow, Gwen inhaled sharply. There stood her father, rolling his own.

No! What's he doing here? Following me? Is that his ghost trying to frighten me? She mentally called to it. *If that's what you're doing, it's not working. You're annoying me!* Squinting, she pressed her lips together. *Why does seeing him upset me so much? This should be a religious moment, a frightening moment, something other than exasperating. Why does seeing him make me so angry?*

With a silent groan, she watched the specter light his cigarette and begin smoking. Instead of dissipating, the smoke seemed to hang about him, suspended, building into clouds of smoke that finally obscured him. Rather than fading away, her father just became less and less visible in the thick smoke until she lost sight of him.

"What do you say, Gwen?"

At the sound of her name, she turned away from the smoky scene. "What?"

"Do you want to have dinner now or eat later?" Percy's eyes went from her ring to her face.

Gwen unconsciously covered her left hand with her right. "What's everyone else feel like?"

"Dinner," said Ruth.

"I'm starving," said Percy.

Chuckling, she said, "Okay, count me in. Let's order." Then she noticed Crow had gone. "Where'd Crow go?"

Percy gave her a sly grin. "I don't think that was tobacco Crow rolled. I think he wanted a less public place to smoke it."

"Oh." Nodding knowingly, she glanced back toward the smoking specter, but it, too, was gone.

As she got into bed, Gwen glanced at her ring. *Why am I wearing it? With all this hiking and climbing, I could catch it on something, break a prong, and lose the stone.* Congratulating herself at her good sense, she unclasped the chain around her neck and added the ring to her mother's crucifix. Immediately, her cell phone rang. Caller ID said it was Art.

It's as if he knew. She swallowed before answering.

"Thought I'd give you a good-night call." Art's voice was warm, caring.

She caught her breath. "Glad you did."

"I miss you, you know."

She squirmed as she chewed her lip, struggling to be truthful. "I miss you, too."

"You sound distant."

"Well, I am three thousand miles away." She chuckled nervously.

"No, you sound," he hesitated, "tired. How far did you walk today?"

"Nearly fourteen miles." She yawned.

"That's what it is. You sound sleepy. Did I wake you?"

"No." Again, she yawned. "Sorry, I was just getting into bed."

"In that case, I'll talk with you tomorrow." His warmth came over the phone. "Sleep tight, my love."

His love. Am I? "Sleep tight."

She disconnected, turned off the light, and lay in the dark, fondling the ring at her neck. *Why did I take it off? Was it really to protect it or not to wear it? Or not to be seen wearing it?*

CHAPTER 6:

The Scallop Shell

"I was like a boy playing on the sea-shore, and diverting myself
now and then finding a smoother pebble or a prettier shell than ordinary,
whilst the great ocean of truth lay all undiscovered before me."
— Isaac Newton

They set out after breakfast, passing through one medieval village after another. At Gonzar, they heard Mass inside the Iglesia de Santa María church. Afterwards, as they continued their pilgrimage. Gwen looked back at the church. Its tall steeple seemed to rise through overhead wires. *Like a mountain rising through a jungle of electric vines.* Near Castromaior, they hiked past a Celtic fort.

When the sun was high overhead, Jaime stopped in front of a small church.

"We're about halfway to Palas de Rei, our stopping point this evening. Ventas de Narón is a good place for lunch. The last village in the Portomarín area, it's a medieval village where a brutal battle between Christians and Moors took place in eight twenty A.D."

"What's that building?" asked one of the pilgrims, pointing to a small stone chapel.

"That's the Madalena Chapel. In ancient times, it was a pilgrims' hospital." Jaime pointed to its wooden door. "Notice the carved scallop shell. As you know by now, the vieira's the symbol of our pilgrimage."

Built of huge green, orange, yellow, and white boulders, the chapel's stones hardly looked natural, yet close inspection proved they were. Gwen ran her hand

56

over their rough-hewn edges, connecting with history. She splayed her fingers, touching the ridges of the carved, wooden shell.

After a quick lunch of fried eel, a local delicacy, Gwen stole a few minutes to explore the town. A wooden door painted Mediterranean-blue caught her attention. The door opened into a quaint shop catering to pilgrims. Inside, she saw displays of walking sticks, necklaces of scallop shells bearing the pilgrim's cross, and gourds bearing the same shell insignia. She fingered a smooth gourd, a rope tied around its middle for easy transport.

"Ancient pilgrims carried water or wine in these," said the shopkeeper in perfect English. "Now, they're souvenirs, symbols."

Symbols. Nodding, she looked at scarves imprinted with the modern shell motif. As she felt the material's silky softness, the shopkeeper said, "The yellow scallop on blue represents the colors of the European Union."

Thanking him, she inspected the scallop-shell necklaces imprinted with the pilgrim's cross. She fingered a shell, noting the two holes drilled through it for the thin leather thong.

"That cross shows a sword with three lilies in the arms and grip. Some say it originated during the crusades, when knights wore small crosses with pointed bottoms."

"Why?"

"So they could nail them into the floor for their prayers."

"Like portable chapels," she said, fingering the cross's sword motif.

He nodded. "The sword's a symbol of St. James."

"I'll take one of these." Handing him a few euros, she picked out a necklace and placed it over her jacket.

She no sooner put it around her neck than she felt a tingling sensation. In a flash of memory, she recalled the first time she had seen a scallop shell, when her parents had taken her to the Jersey shore. As they beachcombed that Saturday, she had discovered it partially buried in the sand. When they got home, her father had drilled two holes in it and used twine for its chain. *I wore that for weeks. Wonder whatever happened to it?*

"You outgrew it, along with your other toys."

At the sound of the disembodied voice, Gwen's jaw went slack. Half expecting to see her father materialize, she looked around, peering up one aisle and down the next. Then she glimpsed the back of a man turning the corner into the last aisle and followed him. When he turned around, she saw it was only another pilgrim from their group.

She felt strangely let down. Though her father's ghost had annoyed her the previous time, she found herself disappointed that he had not shown himself. She laughed at herself as she left the store. *I must be losing my mind. This is just proof.*

Jaime was gathering their group outside the restaurant. "This afternoon, we cross the Ligonde Mountain range that separates the Miño and Ulla rivers. We'll climb Mount San Antonio as we walk through meadows and pine trees."

Gwen groaned inwardly. *And we're only halfway to Palas de Rei. Hope I can do this.*

"You can."

That was unmistakable. I didn't imagine hearing that. Opening her eyes wide, Gwen searched the area. There stood her father at the edge of the group, smiling.

Her hand immediately felt for her pilgrim's shell. Clasping it, she realized it hung over her heart. She looked again at where her father was standing, but he was gone.

On her evening call to Art, Gwen shyly confided the feeling that she had seen her father.

"We've all experienced, that," he said. "Been in a strange place and thought we've seen a familiar face. It's understandable that he's on your mind. You've got nothing but time to think." He paused. "Plus, I'm hoping you're lonely and counting the nights until we meet in Compostela. I miss you. I love you, you know."

She inhaled sharply. Hearing Art's voice, his warmth coming through the miles, made any doubt about him disappear. "And I love you," she said, meaning it. Her hand went to his ring on her chain. After they hung up, she took the ring from her necklace and replaced it on her left hand.

The next day they crossed through a eucalyptus forest on their way to Arzúa. Gwen inhaled deeply. The scent reminded her of when she had had a cold as a little girl, and her father had rubbed Vicks VapoRub on her. She smiled, remembering how much better it had made her feel, and touched the pilgrim's shell on her chest.

That night after dinner, after her call to Art, the four of them gathered in front of the hotel's fireplace for a bedtime snack.

"This is a special cheese," said Ruth, "made only in this area." After pulling apart a loaf of local bread, she handed Gwen a knife. "Try some."

Gwen spread the creamy cheese on the bread and bit into it. "Delicious."

"Here, wash it down with some wine," said Crow, filling her glass.

"Cheers." They toasted and sat back, lolling in the warmth of the fire. "Only two days to Santiago de Compostela," said Gwen.

"Somehow, it seems we've always been on this pilgrimage," said Percy. "That it'll continue, even after Compostela."

Gwen nodded. "I know what you mean. It seems like we've been together months, not days."

They laughed. "Thanks a lot," said Ruth, raising her eyebrows, feigning an offended expression.

"No, I didn't mean it that way." Gwen felt the heat rise in her cheeks. "I simply meant it feels like we're mishpocha, a kind of extended family."

Repeating the word "mishpocha," Ruth chuckled. "Love your Yiddishisms."

"We're together sixteen hours a day," said Gwen. "We eat all our meals together. It's as if—"

"We've bonded," said Percy, sitting beside her on the sofa. "I feel the same way."

"I'll drink to that," said Crow, raising his glass.

"To pilgrimages and bonding," said Ruth, clinking her glass against theirs. Then she stood up and stretched. "Well, that's it for me tonight. Today's hike wore me out."

"How far did we walk today?" Not feeling sleepy, Gwen wanted to keep the conversation going.

"Nearly eighteen miles," said Crow. He set down his glass and stood up. "But I think my age is catching up with me. I'm going to turn in early."

"Not you, too?" said Gwen.

"Our little family's breaking up." Percy's eyes went from one face to the next. "Don't you want one more glass of wine?" He held up the bottle. "See, it's half full."

"You mean half empty, you optimist." Crow grinned at him but shook his head. "Nope, that's it for me tonight. See you in the morning."

As he and Ruth left, Percy looked at Gwen beside him. "What about you? Are you up to another glass of wine?"

"Surprisingly, I am. I've been exhausted the other nights, but for some reason I'm wide awake tonight." She shrugged. "Maybe my body's getting used to this march."

"Could be." Percy chuckled as he refilled their glasses. "They say you can get used to anything."

"I like what you said earlier about the pilgrimage continuing, even after Compostela." She looked at him. "It does feel like we've started a journey that'll go on long past this week."

"They say a pilgrimage is the beginning of a never-ending quest."

"*They*, again." She chuckled as she sipped her wine.

"To continue to grow, we need to find new challenges. We have to try new things that scare us, things we never thought we were capable of starting, let alone completing." Resting his elbow on the back of the sofa behind her, Percy turned to her. "That's what we've begun on this pilgrimage."

She looked into his violet-blue eyes behind his glasses. Sparkling in the firelight, his eyes seemed to glisten. As the pause lengthened, she caught herself, quickly adding, "Yes, I agree."

"So what are your plans after Compostela?" He rested his head on his hand, his elbow still crooked on the sofa. Then his eyes glanced down at her engagement ring and returned to look into her eyes.

"Probably, I'll fly to Paris." She moved her hand so she hid the ring. *Why'd I do that?* She deliberately moved it back where it had been.

His eyebrow cocked, Percy raised his head from his hand. "I thought you were going to Barcelona?"

"My plans have changed." Gwen was purposely vague.

"That's too bad."

"Why?"

He shrugged. "I was hoping to get to know you better in Barcelona." When she stiffened, he added, "I live in Barcelona and wanted to show you around town."

She swallowed. "I've decided to go to Paris."

"Things can always change." Again, he glanced at her ring. "Let me know if anything does," his eyes pierced hers, "change."

She cleared her throat and sat up straight. "I think it's time for me to—"

"Oh, don't go." Chastened, he sat back, out of her space. "Please."

She hesitated, poised between standing up and leaning back. "Why?"

"Actually, I have a favor to ask you."

Still poised between staying and leaving, she asked, "What?"

From beside him, he pulled out a notebook. "I was wondering if you could proofread my notes about the Holy Grail." He opened his eyes wide.

Mesmerized, Gwen stared into them. Then she roused herself.

"Oh, that's right, Bookworm." Grinning, she teased him. "You're writing fairy tales about the Holy Grail, aren't you?"

"That's *folk tales*," he said, pretending to be annoyed, "and I'm trying to publish a hypothesis."

She leaned back. "All right, Mister English Literature professor, let me see it."

"That's Doctor English Literature professor, if you please." He grinned.

She held out her hand as he passed her his notes. Rather than give him her thoughts at the end of the reading, she discussed each page with him as she went along. One page became another, leading into the next chapter.

Before she knew it, light was coming through the window. She blinked, looking about her, trying to get her bearings. The fire had died to ashes, and she realized she had fallen asleep on the sofa. When she saw Percy's head only inches from her own, she jumped to her feet. His notebook clattered to the floor, waking him.

"What—?"

"We fell asleep editing your notes," she said uncomfortably.

He leaned back, groaning. "Sorry."

She sighed. "No harm done, I guess." She looked around, hoping no one was up yet. "But you gotta admit, this does look a bit suspicious."

"Yeah, it does." He glanced at her sheepishly. "Really sorry."

Grimacing, she shrugged. "See you at breakfast." With a wave, she was gone.

She felt guilty, unfaithful, dirty. *But I didn't do anything.* After her shower, she called Art. No answer. Then she remembered the time difference.

When his voice mail picked up, she said, "Wanted my voice to be the first thing you hear when you wake up. Love you."

At breakfast, Gwen never so much as glanced at Percy. When Jaime gathered them for the day's itinerary, she stood with Ruth.

"Today's the last big push," he said, wearing a grin, "nearly eighteen miles."

Ruth groaned. "Why so far?"

"Lavacolla will put us only six miles from Santiago. We'll arrive before noon tomorrow, in time for the Pilgrims' Mass in the cathedral. Buen Camino!"

Gwen's stomach turned a somersault. "Tomorrow's the end of the pilgrimage."

And I'm no closer to finding answers than when I started. She glanced at Percy. *If anything, I'm further from them.*

"Duh." Ruth smiled at her.

"Like we said last night, we know the pilgrimage is coming to an end, but," Gwen sighed, "it's almost here."

"Remember, we still have eighteen miles to cover today and another six tomorrow." Ruth grinned. "Don't count your chickens—"

"Before they're hatched." Gwen and Crow completed Ruth's adage for her.

"You never know what's around the next bend." Percy's eyes found Gwen's as he joined their group.

She turned away and hurried to catch up with Jaime.

The paved lane became a beaten path and then dropped sharply to the bottom of a valley, where a rickety bridge crossed a stream. Gwen tiptoed across the wooden slats, concerned they would give way. Cautious, but anxious to reach the other side, everyone crossed it as quickly as possible. Everyone, that is, but Crow. The longer he hesitated, the more agitated he became.

"Crow, come on." Gwen tried coaxing him from the other side. Taking her eyes off him for a moment as she looked at the rest of the group, she heard a splash. "Guys, Crow fell in!"

Percy and Ruth ran back, and the three of them pulled him out of the shallow water. As he sat on a boulder, his eyes looked dazed, unfocused.

"Are you all right?" Gwen leaned toward him.

Suddenly, he started thrashing about and screaming at Gwen. "Get away! Get out of here, man!"

Percy moved in, pinning his arms to his side. "Hey, hey, Crow, snap out of it."

Gradually, Crow stopped wriggling, and his eyes began to focus. He looked up at Percy first. Then his eyes swept to the pilgrim shell on Gwen's chest, and he took a deep breath. He ran his hand over his face.

"Sorry, man." Taking off his bandanna, he wiped the sweat from his forehead. "I thought you were Vietcong."

Gwen looked from him to the others, not sure what to think.

"I get flashbacks." He shook his head, as if to clear it. "Nam, too much acid." Taking another deep breath, Crow nodded. Then he motioned toward the pointed-cross motif on Gwen's shell. "That looked like a knife. I thought you were VC coming to kill me."

Gwen noticed the bridge had not given way. "Then what made you fall in the water?"

"Snakes."

"Snakes?" Again, she looked from him to the others, not sure what to think.

"During the war, I was in Delta Company, First Battalion, Fiftieth Infantry, One Hundred-seventy-third Airborne Brigade in Phan Thiêt, Bình Thuân Province, South Vietnam."

"That's a mouthful," Percy said.

"Snake capital of the world, it's got Asian cobras, king cobras, coral snakes, kraits, and pit vipers. It's got 'em all." He shuddered. "We were stationed on the marshy area along the coast. I never saw so many snakes in my life. Nam's got a hundred and forty different snake species, and I swear, all of 'em crawled into our camp. Whenever I get a flashback, I see snakes."

"Wow. How often does that happen?" Gwen felt uncomfortable.

"Once every few months or so." He shrugged.

"So you've had your quota for the season." Gwen smiled, trying to cover her uneasiness.

"Maybe, maybe not." He shrugged again. "They sometimes come in twos. Oh, I should warn you."

She took an involuntary step back. "Yes?"

"Following flashbacks, I generally have insights."

"What kind of insights?"

"I don't know. It's like I suddenly get a pair of glasses that lets me see clearly, really clearly. Just for a second, I can see into the future." He wrapped his kerchief around his bushy, straw-colored hair.

"Are you okay now?" Percy helped him up from his perch.

"Yeah, man, I'm fine." But as Crow connected with Percy's arm, his eyelids began fluttering. Then his eyes rolled back in his head. "That book you're writing about the Holy Grail."

Percy exchanged a look with Gwen.

Shrugging, she shook her head. "I never mentioned it."

"What about it?" asked Percy.

"You're going to meet King Arthur." Crow's voice sounded slurred, sleepy.

As Crow got to his feet, Percy let go his arm. "Why would you say such a thing?"

"Say what?"

Crow's eyes appeared focused, but his memory seemed to have skipped a moment. Ruth, Percy, and Gwen exchanged looks. Groaning, grimacing, they turned to catch up with the group.

Crow tagged after them. "Say *what?*"

They followed the path through a wooded glen, emerging at a large round-about. A stone monument stood there, as large as her chest, and had been carved into a shell. Gwen placed her hand on the stone, stroking its cold ridges, as birds flitted about, calling out their welcome from the trees.

"Here it is, my friends," said Jaime, pointing to the signpost. "You've reached the outskirts of Santiago."

"But we must be," Ruth paused, as if calculating, "ten miles away."

A mechanical roar drowned out her voice and the chirping birds. Gwen looked up to see a plane take off.

Jaime wore a half smile. "Yes, my friends, civilization's just over that knoll. Though we've been hiking through the country, Santiago's airport is only steps away."

They climbed the hill to discover the trail followed along the airport's runway, with only a chain-link fence separating them. Gwen ran her fingers over the dozens of stick crosses that had been embedded, woven between the metal links.

"Even here, pilgrims have left their mark." Jaime motioned their group to follow him along a descending path. As they approached a stream, he gathered them together. "This river may be the most historically significant spot in Lava-colla." He grinned. "The town was named for it."

"Lavacolla," said Ruth. "What's it mean?"

Jaime looked at the ladies and hesitated. "For lack of a better definition, it means to wash the . . . uhm," he squirmed, "southernmost, private parts." Turning his attention to the group, he added, "Traditionally, this was the final stop before the Cathedral of Santiago de Compostela. Everyone washed in this stream before presenting themselves at the cathedral."

Gwen looked at the fast-moving water sparkling in the sun. Then she checked her water bottle. *Empty.* She looked back at the stream, listening to it splash against the rocks. "I'm so thirsty. Wish this water was potable."

Ruth glanced at the stream. "I'm thirsty, too, but for . . ."

"For what?"

She sighed. "Thirst's a symptom of a need, a physical need." Ruth paused, seeming to gather her thoughts. "It's our bodies' way of telling us to take action. Ignore the message, and we die. Well, spiritual thirst's also a symptom. Psalm forty-two: 'As a deer longs for flowing streams, so my soul longs for you, O God.'"

She turned her gaze back to Gwen. "This is the last night of our pilgrimage." Her eyes tearing up, she blinked. "I thought by now I'd have gained some insight, gotten some understanding." Half laughing, half crying, Ruth sniffed. "All I've got to show is blisters."

Gwen returned her wry smile. "I'm sure something's moved you these past days—one of the cathedrals, something you've seen in nature." She tried to comfort Ruth but did not know where to start.

Ruth turned sad eyes toward her. "I need God. It's that simple and that," she gestured futilely, "incalculably difficult. I feel my soul's so dried up spiritually, the wind could blow it away."

"What normally quenches that thirst? Going to church, praying, reading the *Bible*?" Gwen made a sour face. "Not that I know personally, but wouldn't any of those things bring you closer to God?"

"Hour-long church services on Sundays, rote prayers, and Biblical quotes only give me small 'sips.'" Ruth shook her head. "I need long draughts of spiritual water. I need an everlasting drink to quench my thirst for God, and I can't seem to find it. Not even here."

Her shoulders sagging, Gwen grimaced. "I'm *so* the last person to ask about these things. I've been away from God for years." She thought of the blessings that had happened along the pilgrimage. "But maybe it's not one long draught but a constant supply of spiritual sips—a combination of many quick prayers, Masses, kind gestures, and actions—that eventually quenches your thirst."

Ruth swiped at the tear that escaped. "Maybe. I'll keep looking." She smiled through wet lashes. "But it's good advice in the meantime."

CHAPTER 7:

Daddy's Girl

"It is much easier to become a father than to be one."
— Kent Nerburn

Gwen found her hotel room disappointing. All glass and shiny surfaces, it reminded her of airports. She thought of the homey rooms she'd had the other nights of the pilgrimage, and reality set in. This was the last night of the journey, the end of the time she had set aside to sort out her thoughts. Tomorrow, Art would meet her. *What am I going to tell him? How do I feel about him, about us?* She groaned inwardly. *I haven't even come to grips with my father.*

She felt rushed, not refreshed, after the pilgrimage. She speed-dialed his cell, and he picked up on the third ring.

"Gwen, am I glad you got through." His warmth came over the phone lines.

Hearing his voice immediately lifted her spirits. "Me, too."

"Your timing's perfect. Our plane's just boarding."

Time. It was closing in. *Tomorrow will be here sooner than I'd like.* "Glad I caught you before your flight left."

"Me, too. They're announcing my section. Got to run, but I'll call you when we land. Love you, Gwen."

"Love you back."

She smiled to herself as she hung up, basking in his love. Talking with Art always made her feel safe. Like clothes just out of the dryer, he made her feel warm and dry. Cozy.

She checked the time and rushed downstairs to the lobby. Slippery marble underfoot, smoked glass and polished aluminum gleamed from every wall.

"There you are." Percy's face lit up when he spotted her. "The restaurant here's geared more toward airline passengers than pilgrims."

"Bad scene, man." Crow shook his head.

"What do you mean?" Gwen looked from one face to the other.

"All hustle and bustle on reflective surfaces," said Ruth, nodding toward the restaurant. "We can't hear each other over the din."

"Then let's find somewhere we can schmooze." Gwen glanced again at their faces, suddenly realizing she would miss their meals together.

Located closer to the airport than town, nothing interesting was within walking distance from their hotel. Instead, they grabbed a cab.

"Old town," Percy told the driver.

The driver looked at him for confirmation. "You mean la zona vieja?"

Percy nodded. "Si."

Within minutes, they were in the historical part of Santiago de Compostela.

"This is more like it." Gwen looked around the narrow alleys lined with cafés, bistros, and coffeehouses. "It reminds me of Barcelona."

One café in particular caught their attention, with its woodwork over plaster and low, arched ceilings. They seated themselves at a round booth with a stone-topped barrel for a table.

Percy grinned. "I dub this the night of the round table."

They were still chuckling when the waiter appeared.

"What was this place before it was a café?" asked Gwen.

"It was the stable of a local palace." The waiter pointed to the arched ceilings, separated by narrow columns. "Each arch covered a stall."

"Now each arch holds a table." Gwen tried to imagine how it had looked with horses.

The waiter handed them menus. "What'll you have?"

"We've got to try vieira while we're here," said Ruth, pointing to Gwen's scallop shell.

Gwen nodded, checking the menu. "Let's nosh, taste a little of everything, get tapas, and share."

They ordered a pitcher of sangría and a sampler of scallops, octopus, crab, and deep-fried squid.

"Does it seem possible this is the last dinner we'll share together?"

"The last supper." Ruth sighed mirthlessly.

"Too bad the party has to end, man." His straw hair bushing out from his red kerchief, Crow shook his head.

"Why have it end?" Percy looked from face to face, lingering on Gwen's.

"What do you mean?" Gwen caught his eye.

"Why don't we rent a car and all drive back together?"

"Right on, man."

"That's a great idea." Ruth raised her glass. "To Barcelona."

Everyone raised their glass but Gwen.

Ruth's smile drooped. "You're not toasting? We're all going to Montserrat."

Gwen shook her head. "Not me."

"But you're going back to Barcelona, aren't you?" asked Ruth.

Gwen wanted to join them, or at least pretend to go along with the idea, not spoil their fun. "I told you my plans had changed." As she fingered the ring on her left hand, guilt consumed her. *I prefer their company to Art's.* Then she caught her breath, trying to rationalize. *I was just swept up in the moment. That's all.*

"Your plans changed once." Percy's gaze was steady from behind his thick lenses. "Maybe they can change again."

Before she could answer, the waiter arrived with a sizzling platter of seafood and a crusty loaf of bread.

Crow ordered another pitcher of sangría as he asked, "What was your favorite spot on the Camino?"

Ruth pulled her guide book from her pocket and pointed to a picture. "The Basilica de San Isidoro in León."

"Why?"

"It was something Gwen said about Gothic architecture raising our spirits. *Understanding*, the second gift of the Holy Spirit, helps us see ourselves in the bigger picture."

"Gives us another perspective." Adjusting his glasses, Percy gave them a wry smile. "You could say that about the whole pilgrimage. It makes us view life differently." He turned toward Gwen. "What was your favorite place?"

Gwen scanned her memories. "León." *Where I first saw my father.* "It's where we started our Camino and where I began photographing the chalice series."

"That's right," said Percy. "Glad you mentioned that. Would you mind if I use one of your photos for the cover of my book?"

She shrugged. "I guess that's okay."

"With all your editing, I wondered if you'd be interested in collaborating with me on this book."

"Possibly."

Percy pulled a business card from his wallet and handed it to her. "Here's my contact info."

She read it aloud. "Perceval Lancelot Gowan, Ph.D." Grinning, she turned toward him. "Could your name have anything to do with you becoming an English Literature professor?"

Percy chuckled.

"Those names sound familiar," said Crow. "Where do I know them from?"

"They're three of King Arthur's Knights of the Round Table," said Percy. "Perceval, Lancelot, and Gawan."

Gwen glanced again at the card. "It's spelled Gowan, not Gawan."

"According to family history, Gowan, which means blacksmith, is a variation of Gawan and Gawain."

"With a name like that, no wonder you're fascinated by the Holy Grail." She silently read the rest of his contact information and then looked up. "I didn't know you lived in Barcelona. I thought you were from New York. We came over on the same flight."

"I was returning from a visit."

"So you're not American?" Tilting her head to the side, Gwen studied his features.

"Nope." He shook his head.

"You're Spanish?"

Again, he shook his head. "Catalonian."

"But you don't have any accent." She grinned. "I'd never have guessed you weren't American."

"I spent a lot of my childhood in the States with my mother."

Crow scrutinized him. "You're Catalonian? Not Spanish?"

Shoulders back, Percy sat up straight, an unmistakable gleam of pride glinting from behind his glasses. "Born and, for the most part, raised there."

"How can you Catalans be such nationalists, man?" Crow set down his glass with a thud. His arms braced on the table, he leaned forward, poised to debate. "If Catalonia gains its independence, it opens a Pandora's box. Separatists in Scotland, Bavaria, Flanders, and who knows where else will scramble to secede."

"Catalonia's already recognized as a nationality." Percy spoke calmly, but his eyes narrowed. "We've had a statute of autonomy since 1979. Separating from Spain is simply the logical next step."

"What do you mean, 'separating from Spain'?" As Crow's left eye began to track independently, his right eye wandered. "You *are* Spain."

"If you mean financially, yes, we are." Percy's eyes flashed. "Catalonia supports Spain. Every year, Madrid forces us to pay seventeen billion euros in taxes. Those demands have pushed us into debt to provide even basic services."

Crow downed his glass of sangría. His voice becoming high-pitched and whining, he said, "It's a partnership, man."

"A lopsided partnership. It's taxation without representation. Catalans want a change. Fifty-seven percent of us want independence."

"That's separatism, man, and it's—"

Watching Crow's eyes and listening to the growing agitation in his voice, Gwen held up her hand. "Guys, how 'bout an amicable agreement to disagree?"

"We're not arguing." Percy shrugged. "We're dialoging."

"Just having a friendly discussion." Crow grinned as his eyes synched again, locking onto Percy's. "Ain't that right man?"

In answer, Percy clinked his glass against Crow's.

Rolling her eyes, Gwen muttered, "Fine." Moving her glass where Crow was seated, she said, "Then you sit next to Percy so Ruth and I can talk."

"Yeah, man, sure. But first, let me order another pitcher of sangría."

As the political discussion resumed, Gwen turned to Ruth. "Never got into politics much. Did you?"

Ruth made a sour face. "Not really."

Gwen poured the last of the sangría into Ruth's glass as the waiter brought a fresh pitcher. "This may not quench your spiritual thirst, but it'll wet your whistle."

"How about you?" Ruth studied her face. "Have you found what you were searching for on this pilgrimage?"

Gwen took a long breath, asking herself the same question. "Don't know. I've had . . ." She paused, shy about confiding that she saw. *What? Ghosts?* She took another deep breath. Lifting up her glass, she said, "Before I tell you this, I want you to know I'm not drunk."

Ruth laughed, clinking her glass against Gwen's. "I'll drink to that."

Chuckling nervously, Gwen sipped and then started again. "At least three times this past week . . . I've seen what appears to be my father's ghost." She peered into Ruth's face, waiting for any hint of sarcasm or scorn.

Ruth shrugged. "So?"

With a silent sigh of relief, Gwen continued. "I saw him the first time at the Basilica de San Isidoro, the second time when Crow rolled a cigarette, and the last time in the gift shop, where I bought this." She fingered the pilgrim's shell around her neck.

"The day I met you, you mentioned having trouble dealing with, as you put it, the whole father/Father metaphor."

"That's true."

"When Crow compared you to Dorothy in *The Wizard of Oz* and asked you where home was, you said you didn't have any place to call 'home,' and I called you an orphan spirit."

Gwen nodded. "I remember."

"And at the bridge you admitted you'd been a 'daddy's girl,' born on Father's Day, but that you'd become estranged from both your fathers." Ruth peered into her face. "Maybe this is your way of making peace with both."

Gwen squinted, trying to understand. "What do you mean, making peace?"

"I'm no psychologist, but it certainly seems you've got daddy issues. Maybe this is your psyche's way of role-playing. Your brain fools your eyes into thinking you're seeing your father's ghost, but actually it's your subconscious working out your issues."

Gwen thought for a moment. "So you think it's just a manifestation of my thoughts, not a ghost?"

Ruth shrugged. "Something like that."

"You don't think I'm losing my mind?"

Ruth laughed out loud, turning Crow's and Percy's heads. "No, like I said before, I think you're an orphan spirit."

"What is that?" Gwen asked.

Pursing her lips, Ruth thought for a moment. "A spiritual orphan's someone who feels alone. They don't feel they have a secure place in their Father's heart, where He can express His love. They're anxious, insecure. They feel on the outside, looking in, that they don't belong."

"So far, that pretty much describes me." Gwen sipped her sangría, thinking. "But why? I've asked myself that a thousand times."

"There can be many reasons." Ruth's forehead crinkled. "Spiritual orphans often can't accept their heavenly Father's love because their earthly fathers have hurt or rejected them. They can't bring themselves to trust God because the ability to trust involves vulnerability."

Gwen sniffed. "That's me, always proving I can do it without anyone's help." She instantly thought of her career. *I made it to where I am without anybody's help—not a father's, not a husband's.* She gasped. *Just listen to me.* Shaking her head, she cringed.

"Trust includes receiving. Spiritual orphans can't trust, so they can't receive until their core of pain's healed. Basic trust is a real issue for spiritual orphans."

Gwen snickered. "Tell me about it."

"Trust implies opening up to others, but spiritual orphans can't do that. They're so afraid of being hurt, their spirits shut down. They won't let themselves be vulnerable."

Arms crossed, Gwen thought of the relationships she had missed, the dates she had turned down, over the years. *I was always afraid to let anyone get close. Saying no before getting started was easier than taking a chance. Safer.* She glanced at Percy, deep in conversation with Crow. Then she looked at Ruth.

"Yeah, I've always closed myself off to relationships with men. Never let myself get involved."

Ruth pointed to her engagement ring. "Then what do you call that?"

"I don't know." Gwen squirmed, unable to explain it to herself, let alone to Ruth. "Art just makes me feel safe, secure. He's the only man other than . . ." She caught herself before she said it.

Ruth gave her a sly grin. "Other than who?"

She laughed. "Other than my father."

"Back to your father, again." Ruth raised an eyebrow, as if to say *See?*

"What are you, a psychoanalyst or something?"

Shaking her head, Ruth smiled. "Nope, but I've been a social worker for years. I've seen this kind of behavior in dozens of women."

Gwen raised her eyebrow. "Only women? Not men, too?"

"Mostly women, at least in my experience. Spiritual orphans shut themselves off from any relationship, even one with their heavenly Father."

"Why?"

"Because they don't trust God any more than they trust their earthly fathers. I've read a lot of books on the subject. Because they lack trust, spiritual orphans struggle with control issues, independence, and pride. They're incapable of intimate relationships because they simply can't accept love."

Ouch. Gwen grimaced.

"Spiritual orphans think they'll never measure up to God's standard because they can't do enough to earn His love. They're still trying to earn Daddy's approval. They're God's servants, not daughters. Servants perform tasks, but daughters accept their Father's love."

Gwen sighed. "How do I do that? Accept God's love?"

"Let the Holy Spirit heal your heart. Ask God to heal you, lead you to a deeper relationship with Him."

"But how?"

"Through prayer . . . for yourself and your father." Ruth smiled gently. "From what you've told me, your father needs healing just as much as you."

Scowling, Gwen said, "He's dead."

"Just because he's dead doesn't mean his soul's at rest."

Gwen started to respond, but Percy interrupted. "What are you two whispering about?"

She interpreted his remark as a thrown gauntlet. Raising her eyebrow, she accepted his challenge.

"What? You think you're the only ones who can discuss conversational taboos? Since you two monopolized politics, we chose religion."

Crow hooted. "Guess she told you, man. Got anything to say for yourself?"

Percy grinned sheepishly. "Not if I'm interested in Gwen collaborating with me on my book."

Ruth again raised her eyebrow, as if to say *See?*

Gwen groaned inwardly. *When will I learn?*

"Just kidding." She forced a begrudging half smile. "You serious about collaborating?"

"Absolutely. I wouldn't have asked otherwise."

She searched his face for sarcasm, but his eyes were earnest, sincere. She gave a silent sigh.

"Sure, I'd be happy to finish editing your manuscript, if that's what you mean by collaborating."

"Great! Well, editing *and* incorporating your chalice pictures." He reached for his backpack hanging on his chair. "As a matter of fact, I just happen to have my notes with me."

"Okay, folks, this is where I bow out." Crow pushed his chair back from the table and stretched. "My eyes are too tired to read print."

"Just a second." Ruth pulled on her jacket. "I'll share a cab back with you."

Gwen turned in her chair. "You're both leaving?"

Ruth leaned over, so only Gwen could hear. "Two's company."

Feeling the heat rise in her cheeks, Gwen was glad for the dim lights. "Actually, this light's not the best for editing." She turned toward Percy. "Let's go back with them. The light in the hotel lobby's got to be better than this."

Ten minutes later, she and Percy found a quiet spot on the hotel's second floor. Practically deserted, the area boasted a reading table with a desk lamp.

"Perfect," Gwen said.

Their heads close as they edited the manuscript, Gwen could not help observing details about Percy she had not previously noticed. As he moved, he gave off the subtle scent of lime. She inhaled deeply each time he turned his head. His narrow sideburns tapered to blunt tips that met his five o'clock shadow. On second glance, she saw the day's growth had become a bristly stubble.

Wonder what that would feel like in a kiss?

"Anything wrong?" he asked.

"What?" Sitting up straight, it occurred to her that she had been staring at him. She cleared her throat. "No, why?"

"You were looking at me."

"No, I . . ." Searching for an excuse, her eyes rested on the manuscript. "I just wanted to ask you why you chose to use a semicolon here." Pointing with her red pen, she asked, "Shouldn't it be a colon?"

"Right you are." He chuckled. "That's why you're paid the big bucks."

She smiled, then yawned and stretched her back, rotating her neck.

"Shoulders stiff?"

"Oh, yeah."

"Turn around," he said, flexing his fingers. "If I do say so myself, I give great shoulder rubs."

"No, that's okay." She pursed her lips in a grimace. "I'm good."

His hand already on her shoulder blade, she felt his thumb dig into a sore spot. Immediately, the tension began slipping away. Sitting up straight, she pulled away, but his fingertips seemed to find one knot after another.

"No, I'm fine. It's—" A sigh escaped.

"Just relax. Let Doc Percy's fingers work their magic."

She felt an odd mixture of uneasiness and relaxation. Then her eyes rested on her ring, and she scrambled to her feet. Gesturing toward the manuscript with her red pen, she said, "Why don't you email me the rest?" She looked at her watch. "Speaking of rest, I need to turn in if we're having an early start in the morning." Without waiting for an answer, she turned away, calling over her shoulder, "Night."

Back in her room, she double-locked the door, leaned against it, and drew a deep breath. *What was I thinking?*

She looked at her ring, fingering it. *Tomorrow I'm meeting Art, going to Paris with him. Then what?* She tried to put it out of her mind. *Tomorrow will take care of itself.*

She showered and climbed into bed. Lying in the dark, she could not fall asleep. Her guilt-tinged thoughts kept cycling from Percy to Art to her father and back. She recalled another sleepless night when she had been eleven.

Her mother had taken her to the Metropolitan Museum of Art, where they had spent Saturday afternoon looking at the Egyptian collection. The mummies had captured her imagination, but it was the first time she had been confronted with mortality. And immortality. There lay the bodies of people dead for thousands of years.

Where were their souls?

Worried about her father's soul going to hell, she could not sleep that night, either, as she mentally listed his sins. He never went to church. He had never been confirmed or taken First Communion. She doubted he had been baptized. Finally, she had gotten out of bed. Choked up with tears, she could barely talk as she struggled to put her worries into words.

Her father had sat at the kitchen table, smoking, watching her from behind narrowed eyes. Though her father had been impassive at first, it had seemed the harder she tried to express her fears, the more annoyed he became.

Finally, he had rolled his eyes and then stubbed out his cigarette. "Get to the point."

Not knowing how else to phrase it, she had blurted out her thoughts. "I'm afraid you'll go to hell when you die." Then an idea had occurred to her. Sniffling, she had asked, "Do you at least believe in God?"

He had said he did, and she had gone back to bed. *But I didn't believe him then any more than I do now.*

The letter. Gwen turned on the light. *Maybe that's the clue.*

She jumped out of bed and rifled through her backpack, trying to find her father's tattered, yellow letter from the safe deposit box.

She carefully unfolded it, holding the two dog-eared halves together. Again, she studied the date. February twenty-eight, 1938.

Clark,
You can't understand now, but please try to forgive me someday.
Love,
Mother

My father had been eight years old, the same age I was when he emotionally abandoned me. She reread the letter. *What had his mother done to him?*

She fell into a deep sleep, dreaming of a little boy with light-brown hair and hazel eyes. Sniffling, shaking, his eyes brimming over with tears, he stood tall, trying not to cry.

"Be my brave little man." Tears in her eyes, a woman with a bobbed haircut, wearing a floral print dress, stooped down to hug him. Grasping him tightly with one hand, she swiped at the tears spilling down her cheeks with the other. "Your grandma needs you to look after her now." Then, clearing her voice, the woman let him go and rose to her feet. "Now that your mother has Bill to look after her, you'll be the man of *this* house." The woman looked to the older woman, tears falling. "Isn't that right, Mom?"

The older woman looked from the boy to the young woman. "You sure you're doing the right thing?"

"I've got no choice. Bill . . ." A sob escaped as she shoved an envelope into the older woman's hands. "Give him this after I go."

Again, the older woman looked from her to the boy and back again, her chest silently heaving.

"Please!" The younger woman broke into tears and ran out the door as the little boy cried after her.

"Mother! Mother!"

He tried to run after her, but his grandmother caught him by the shoulders.

"Clark, like your mother said, you've got to be strong. You're the man of the house now, and men don't cry."

The woman held him against her until she felt his tears subside. Then, still holding him by his shoulders, she knelt down until she was eye level with him.

"These are hard times, Clark. Your momma did what she had to. She's going to live with Bill now."

"But why can't I live with her and Bill?" His cheeks tear-stained, his eyes red, he studied his grandmother's face. "Why?"

She tried to answer, but tears choked her words. Instead, she handed him the letter and stood up. Clearing her throat, she said. "You go on to your room now. I'll call you when supper's ready."

"Yes, Ma'am." Clasping the letter to his chest, he turned and trudged toward the sewing nook that had been converted into his bedroom.

He sat on the bed, slowly opened the sealed envelope, and read it as tears rolled down his cheeks.

> Clark,
> You can't understand now, but please try to forgive me someday.
> Love,
> Mother

Gwen woke with a start. Still half asleep, an early memory slipped into her mind. She recalled overhearing her aunt Irene whispering to her mother how her grandmother had divorced her first husband on the grounds of physical abuse. Blinking, she remembered her father once mention that his grandmother had brought him up, not his mother. *Ohmigosh. Grandma deserted him when he was eight, so she could remarry.*

Suddenly, Gwen saw her father in a new light. No wonder he'd been distant after her eighth birthday. Abandoned at eight himself, he'd been emotionally stunted. With no father figure, he'd had no role model. He hadn't been taught how to be a father. His birth father had abused his mother and probably him. Then, to remarry, his mother had dumped him on his grandmother.

Poor kid, he'd been left to fend for himself. Who says the sins of the father aren't inherited? Because of my grandmother's decisions, my father was stunted. Because of my father's decisions, I . . . It all became clear. *Because of my father's decisions, I've been incapable of loving. I don't trust people. I don't believe in God. Dysfunction's been passed down like a family heirloom.*

As she drew a deep breath, she closed her eyes to better absorb the idea. *Choices we make affect not only us but future generations.*

I'm still trying to earn my father's approval. Maybe he's still trying to earn his heavenly Father's approval, so where does that leave him? Not heaven. Not hell. But where? Purgatory?

And what if Art and I have children? Would I be as emotionally distant from them as my father and grandmother were from their children? Maybe it didn't start with my grandmother. Who knows for how many generations this flawed father/daughter cycle's continued?

I have to break it. But how? Ruth's words came to mind.

"Pray for him. Your father needs healing as much as you."

CHAPTER 8:

King Arthur

"Deeds in themselves are meaningless
unless they are done for some higher purpose."
— David Franzoni

They left Lavacolla early the next morning. Unsure if she wanted to sleep an extra half hour or just wanted to avoid Percy, Gwen skipped breakfast, meeting the group as Jaime addressed them.

"Today's the final stage of the pilgrimage, but keep in mind, your inner journey's just begun."

Gwen caught her breath. *Hope so.*

"From here, we'll climb Monte de Gozo, Mount Joy. Traditionally, pilgrims race up the five-kilometer slope to catch their first glimpse of Compostela's spires." He grinned. "Anyone here named Leroy, Kroll, Koenig, Rex, Rey, or anything else meaning *King*?"

The group looked at each other, shaking their heads. No hands went up.

"No? In the past, when people made the pilgrimage there and back on foot, the first pilgrim to reach the top was proclaimed 'king.' The name stuck." He grinned. "You'll be glad to know, after Mount Joy, it's all downhill."

The group chuckled.

"Literally, it's an hour's descent into Santiago de Compostela, where we'll visit the Apostle James's tomb in the cathedral, get your certificates, and attend the Pilgrims' Mass. Buen Camino!"

And see Art. Gwen felt a combination of excitement and dread. *Why would I dread seeing my fiancé?* She sighed.

"What's the matter?" Ruth wore a lopsided grin. "Sorry the pilgrimage is ending, or sorry you're returning to reality?"

Gwen flinched. "Ouch, you nailed it."

"Which, ending or returning?"

"Returning." She held up her left hand, staring at her ring. "My fiancé's meeting me in Compostela this afternoon."

"What's wrong with that?"

"That's exactly what I was asking myself." She wrinkled her brow. "I should be happy. Ecstatic. Why am I so conflicted?"

"Could it be you're not sure you want to marry him?"

Gwen scratched her head. "He's the perfect man for me—intelligent, thoughtful, considerate. And he listens to me. Really listens!"

"You're trying hard to sell yourself on the idea, but I'm just not buying it."

Gwen frowned, trying to understand. "Why do you say that?"

"You never mentioned the word *love*." Ruth's lopsided grin deepened into a smirk. "Some people can't see past the tip of their nose."

"What do you mean?"

Ruth rolled her eyes and then gestured toward Percy with her chin.

"Percy?" Gwen glanced at him and quickly turned away. "You've got to be kidding."

"Me thinks the lady doth protest too much."

"No, no, no." Shaking her head, Gwen said, "We're just friends. That's all."

"Like I said, some people can't see the forest for the trees." Ruth smiled sympathetically, then she started after Jaime, calling over her shoulder, "Race you to the top of Mount Joy."

❄

The path became a paved walkway, surrounded by creeping suburbia. Trees gave way to apartment complexes, hotels, hostels, and campgrounds. When they reached the top, tall structures interfered with the view.

Gwen's disappointment only added to her growing agitation about seeing Art. Her day of reckoning was close at hand.

What do I do? Give him back his ring? Say I'm not ready. Say I don't know? She heaved a sigh. *I'm not ready. I don't know, but . . .* She scratched her ear. *I like him, admire him.* Then Ruth's words rang in her ears. *But love? Maybe I'm simply incapable of loving anyone.*

She looked at her hand, turning her fingers this way and that to see Art's ring better. *The easiest solution is to keep wearing this, follow the natural progression, and in a few months, marry him.* She sighed again, this time congratulating herself on finding the logical solution. *Who knows? Maybe, by that time, I will love him.*

"What are you sighing about?" asked Percy.

Caught off guard, she flinched. Then, looking for an excuse, she craned her neck, pretending to look for the cathedral's spires. "I can barely see Santiago de Compostela."

"Yeah, the treetops really obscure the view." He pushed his glasses up the bridge of his nose. "The gray day doesn't help, either."

She gazed overhead. Several cirrus clouds rolled by, but otherwise, the sky was blue.

"What do you mean?"

Grinning sheepishly, he shrugged as he glanced at Crow and Ruth. "This is the last day our little group will be together."

"I thought you were all driving to Barcelona tonight."

"That's tomorrow, and it's just the three of us, while you're flying off to Paris and marriage."

"Oh, yeah . . . well." She stepped away, starting down the hill. Percy's nearness made her uncomfortable. Hearing him talk about her marriage to Art was unnerving.

He caught up with her. "You left so quickly last night, you didn't give me your email address."

"Oh, that's right. Got a pen?"

He dug in his backpack, producing his notebook and handing her a red pen. "You should have red ink for all your editorial comments. Even your email."

Chuckling, she scribbled her address and handed him back his pen.

He covered her hand with his. "Keep it." His violet-blue eyes smiled behind his thick glasses. "I hope you make every day a red-letter day."

She opened her mouth to speak, but no words came out. Her jaw slack, she blinked, not sure what to say. Finally, she found her voice.

"Thanks." Pulling her hand from his, she held up the pen. "I'll try not to slash your manuscript with so much red ink it bleeds."

❄

An hour later, Jaime gathered their group in the huge square before the cathedral Santiago de Compostela. As they gazed upward at the massive structure of Galician granite, he said, "Congratulate yourselves. You've joined the ranks of millions of pilgrims who've made this spiritual journey for over a millennium. Now that you're here, here's what to do next."

He pointed to the Pilgrim's Office. "First get your Compostela certificate, proving you've followed the Camino de Santiago pilgrimage." Then, he pointed to the cathedral doors. "After climbing that stairway, you'll enter the carved Portico de la Gloria. Completed in 1188, it's considered a masterpiece of medieval art. You'll see the figure of St. James in its center column. Place your hand on the pillar, finding the grooves made by the many pilgrims who've come before you. Say a prayer of petition or thanksgiving. Then climb the stairs behind the altar and hug the gilded statue of St. James, wrapping your arms around him from behind."

Gwen chuckled at the idea of hugging a saint. "It seems so personal," she whispered to Ruth.

"Doesn't it, though?" Percy caught her eye.

Again, she flinched, thinking she had been standing beside Ruth. With a stiff smile, she turned back to listen to Jaime.

"We'll meet back here at noon for the Pilgrims' Mass. Buen Camino!"

Chuckling, the group answered in unison. "Buen Camino!"

After receiving her Compostela, Gwen took off by herself, wanting to get her thoughts straight before meeting Art. When she put her fingers in the grooves of St. James's pillar, she prayed for two requests.

Please let my father's soul be at rest. She recalled her dream of the abandoned little boy. She thought of him becoming a hen-pecked husband to Mildred, and she grieved for her father.

Please help me work out my issues with . . . She meant to name one person, but images of her father, Art, and Percy kept cycling through her mind. Then it occurred to her. *Early issues with my father made later relationships with men difficult. Please help me work out my issues with men.*

She peered down the long central aisle. The luminous Baroque altar, blazing with gold beckoned her with its portrayal of St. James as teacher, pilgrim, and knight.

In the muted sanctuary, she breathed in the air of holiness, inhaling the incense of centuries. The devotion was palpable. Listening to Gregorian chant in the background, she watched the pilgrims kneeling in prayer, their lips moving silently. She imagined she heard their hushed dreams, hopes, pleas, and prayers, all vying for God's attention. For Saint James's intervention.

Deep in thought, she stood in line, waiting her turn to hug St. James. When she put her arms around him, she felt a cool peace enter her heart. Then, deep in thought, she descended into the Roman mausoleum beneath the high altar to pay her respects to the Apostle's relics.

When she emerged, she felt invigorated, refreshed, filled with a sense of purpose. Though still unsure how she would resolve her relationship with Art, she now looked forward to meeting her future head-on. She turned on her cell phone and saw three messages from Art. Skipping the earlier ones, she opened the most recently time-stamped text.

Am across the street from the cathedral. Then it noted the address of a restaurant.

BRT, she texted.

Moments later, she entered the café, her eyes drawn to the black-and-white, marble-tiled floor. It seemed so clinical, reminding her of an old-fashioned pharmacy. Then her eyes searched the linen covered tables for Art. There he was, rising to his feet. Eyes locked on hers, he rushed toward her, enveloping her in his arms.

She breathed in his scent with a deep sigh of relief. He felt so good, like she was coming home. *How could I ever have doubted he's the one I love?* Meaning it, she hugged him back.

"It's good to see your smile," he said, giving her hand a parting squeeze as he led her to their table. "Good to see *you!*"

"Seems like a whole lot longer than ten days since I saw you."

"Tell me all about your adventures." He held her chair and then sat across from her, leaning toward her, as if hanging on her words.

He makes me feel so special. Basking in his undivided attention, Gwen studied his face. Light-brown eyes, thick eyebrows, cropped dark hair, pointed ears, he looked like he was always listening, watching, alert to her needs. She breathed in again, flattered and satisfied in her security.

She did not turn her head until she heard her name a second time. "Gwen!"

Startled, she spun around. There at the door stood Ruth and Crow, waving at her. A third person accompanied them, and she did a double take, not immediately recognizing Percy.

Instead of glasses, Percy was wearing contacts. His violet-blue eyes that had been minimized behind thick lenses now twinkled, mesmerizing her. She found it difficult to take her eyes off his. Then, remembering her manners, she waved, and they started toward the table.

Ohmigosh, do I really want Percy to join us?

Too late. Art rose to his feet, leaving her no choice but to introduce him to her friends.

"This is Ruth, Crow, and Percy." Barely whispering, she swallowed his name, consciously avoiding Percy's eyes as she focused on Art.

The group stood waiting until Art held out his hand, smiled graciously, and took matters into his own hands.

"Glad to meet you. I'm Gwen's fiancé, Art. Won't you sit down?"

Gwen felt the blood drain from her face. She took a cleansing breath, trying to ground herself.

This is ridiculous. Why do I feel so giddy? So guilty? It's not like I've done anything wrong.

"We don't want to intrude." Percy stepped away from the table, but too late. Crow had already sat down.

"Nonsense," said Art, pulling out a chair for Ruth. "Please join us."

Gwen had to admire his style. *Art's the perfect host.* She gave him an appreciative half smile, feeling sheepish after her earlier thoughts. Imitating his example, she began to relax.

"This is the motley crew I told you about in our phone calls. We've shared every meal, as well as sangría, stories, sore feet—"

"And blisters," interjected Crow.

"And blisters, since we left Léon," finished Gwen, chuckling.

"I'm going to miss our little group," said Ruth, looking from one face to the next. "You can close your eyes to reality, but not to memories."

"This pilgrimage isn't over yet," said Crow, rising to his feet. "In fact, this meeting calls for a toast." He waved over the waiter. "Hey, man, bring us a bottle of wine."

"Albariño?" asked the waiter.

"What else?"

Within moments, the waiter was back with the wine and five tiny ceramic bowls.

Picking up one of the cups, Gwen turned it in her hand. "These look like rice bowls."

"In Santiago, it's traditional to drink Albariño from these bowls." He surveyed them as he poured the wine. "Peregrinos?" All but Art nodded and responded with enthusiasm. He placed a bowl in front of each. "Enjoy! Buen Camino!"

In response, they all raised their white bowls and toasted his health. "Salud!"

"To our motley crew," said Gwen, raising her bowl, glad now the group had joined them. She tilted her head and grumbled. "I'm going to miss you guys." She raised her bowl. "Buen Camino!"

After toasting, Percy scrutinized her. "One journey's ending for you, but another's beginning. You're getting married and going . . . *creating* a home." Then he turned his eyes toward Art. "You're a lucky man."

"Thank you." Art beamed as he glanced sideways at her. Putting his arm around her shoulders, he hugged her. "I couldn't agree more."

Gwen smiled brightly but through clenched teeth, mentally shrinking from his touch. *At least in front of Percy.*

"To the happy couple," said Crow, raising his bowl.

The group toasted, and then Percy glanced at his watch. "The Pilgrims' Mass starts in fifteen minutes."

"We don't want to be late." Ruth finished her wine and started buttoning her jacket. "They read the names of the pilgrims who've received their Compostelas in the last twenty-four hours."

"That's us!" Gwen jumped to her feet.

"Hey, man, come on!" Crow downed his wine in a gulp, left money for the waiter, and jumped out of his seat. "Let's go."

The five of them squeezed into a pew, Art in the lead. Gwen followed him, then Percy, Ruth, and Crow. When Gwen heard her name read aloud, the finality of the journey sank in. Bowing her head, she said her final novena, following it with a silent prayer of thanks for having completed the pilgrimage.

Am I any closer to understanding what I needed to learn, what I need to do, than when I started? She glanced sideways at Art to her right. Glancing sideways at Percy to her left, she sighed. *If anything, this pilgrimage has only muddled the issues.* Shutting her eyes, she prayed silently. *Please help me, Lord. Please.*

Without warning, Gwen felt her worries slip from her shoulders like a heavy cape. Filled with a buoyant peacefulness, she knew God had heard her prayer and would answer it.

What's changed? She opened her eyes. What she saw was bowed heads, but she visualized the individual prayers ascending collectively. As she followed them with her mind's eye, she imagined them rising to the ornate ceiling and then above to heaven. *God's listening. That's what's changed.*

Convinced her prayers were being answered now, she felt inspired to pray for her father. It took several false starts, but she found it easier to pray when she pictured him as the lonely little boy, not the detached father.

Adding to her reverence was the congregation's hushed stillness. Suddenly, a Baroque organ reverberated throughout the sanctuary, its sound waves crashing over Gwen like breakers. Feeling the vibration more than hearing the music, she turned toward the collection of pipes. Half expecting her mind's eye to envision the tones, the only movements she saw were the pipes' vibrating flaps.

"The Apostle's Anthem," Percy whispered.

She nodded, silently acknowledging him in the awe of the moment. Then she felt Art's eyes on her. She turned toward him, her eyebrow arched in a question. *What?*

He shook off her query with a bland smile.

She leaned into his space. "That's the Apostle's Anthem playing," she whispered.

Art nodded, this time his smile warmer as he took her hand in his.

After Communion, several men lowered an immense censer from near the ceiling and filled it with charcoal and incense. Then, using ropes, they began swinging it side to side, farther and farther, way overhead, until it reached the lengths of the cathedral, from one end to the other.

"That's the Botafumeiro," Percy whispered.

Gazing overhead, Gwen's jaw was slack. Again, she nodded silently as her head followed the swinging incense burner, whipping past the priests and then back up into the air again. At the speed it was traveling, she was certain the censer would either crash into someone or fly off the end of the rope. It was awe inspiring.

Afterwards, they filed outside.

"I'm starving," said Crow.

"There wasn't time for more than a drink before Mass. Let's have a late lunch." Ruth glanced at them, chuckling. "Okay, last night didn't count. *This* is the last supper."

"The last hurrah," said Percy, his eyes on Gwen.

She met his eyes briefly. "Guys, I haven't had time to even ask Art when our plane leaves." Then she turned toward him. "What time's our flight to Paris?"

"Not until early tomorrow." Art focused a private smile on her. "We'll have plenty of time to . . . talk schedules later." Then he turned to the group. "How 'bout lunch?"

Gwen loved the way he lavished attention on her. Now that he was here, she wanted to spend time alone with him, but she was not ready to leave her friends just yet. She jumped on his offer.

"That's a great idea!"

They found a restaurant near the cathedral. From its second-floor dining room, it overlooked four streets.

"This is like being at an outdoor café, but better," said Ruth. "All the perks, but none of the discomfort."

Over an array of seafood tapas, crusty bread, and two bottles of Albariño, they shared their adventures with Art, mentioning every steep hill, every good bottle of wine, and every basilica, cathedral, chapel, church, and monastery.

Art's expression never changed, but his eyes tracked the conversation. Every time Gwen glanced at him, he was watching her. At first, she dismissed it. *Art's just being attentive.* Then she noticed he had become very quiet, barely joining the conversation. His eyes never seemed to move off her, except to glance occasionally at Percy.

When the topic of chalices came up, Percy half turned in his chair, tilting his head toward her. "I finally decided which photo I'd like for the cover."

She watched Art's expression flicker and then return to his bland smile.

"Which one?"

"The first one you took in the Basilica de San Isidoro."

"Oh, yeah, in León." She chuckled, recalling it. "That was the day we all met at Peregrino Paths." Then turning toward Percy, she corrected herself. "Actually, *we* met that morning on the train."

"No." Shaking his head, chuckling, Percy's violet-blue eyes glinted as he playfully challenged her. "Don't you remember? We ran into each other at the top of the Mirador de Colom the day before that."

"Oh, that's right. *No,* that's not where we *met.*" Giggling, she corrected him. "We met on the Barcelona shuttle bus from the airport. No, no, wait a minute!" Caught up in the moment, she rested her hand on Percy's shoulder. "It was the flight over from Manhattan. Believe it or not, we were seated in the same row."

Her giggles beginning to subside, she put hand on her chest and caught her breath. Blinking, thinking, her smile faded. "We've been together almost the entire time in Spain."

"Ten days," said Art, wearing a stiff smile. "But then, who's counting?"

Reacting, Percy's violet-blue eyes lost their twinkle as he dropped his smile.

"Gwen's been kind enough to begin collaborating with me on a book about the Holy Grail."

"Is that so?" Again, Art's expression flickered. A sneer momentarily curled his lip before he resumed his easy-going smile, but his eyes looked dark as coal.

Percy tried again. "It's just a coincidence that—"

"So," said Crow, jumping in. "How about that Catalonian vote for independence?"

Normally, Gwen would have rolled her eyes at the introduction of politics, but this time she breathed a sigh of relief when Crow changed the topic, and Percy grabbed the bait.

"Yeah, the rally's tomorrow night, and the vote's Sunday," said Percy. "This will make history."

"You seem pretty sure of history before it's happened." Art's eyes glittered like black ice. "Isn't it a bit premature to presume what will make headlines and what will be forgotten?"

"Catalans will never forget their basic need for independence." Percy's bright-blue eyes darkened, like a storm breaking at sea.

"You sound passionate, my friend." Art's mouth lifted in a half smile, but his eyes remained icy.

"I am. Catalonia deserves independence." Percy glanced at the group. "We've discussed this before."

Crow jumped in, wearing a devilish grin. "Catalonia's part of Spain, man."

"It's a Spanish autonomous community," said Percy. "There's a difference. Catalonia already has a high level of self-government."

"Breaking away could trigger a dangerous potential for conflict." A grim twist to his mouth, Art's expression became serious.

"The Second Spanish Republic granted Catalonia autonomy in 1932," said Percy. "It *is* autonomous."

"Don't forget what happened between 1936 and 1939." Art's words were somber.

Percy dismissed the idea with a wave of his hand. "The Spanish Civil War was unrelated."

At the word *war*, Crow turned toward him.

"Don't be so sure, my friend," Art said, his dark eyes watching him. "The war began after a group of generals made a declaration of opposition."

Again, at the word *war*, Crow turned, this time his eyes fixed on Art.

Gwen caught Art's eye. "Maybe this is a subject *Trails n' Treks* or one of your other publications should cover?"

Art nodded thoughtfully. "Maybe it is, at that."

His eyes blinking, Crow asked Art, "What was your last name again?"

"Pendred. Why?"

"Art . . ." Crow's eyelids began fluttering. "Could that be Arthur Pendred?"

Art nodded. "Again, why?"

His eyelids still fluttering, Crow turned toward Percy. "That book you're writing about the Holy Grail. Arthur Pendred . . . Arthur Pendragon."

Percy exchanged a look with Gwen.

"I told you you'd meet King Arthur." Crow's voice sounded slurred, sleepy.

Art's eyebrows gathering into a V, he turned to Gwen. "What's this character talking about?"

"Crow gets flashbacks." Wincing, she glanced at Percy before answering. "As well as what he calls 'insights.'"

His eyelids trembling, Crow pointed at Percy. "Perceval Lancelot Gowan, named for three of King Arthur's Knights of the Round Table: Perceval, Lancelot, and Gawan." Turning toward Gwen, he added, "You're Guinevere." Then turning toward Art, he said, "You're Arthur Pendragon, King Arthur. *Me?* I'm Merlin, the soothsayer." Again, he turned toward Art. "Be careful not to lose your Guinevere, Arthur." Crow then fell back in his chair, laughing, self-satisfied with a job well done, a message delivered. He lifted his wineglass and drained its contents.

"Okay, pal, time to check you into your room." Percy helped Crow to his feet.

Ruth shouldered him on the other side. "Let me help." She splayed her fingers in a wave. "Nice meeting you, Art. Gwen, hope to say goodbye before we take off in the morning."

Finding herself alone with Art, Gwen felt self-conscious. She glanced at him sideways. He was staring at her. Unable to meet his eyes, she looked down at the ring on her left hand. A sniffle passing for a laugh. She joked, "Thought they'd never leave."

He took a deep breath. "We need to talk."

She nodded.

"What was that all about?"

"That's just Crow being himself, an aging hippy with flashbacks and 'insights.'" She mimed making quotation marks with her fingers.

"That's not what I'm talking about." He paused until she looked up at him. "You know what I mean."

Biting her bottom lip, she shook her head. He kept staring until she answered. "Haven't a clue." Right hand behind her back, she crossed her fingers.

"How do you feel about us?"

Again, she looked at the ring. "We're engaged."

"That's an observation, not a feeling." He leaned into her, taking her hand in his, fingering her engagement ring. Then he looked into her eyes. "Do you love me?"

She took a deep breath and swallowed. "Sure."

His chuckle was mirthless. "You seem to lack . . . conviction." Letting go her hand, he sat back in his chair. "Maybe it's my fault. Maybe I rushed you into this. Maybe you need more time."

"Time for what?"

"To think us over."

"What do you mean?" She felt she was losing him. She sensed him drifting away, but she could not muster the energy to stop it. *Why do I feel so tired?*

"I saw the way you looked at Percy, the way he looked at you."

Her eyes narrowed as she searched his face for clues. "What are you talking about?"

"Can it be possible you're not aware?" He shook his head. "Your eyes light up when you're around him. Your whole face animates, comes to life, when you look at him." Staring into her eyes, he added, "I don't see that expression when you look at me."

She scoffed. "I hardly know him."

"What was that you said? You'd been together ten days in Spain."

"So?"

He took a deep breath. Then, in a patient tone of voice, he said, "Whether you know it or not, you're attracted to Percy."

"No." Frowning, she hunched her shoulders and spread out her hands. "We're just buddies, part of the foursome."

He raised his eyebrow. "Maybe, maybe not." Leaning back farther in his chair, he crossed his arms. "Tell you what. You decide. Think it over tonight. If you want to be with me, come to Paris with me tomorrow. If you don't . . ." He paused, seeming to choose his words. "If you still need more time to decide, go to Barcelona with your foursome. You can cover the independence rally and vote. Heck, stay until Christmas if you need more time to think it over. You're on the payroll."

Still unable to meet his eyes, she glanced at him and then down at her ring.

"That's awfully generous of you, Art." She chewed her lower lip. "I don't know what to say."

"I know." Grimacing, he pressed his lips together. "You're conflicted." His tone was sarcastic.

"No—"

"It's obvious. To me, at least." He took her hands in his and stared at her until she lifted her eyes to his. "I love you, Gwen. I want to marry you, but I want you to be just as certain as I am that marriage is right for us." Turning over her hands, he kissed her palms tenderly.

The gesture touched her heart. At that moment, a love welled up in her so strong, she tried to speak, tell him how she felt, but the lump in her throat strangled the words. Instead, she reached out and kissed him.

When they broke apart, his eyes lit up. "So does this mean you're coming to Paris with me in the morning?"

She wanted to say yes, tried to. She opened her mouth, but something inside prevented the words from coming out. Nodding, she grimaced. Then she shook her head.

"I don't know." She looked into his eyes. "I'm sorry, Art. I just—"

"Need more time," he said, finishing for her.

"No, well, a break to regroup, to think things over, would help, but . . ." She groaned. "I really need a sign, some indication that'll prove marrying you is the right thing to do. For both of us."

"A sign." He tugged at her left hand, turning it to display her ring. "Isn't this a sign enough?" He gently kissed her lips, her eyelids. "Aren't these indications enough?"

Pursing her lips, she sadly shook her head.

"Come back to my room with me. Let me convince you."

Her eyes widened as she imperceptibly shrank away from him. "I . . . I have my own room."

Pursing his lips, he nodded. Then he dropped his hands from her shoulders. "In that case, sleep on it. Let me know in the morning."

Art started to walk her home, but she begged off in front of the cathedral.

"The hotel's only a few steps away. I need to think." Shaking her head, she corrected herself. "I need to pray about this."

"If you decide to come with me, I won't leave for Paris 'til eight in the morning. I'm in room three-forty-two. I'm also a light sleeper if you want to stop by earlier to . . . talk." With a dubious smile, he lightly kissed her lips. "Please keep in mind, I love you, Gwen."

Nodding, she raised her hand in a listless wave. Then she walked into the immense cathedral, feeling small. Every sound was magnified, even her footsteps. Even her thoughts. They seemed clearer, somehow amplified in the sanctity of its walls. She knelt in one of the pews and mentally told God everything going through her mind.

Her hands cupped in prayer, she weighed the pros and cons of marrying Art.

He loves me. I feel love for him, just not that kind of love, and if I ever thought I did, I don't, anymore. She pressed her fingers into her temples. *Why am I questioning this? Percy's never even asked me out. It's not a relationship. Yet, if I question my relationship with Art over this . . .*

She sighed, feeling her shoulders heave. Unsure what to do, she simply whispered, "Please give me a sign." Then, crossing herself, she noticed something rolling under the pew. Reaching down, she picked up a coin.

As she weighed it in her hand, she chuckled inwardly. *Is this the answer to my prayer? Toss a coin? Heads, I go to Paris with Art. Tails, I go to Barcelona.*

Then she looked at it more closely. A penny. *What's a US penny doing in a Spanish church?*

Suddenly, a little poem her father had taught her came to mind:

> *When an angel misses you, they toss a penny down.*
> *Sometimes just to cheer you up, to make a smile from your frown.*
> *So don't pass by that penny when you're feeling blue.*
> *It may be a penny from heaven your guardian angel's tossed to you.*

Gripping the penny tightly, she looked around the quiet nave. *Dad? Are you my guardian angel?*

The only other person nearby was a monk wearing a cowl hood in the next pew. He turned toward her, his face nearly hidden in the folds of material, but she recognized the eyes peering out at her

Dad? She blinked, hoping to clear her vision, hoping her tired eyes were seeing nothing more than a figment of her imagination. After the second, third, fourth blink, the figure remained. She swallowed hard, then blinked again, hoping it would disappear. Still it remained.

Though its mouth never moved, she heard its words in her inner ear. *Marry for love.*

She mentally replayed the words, trying to guess their meaning. *Are you saying marrying Art would be a marriage of convenience?*

She looked back at the figure. It had gone.

Scrambling to her feet, she crossed herself and bolted out the door. Still holding the coin firmly, she rushed to her hotel, stopping only long enough to pick up her key at the front desk. She wanted nothing more than the safety of her room.

She took the elevator to the third floor and found her room directly across the hall from Art's. She tiptoed past his door, not yet ready to face him. After she secured both locks, she examined the penny under the desk lamp.

She gasped as she saw the year: 1943. *Ohmigosh, this is the elusive 1943 copper cent my dad and I tried to find. We completed the entire penny collection, all except this one.* She turned it round and round under the light, wondering if her father had anything to do with its appearance.

The desk phone rang, jarring her thoughts.

"Hello?"

"Gwen, I wanted to check with you about tomorrow," said Ruth's voice. "Can we meet for breakfast to say goodbye before your flight?"

Gwen sighed. "That would be great, but I'm not sure about anything in the morning yet. Hey, you got a minute? I'd like to show you something I just found. Get your take on it. I'm in room three-forty-one."

"Sure, I'm two doors down from you. Be right over."

Before Gwen hung up, she heard a light tap at her door.

"Ruth?" She checked the peephole.

"It's me."

Within minutes, Gwen had brought Ruth up on the afternoon's happenings with Art. Then she showed Ruth the penny.

Ruth gave a low whistle. "And this is a wheat penny. It could be worth a fortune."

"What do you mean?"

"I've got an uncle who's a numismatist." At Gwen's blank stare, she added, "A coin collector. We can check with him in Barcelona, but I know the wheat penny's rare." She examined it again and looked up at Gwen. "And you say you found this in the cathedral?"

Gwen chewed her lip, debating whether to confide all the find's details. Finally, she told Ruth how the penny had rolled toward her, and the only other person nearby had been a monk.

"It's a 'heaven cent,'" said Ruth, spelling out the difference. "There's a poem about it. I forget the rhyme, but supposedly heaven cents are signs from departed loved ones."

"Signs." Gwen grinned. "That's what I'd asked for, although I'd been taught pennies are from guardian angels."

"Either way, it sounds like someone, something's, looking out for you." Then Ruth's smile faded. "So what are you going to do in the morning? Go to Paris with Art, or come to Barcelona with us?"

Gwen took a deep breath. "After getting our Compostela certificates yesterday, I wandered around the cathedral, hoping for guidance, inspiration." She rolled her eyes. "*Something!* At one point, I felt compelled to pray for my father. I discovered if I thought of him as the abandoned little boy he had once been, rather than the distant father I recalled, it was easier to pray for him, easier to feel compassion for him."

Ruth chuckled. "Knowledge is a gift of the Holy Spirit. It lets us see the circumstances of our lives as God sees them. It lets us realize His purpose for us, His reason for putting us into specific situations. More than an accumulation of facts," said Ruth, "it's the science of the saints. I do believe you've stumbled on another gift of the Holy Spirit: knowledge."

"I don't know about that, but something else occurred to me in the cathedral. My relationship with my father has influenced all my other relationships with men. I have to work out my daddy issues before I can decide whether or not Art's the man to marry."

"Sounds to me like you need more time to think." Ruth flashed her teeth. "So does this mean you're coming to Barcelona with us?"

Gwen gave a surprised laugh. "You know, talking with you has made my choice clear. Until this moment, I'd had no clue what to do, but you're right.

The wise thing is not to rush into anything. Yes! I'm going with you. When are we leaving?"

"Eight in the morning."

"Same time as Art's leaving for Paris." She looked at the time. "I'll catch him first thing when I get up."

CHAPTER 9:

Paris or Barcelona

"To travel is to live."
— Hans Christian Anderson

That night, she dreamt she was talking with Art, trying to explain why she needed more time, why she was going to Barcelona instead of Paris.

In the dream, Art met each of her excuses with a logical argument.

"You'll have time to think in Paris. While we're there, let me spoil you."

"But I'm not sure I'm ready for marriage."

"You're just getting cold feet. I love you, Gwen."

With the words "I love you, Gwen," her father's spirit suddenly animated Art, as if his ghost had invaded Art's body. The face was a juxtaposition of both their features, but the words that came out were her father's. It was based on what she had heard earlier in the cathedral, of that she was sure: "Marry for love."

The conversation continued, but with her father's dialogue.

"I love you, Gwen. You're wise not to rush into anything. Don't make the same mistake I made and my mother made before me—marrying the wrong person. These decisions affect more than just you. They affect your children and your children's children. Marry for love, Gwen. Marry for love."

With that, she woke up and looked at the time. She splashed water on her face, ran a brush through her hair, and dressed, slipping the penny in her pocket. Five minutes later, she was tapping at Art's door.

Still in his bathrobe, he invited her in. Two carafes and two cups and saucers were setting on a linen covered tray.

"Come on in," he said, holding open the door. Gesturing toward the coffee, he added, "I've been expecting you."

She gave him a warm smile, paraphrasing his words in her dream. "You're spoiling me."

"Not as much as I'd like to." He pulled a second chair closer and began pouring. "Have a seat. As I recall, you take cream and sugar."

Sitting down, she nodded. "You've got a good memory."

"Better than you think." For a moment, his eyes flickered coldly, but then he returned to his jovial host persona. Pouring from the second carafe, he touched his hand to the silver pot, feeling its temperature. "Warmed milk." He smiled at her. Then, using tongs, he placed two raw sugar cubes in her coffee and stirred it with a demitasse spoon.

"What a luxury." She took the diminutive cup from him and sipped slowly, rolling it over her tongue, savoring it. "Seriously, this is the best coffee I've ever had."

He grinned. "It's just coffee, but if it's pampering you like, wait 'til we get to Paris."

Sighing, she remembered why she had come and set down her cup. *Face it. I like the way he makes me feel—warm, safe, snug.*

Then a chill passed over her as she looked at Art. She knew what she was about to say could drive him away. She glanced at the comfortable life she most likely was giving up, realizing she could never afford this lifestyle, nor could a professor. *A professor? Where did that come from? I simply have to think this through better, know I'm making the right decision.*

"Art—"

"Here it comes." A grim twist to his mouth, he drank the last of his coffee and set down his cup.

She wanted to reach out, take his hand in hers, but he was sitting across the coffee table from her. Instead, she fingered the penny in her pocket and looked up at him.

"Art, yesterday when you dropped me off at the cathedral, I prayed for a sign." She held up the penny. "This came rolling toward me in a nearly empty nave."

He wrinkled his nose. "A penny?"

"Not just any penny." She held it out for him. "A rare, nineteen-forty-three copper cent, something only my father would have known about."

He took it from her, glanced at it, and gave it back, looking suddenly tired. "What's your point, Gwen?"

She started, sighed, and then started again. "I think this is a message from my father."

"And what's he telling you, Gwen?" Squinting, he crossed his arms, scrutinizing her.

"That I should be sure I love the person I marry."

"The person you marry. Not necessarily me, but someone, anyone. Am I hearing right? Correct me if I'm wrong." His sarcasm was palpable.

She swallowed, disliking this contest of wills. Still fingering the penny, she took a deep breath and faced him. "Yes, you heard right. I do love you Art, but . . ."

"But what?"

"I'm not sure I love you for the right reasons. That it's enough. I respect you, admire you, like you immensely, but I have to be sure that's the basis for marriage."

"And all of this just happened to occur during the past ten days?" His eyes pierced hers as he rose to his feet. "You sure it's not someone you met recently who's making you rethink our engagement?"

"Be fair, Art, we never had a chance to discuss our engagement. You surprised me with this ring, and I've struggled with my feelings ever since."

"Struggled?" He snorted derisively. "I never realized what a hardship my proposal of marriage was to you."

She stood up. "No, Art, it's nothing of the sort." She took a deep breath. "I just need a little time, some space to sort out my feelings. You said so yourself yesterday. And when you proposed, you agreed that it was sudden, and I could have some time to think about it. I never even gave you a real answer. This is all very overwhelming for me." She walked around the table and hugged him, then pulled away to look him in the eyes. "Please, I'm only asking for a few weeks. Like you mentioned, I can cover that political story in Barcelona."

His arms hanging limply at his sides, he did not respond. Again, Gwen felt a chill. Loosening her grip, she backed away. Unable to look at him, her eyes fell on her ring, and she began twisting it off her finger.

"If you'd feel better taking back your ring, I understand." Her eyes dry, she handed it to him.

He took the ring from her, looked at it, and then looked into her eyes. Gripping her tightly, he whispered in her ear. "Gwen, I love you. I can't say I understand what you're doing, but it's obvious you need to do it." Letting go his grip, he held her at arm's length and placed the ring back on her left hand. "Take as long as you need, Gwen. Just remember, I love you."

She felt the tears running down her cheeks now, tasted their saltiness on her lips. She kissed him and held him against her, teetering between leaving for Paris with him and driving off with her friends, between going his way and going her own. Only the penny in her pocket reminded her to be true to herself.

*

An hour later, she was on the road again, this time in a rented car headed for Barcelona. Percy was driving. She was in the passenger seat. Crow and Ruth sat in the back. The deal was everyone would take turns, each driving for two-and-a-half hours. In ten hours, they would arrive in Barcelona.

Gwen called to confirm her reservation at the hotel.

"Cancel it." Ruth leaned forward from the back. "I've got an extra bedroom you're welcome to use."

"You're sure? I'm drawing per diem. At least let me pay weekly rent."

"Tell you what. You buy the groceries," said Ruth. "And I'll cook for us both."

"Deal."

Percy had his own apartment in Barcelona, and Crow would stay with friends. They exchanged phone numbers and planned to visit Montserrat together.

"What about the cathedral and basilicas?" asked Ruth. "Wouldn't it be fun to tour them as our gang before we go to Montserrat? Let Montserrat be the grand finale?"

Keeping his eyes on traffic, Percy glanced at Gwen and then spoke into the rearview mirror. "It would, except I'm volunteering for the independence rally and vote. My free time will be limited this week, but I'd like to join your travels after that."

Gwen watched him. "When are they holding them?"

"Tomorrow night's the rally. Sunday's the vote."

Gwen half turned in her seat. "Why don't we join the rally tomorrow? Where are they holding it?"

"Espanya Square, the heart of Barcelona, the symbolic heart of Catalonia."

❄

The next night, their group met at a predetermined address, a bakery two blocks from the Plaça de Espanya, and walked to the square together. Gwen surveyed the sea of people wearing yellow and red.

"No way would we have found each other in this crowd."

She snapped shots of a double-decker bus, painted to resemble a massive Catalonian flag, dropping off more supporters in view of the square. Motor traffic was blocked closer to the event as hundreds of thousands of people crammed the streets between Espanya Square and the Catalan National Art Museum.

Waves of people carried Catalonian flags, wore Catalonian flags like capes, or painted their faces red and yellow to look like Catalonian flags. Red and yellow stripes hung from every building and flew from every pole, with some banners and flags bearing an additional white star on a blue triangle.

Percy led them to the east side of Espanya Square, where he joined a group of people carrying oversized letters. Someone handed him a large C, and he lined up with the others across Avenida Maria Cristina to spell out "INDEPENDENCE." Gwen recorded the event just as the television crews moved in.

She accepted a "Yes, We Catalan" button from one of the volunteers, attaching it to her lapel.

"It seems everyone's supporting the secession," she said.

They climbed the steps and gathered around la Fuente Mágica de Montjuïc, listening to impassioned speakers promote Catalan independence.

"The excitement's contagious." Despite her limited Spanish, Gwen found herself sympathizing with the movement. She turned toward Ruth and Crow. "I've never been involved in a political crusade before."

"It's a happening, man," Crow grinned. "Takes me back to the sixties."

Afterwards they met up with Percy and found a pub where they shared a bottle of Cava.

It reminded her of Art, the night he had proposed. She looked at her left hand, wondering if she had made the right decision in choosing Barcelona over him and Paris.

"To Catalonia," said Percy, raising his glass. Blinking, Gwen consciously put on a smile. They all clinked glasses.

"To independence," said Crow.

Wide-eyed, they studied him and then looked at each other.

"What's the matter?" he asked, slowly lowering his glass.

"Aren't you the one who's always arguing for Spanish rule?" asked Gwen.

"Yeah, man, I like a good debate, but when push comes to shove, I always back the underdog." He raised his glass again. "To independence!"

Chuckling, they clinked glasses. Their party did not break up until eleven o'clock when Crow announced he had to catch a train to the suburbs. They walked him to the subway, and then Percy walked them to their apartment.

"Let me show you a shortcut through this alley," said Ruth. "It saves ten minutes."

As they passed a garbage dumpster, Gwen thought she heard a soft mew. She looked around but saw nothing. Suddenly, a shadow ran out from under the dumpster, nearly tripping her, and then began purring and rubbing against her legs.

"Oh, look, a kitten." Gwen leaned down to pet it, and the purring got louder. "Don't want to scare the little cutie." She gingerly picked it up, but the kitten did not seem to mind at all. As she held it up to see its face, it climbed on her shoulder, seeming content from its vantage point.

"I think you've found a friend." Ruth chuckled and scratched behind the kitten's ears as it bunted her hand, seeming to enjoy the attention.

"It's a she," said Percy, checking. "And she sure seems to like you two."

A store's back door opened, and a man brought out a garbage bag for the dumpster.

"Is this your cat?" Gwen asked him.

"No, but I've seen it here the past two nights." He pointed to several empty cat food cans. "I've been feeding it, hoping someone would take it in."

"So no one owns her?"

"You're the only ones who've shown any interest."

"I haven't even seen her face. She climbed up here before I could get a good look at her." Gwen tried to pry the kitten from her perch, but she would not move, holding on to Gwen's shirt with her claws. Gwen laughed. "Talk about passive resistance."

The man smiled at the kitten resting on her shoulder. "Looks like she's adopted you."

"Now what?" Gwen said, looking at her friends.

"Why don't we keep her?" Ruth's face lit up, even in the dim of the alley.

"It's your apartment, but I'll only be staying there a few weeks." Gwen scrutinized her. "Are you sure you want to adopt a kitten?"

"She'll be good company after you leave."

"As long as that's okay with you." Even when she shrugged, the kitten held on, never budging from her collar bone.

"What'll we call her?"

"What about Catalonia," asked Percy, "in honor of the independence rally tonight?"

"I like it." Gwen turned toward Ruth. "What do you think?"

"Catalonia, it is."

"That all right with you, Miss Kitty?" Gwen reached up to pet the kitten.

"Me-ow-ow," said the cat, and they burst out laughing. "Me-ow-ow."

"What a weird sound," said Percy. "Guess she likes her name."

"Yeah, but which one?" Gwen said. "Catalonia?"

The cat was silent.

Gwen said, "Miss Kitty?"

"Me-ow-ow."

"Let's compromise," Ruth said. "Let's call her Miss Kitty Catalonia."

The cat was silent.

"How 'bout Kitty-Cat, for short?" Gwen grinned as she addressed the cat. "Kitty-Cat."

"Me-ow-ow."

"She likes it!"

Suddenly, Gwen's smile faded as she recalled the first cat she had named. When she was thirteen, her parents had moved to an apartment that allowed pets. Finally, she could have a cat. She had been thrilled when they adopted a kitten, and her mother let her name it. She had researched it, given it a lot of thought, and come up with the perfect moniker: Ginger.

The name lasted two days until her father had said, "Simms is a better name. You don't mind, do you?"

Not really a question, but a statement. No response was expected or tolerated. Gwen bit her lip, but with that act, the rift between her father and her became an abyss. The distance between them had become too wide for any bridge to span it.

Overnight, the cat became her father's property. Instead of being allowed to sleep with her as it had the first two nights, the cat was put outdoors before going to bed. Each morning it had limped home, scarred and bleeding from cat fights. Nothing Gwen said could change her father's mind about it being "an outdoor cat." One morning, the cat did not return.

Gwen took a deep breath. *Ginger was the first and last pet I ever owned.* She gently took the kitten from her collarbone perch and placed it in the crook of her arm.

"Kitty-Cat, tomorrow, I'm taking you to the vet's. You're going to be the best-loved, best-cared-for kitten in all of Barcelona."

In the dark, Gwen noticed the ember glow of a cigarette tip as someone took a deep drag. Judging from the kitten's lowered ears and hiss, it saw the glow, too. As they passed by, Gwen caught a glimmer of her father's eyes, watching.

First thing the next morning, Gwen purchased kitten food and set up a litter box, which Kitty-Cat used immediately. She also bought a cat carrier and took the kitten into the veterinarian's. In the light of day, Gwen had noticed two dark-brown patches around Kitty-Cat's blue eyes, two dark-brown ear tips, and a kinked, dark-brown tail in an otherwise cream-colored coat.

"Looks like she's wearing a mask," Gwen said.

"Pequeño bandido," said the vet tech. "She looks like a little Siamese bandit. What's she here for?"

"She's a feral that needs a general checkup and vaccinations."

After a thorough exam, the vet said, "Just the usual, worms and ear mites, both easily treatable. Otherwise, she's a healthy kitty. Is she using a litter box properly?"

"Yes, thank goodness. How old is she?"

The vet checked her teeth. "Five weeks, maybe six. Bring her back when she's four months old to get spayed."

"Oh, I won't be here then."

"Kittens can become pregnant at five months. A responsible pet owner—"

Gwen interrupted the lecture before it began. "My roommate will bring her in to get spayed. I promise."

❄

The kitten took to sleeping with Gwen. Although both she and Ruth left their bedroom doors open, Kitty-Cat curled up with her.

Gwen enjoyed the company, as well as the "early warning" indications. After Kitty-Cat started sleeping with her, Gwen began seeing her father, or at least being aware of his presence, every night. *But is it because Kitty-Cat can see my father, or is she somehow attracting him?*

Something else Gwen noticed was how her last thoughts at night and first thoughts in the morning were about Percy, not Art.

Art had not called her since she chose Barcelona over Paris. Friday, she blew it off. *He's busy.* Saturday, she was concerned but did not want to appear anxious. By Sunday morning, she was worried enough to call him. He picked up on the third ring.

"Art, are you all right?"

"I'm fine. You?" His voice was cordial, but cool.

"I'm a little concerned about you."

"Really? Why's that?" His tone was flip, superficial.

"We left under less than the best of circumstances. I just want to make sure nothing's wrong."

"How kind of you." His sarcasm stung.

"Art, you're pouting, aren't you?"

"Look, I'm not exactly jumping for joy after you took off with your friends, preferring Sir Perceval's company to mine."

She counted to five. "We'd discussed this. One, I need time to think, and two, I'm covering the Catalonian vote."

His tone changed to professional. "What have you learned?"

She smiled to herself, feeling his icy attitude begin to thaw. "Got clips and photos of the independence rally Friday. Later this morning, I'll interview voters as they leave a local polling station, a neighborhood primary school. Then tonight, I'll wait for the results in a local pub and capture the mood on camera. How many words do you need, and when do you need them?"

"Gwen, how can I stay mad at you? You're too damned good at what you do."

His chuckle warmed her heart. As she inhaled, it suddenly occurred to her— she had been holding her breath, waiting for his approval. *Oh, no. No! I used to do that with my father. I needed his praise, his endorsement.* Groaning, she let her head fall on her chest. *What am I doing? Still trying to earn my father's approval? Is Art my—?*

"So can you deliver?"

"Sorry, you cut out there for a minute." She fibbed, trying to mentally rewind his words.

"I said, can you email the photos and copy by six tonight?"

She scratched her head, thinking. "I'll do my best."

"That's all I ever ask—your best. Gwen, that wasn't idle praise a moment ago. You're really talented. All I want for you is to live up to that potential." The smile came through his voice. "That's part of your attraction. I want to be there for you, mentor you. I want to help you reach your potential."

She silently sighed. *This is more complicated than I thought.*

"Art, deep down, I think I knew that, but thanks for reminding me. I . . ." She chewed her lip, debating how much to disclose. "I have to admit, that's part of your charm, too."

"Gwen, we're a team professionally, and I believe we'd make a good match romantically." His warmth came over the phone.

She mentally groaned, more conflicted than before.

When the pause lengthened, he added, "Don't mean to rush you. Take as much time as you need, but keep one thing in mind. I do love you."

Inside she melted, crumbled, caved. She wanted to say, 'I'll take the next flight to Paris.'

What's stopping me?

Again, when the pause lengthened, he said, "Okay, I get the hint. I'll call you tomorrow. Bye."

The phone clicked before she could say anything. "Bye," she said to a dead line.

What is wrong with me? Why is it so hard to tell Art how I feel?

"Are you ready?" called Ruth through the bedroom door.

"What?"

"Are you ready for church? Remember, we're meeting Percy and Crow at the cathedral."

"Oh, that's right. I forgot. One sec." She ran a brush through her hair, found a scarf that added a touch of color to her black pullover, grabbed her camera, and opened the door. "Ready as I'll ever be." She petted the kitten on the bed. "See you in a couple hours, Kitty-Cat."

"Me-ow-ow."

"She's so funny. I never heard a three-syllable meow before." Ruth scratched Kitty-Cat's head.

Still chuckling, the two headed north along La Rambla, turning onto Ferran as they worked their way through the Gothic Quarter toward the cathedral.

"Did you know," said Ruth, "its full name is the Cathedral of the Holy Cross and Saint Eulàlia?"

Gwen glanced at her as they walked. "Why two names?"

"It's the Holy Cross because one chapel contains the crucifix from a ship that fought at the Battle of Lepanto. According to Catalan legend, during the battle, the body of Christ actually *moved* on the crucifix to avoid an oncoming cannonball. They took it as a sign from God that they'd defeat the Ottoman Empire."

"Did they?"

"Oh, yes, they stopped the Ottomans from expanding into Western Europe. That battle was a real turning point in history."

"But this is all folklore, right?" Gwen said. "I mean, the body of Christ didn't actually *move*. People just imagined it, right?"

Ruth lifted her shoulders in a shrug. "Judge for yourself. After Mass, let's look at the chapel's crucifix. You explain how the body of Christ got tilted to the right."

Rather than argue, Gwen changed the subject. "Okay, then why is the cathedral named after Saint Eulàlia?"

"According to tradition, a thirteen-year-old girl was martyred in Barcelona for refusing to worship Roman gods. She suffered thirteen tortures, including being rolled down a hill in a barrel studded with knives."

"No!" Gwen stared at her, grimacing.

"Yes." Ruth nodded. "It happened on Baixada de Santa Eulàlia."

"Is that near here?"

Turning left onto Carrer d'Avinyo, Ruth said, "Not this alley, but at the next one, we'll make a right onto the street where it happened."

Five minutes later, they turned onto Baixada de Santa Eulàlia, pausing in front of a tile inscription on one of the buildings.

"This is it," said Ruth, translating the inscription.

As they began walking northeast toward the cathedral, Gwen began breathing more heavily. "I'll say one thing. This is definitely an incline." She turned to look where they had just climbed. "I'd sure hate to roll down this hill in a barrel."

"Especially with knives stuck in it."

Gwen shivered. "Eww!"

"For centuries, they've kept thirteen white geese in the cloister."

"Why?"

"It's a reminder of Eulàlia's age when she was martyred."

They turned another corner, and in front of them was the cathedral.

"Oh, that's gorgeous." Catching her breath, Gwen stopped to admire it. "Wait one second? I've got to get a picture of this Gothic architecture."

A moment later, they caught up with Percy and Crow and filed into church. The pews were filled to capacity with believers and tourists. The only seats available were behind one of the columns. To measure, Gwen tried to put her arms around it, stretching.

Chuckling, Percy shook his head. "You're not making half its circumference."

"Not a third," said Crow.

"Those columns are huge." Gwen eyeballed it. "It's wider than the four of us sitting here. It's blocking half the altar for us."

"Just look up at the weight it's supporting."

Their eyes traveled up the length of the column, where it branched into an arch meeting with another arch and another. Above those rose vaulted ceilings.

"Amazing architecture." Again, Gwen captured it with her camera.

When Mass began, Gwen was relieved to hear it was in English. During the homily, the priest discussed the teachings of St. Leo the Great.

"Dare to call God 'Father,'" he said. "If you call yourself a Christian, realize you're privileged to recognize your true parentage. Born of the flesh, you can be reborn by the Holy Spirit. You can obtain by grace what you lacked at birth. As long as you acknowledge yourself as the adopted child of God, you can call God 'Father.'"

Father. Gwen considered the idea. *God's my heavenly Father, not the person I resented from my childhood. Why did I stop going to church after my biological father turned his back on me?* She shook her head, wondering at her logic. *I was young. What else can I say?*

After Mass, they walked around the cathedral, marveling at the architecture and artworks. Gwen pulled Ruth aside, wanting to hear her opinion of the homily.

"I thought it was a wonderful discussion of the fruits of the Holy Spirit."

"What do you mean?"

"Basically, the homily was about the gift of amazement. Here we are, imperfect beings adopted by God through the Holy Spirit. Think what that means." Ruth sang a few lines from George Gershwin's "Summertime."

"Your daddy's rich, and your mamma's good lookin'." Ruth laughed. "We have the richest Father in the world."

Gwen scratched her ear. "I still don't get it."

"Piety's the gift of reverence. When we're pious, we recognize our reliance on God for everything. Worshiping and loving God *as our Father* is another gift from the Holy Spirit. Does that make sense?"

Frowning as she concentrated, Gwen rephrased Ruth's words, trying to absorb the idea. *Loving God as my Father.* Then, from the corner of her eye, she spotted a man watching her so intently she was compelled to turn toward him. As her eye caught his, she gasped. It was her father. Smiling. *Loving God as my Father. Is that what you're trying to tell me?* He nodded.

She turned back to Ruth. "And that's piety?"

"Yup." Ruth grinned. "If I'm counting right, this is your third gift from the Holy Spirit. Piety, Knowledge, and—"

"Understanding." Gwen's chest rose in a silent sigh. "Hopefully, it'll begin to sink in."

"What will?" asked Percy.

"Understanding." Suddenly, Gwen remembered. "Don't forget to take me by the polling station. I need to interview a few voters, capture their opinions."

"Not a problem. It's a neighborhood school just a few blocks from here." His blue eyes lit up. "But first you've got to see the folk dancing."

"Folk dancing?"

"Yes, every Sunday after Mass, they hold traditional Catalan folk dancing in the Plaça de la Seu, Cathedral Square."

"Where?"

"Right out front." Grabbing her hand, he said, "Come on!"

Just outside the cathedral, a brass band was playing Catalan folk music. In the square below them, hundreds of people had formed informal circles and were dancing together. Mostly older people, some young adults, and a few children also joined the fun.

"This is the Sardana. The only requisite to join is to know the steps." Percy's eyes were blazing.

"Why do they do this?"

"Aside from its being fun?"

She nodded.

"It's a symbol of Catalan unity." He winked. "With the vote today, more people are here than usual."

Again, grabbing her hand, he pulled her toward the nearest circle of dancers, but she held back. "No, no, I can't. I don't know this dance."

He laughed, his white teeth contrasting against his tanned complexion and five o'clock shadow. "I'll show you. It's easy." Still holding her hand, he led her through the dance steps until she felt comfortable. "Ready?"

She giggled, holding back.

"No holding out. You're ready this time." With that, Percy led her down the cathedral's steps, past the musicians, and with a smile, joined a circle of dancers.

They step-step-hopped, held hands as they lifted their arms in unison, turned left, turned right, and step-step-hopped in time to the music.

Gwen saw Ruth and Crow watching them from the steps. At a break in the music, she waved them over, but both shook their heads. Before she could catch her breath, the music started up again, and she was caught up in the moment. No longer the dancer, she was the dance.

When the music finally stopped, Gwen was breathless. The beat had kept her going, but now her lungs cried out for air.

Between gasps, Percy said, "Now you understand the solidarity of the Catalans. Dancing to the same drummer, you feel one with each other. But now you've got some interviews to tape."

Gwen held back long enough to invite Ruth and Crow. "Are you coming with us?"

"How long are you going to be?" Ruth asked, glancing at Crow. Gwen looked to Percy.

"An hour," he said. "The school's literally around the corner."

Ruth and Crow shook their heads as Crow pointed across the street. "See that bistro? We'll be in there having sangría. See you in an hour, man."

❄

They were back in forty-five minutes.

"That was fast." Crow ordered another pitcher of sangría and two more glasses.

"Percy knew right where to go, and then he set up the interviews: one, two, three." Gwen smiled her gratitude. "It went so smoothly, this article's practically writing itself."

Percy returned her smile. "Any time." His eyes rested on hers, lingering.

"So, wasn't the cathedral beautiful?" Crow asked loudly.

Percy and Gwen's heads turned toward him.

"Gorgeous architecture," said Gwen.

"I have an idea." Ruth held up her left index finger, as if making a point. "Why don't we attend a different basilica, monastery, or cathedral each Sunday for Mass?"

"And then discuss it afterwards over lunch?" suggested Gwen. She smiled gleefully. "Maybe I can develop another article from our discussions."

"Always an angle," Percy pretended to tease her.

"Angle or angel?" She returned his grin.

"Seriously," said Ruth. "Counting the cathedral, there are four major basilicas in Barcelona. There's Santa Maria del Mar—"

"Four, you say." Crow became quiet.

"What are you thinking?" Gwen chuckled. "I can almost see the wheels spinning in your mind."

"Four churches, four elements."

"I'm not following." Gwen shook her head.

"Earth, wind, water, and fire—the elements can be your angle," said Crow. "Santa Maria del Mar is obvious."

"Mar is water, the sea," said Ruth. "Then Santa Maria del Pi could be fire since that one was gutted by fire during the revolution. It's been rebuilt, but Mass isn't said there."

"But it's a great venue for musicians," said Percy. "Maybe we can catch a concert there."

"Okay," said Crow, counting on his fingers. "We have water and fire covered. What about earth and air?"

"The cathedral's obviously earth," said Gwen.

"Why?" Percy's head back, he gazed at her.

"It's so down-to-earth. Those immense columns seemed to root the vaulted ceiling into the ground itself. It's where heaven meets earth."

The three glanced at each other, agreeing.

"All right," said Crow, "then the last one would be wind."

"Easy one." Percy grinned. "La Sagrada Família."

"Why should it be wind?" Gwen challenged him.

"The light, the windows, the stained glass windows." His blue eyes sparkling, he looked from one to another. "In the morning, the rays come through the green and blue side of this immense basilica, creating an ethereal kaleidoscope of color. In the afternoons, the sunshine pours through the yellow, orange, and red side. The hues are so intense, so saturated, it's as if the air's on fire."

"If not the wind, the air," said Gwen, visualizing it. She turned toward Crow. "What a fabulous idea to describe the four churches by the four elements." She grinned. "Crow, you're a genius."

"If you like that categorization," said Ruth, "what about classifying the churches by the seven gifts of the Holy Spirit?"

Percy and Crow had blank looks on their faces.

Gwen chuckled. "Why don't you explain?"

"There are seven gifts from the Holy Spirit. At the cathedral in León, Gwen received the gift of understanding. At the cathedral in Compostela . . ." Ruth looked to Gwen to finish.

"I was given the gift of knowledge."

Percy looked at Crow, and Crow rolled his eyes.

"Guys, this is a serious subject." Gwen gave them a stern look, and Crow smirked at her.

"Never mind them," said Ruth. "Lessons aren't given, they're taken."

"Good one," said Gwen. "I think the seven gifts are a great way to classify the churches. Three already fit into this category. Only four more to go."

"Another good angle," said Crow, tongue-in-cheek, rolling his eyes again and laughing.

"All right, all right, enough sangría." Gwen called over the waiter. "Time to order food."

❄

After their late lunch, Gwen interviewed a few of the patrons, recording their opinions for her article. At quarter to three, she excused herself.

"Guys, I've got three hours to write and submit this article. I'd better get back to the apartment."

"I need to get back too," said Ruth. "Meet you two next Sunday at Santa Maria del Mar."

Twenty minutes later, Gwen was typing in bed, Kitty-Cat dozing at her side. At five fifty, she uploaded the article and photos and then called Art.

"I was just about to call you," he said.

Gwen smiled to herself. "I didn't feel like waiting."

"Really?" She heard the skepticism in his voice.

"Why should that surprise you?"

"Lately, that's all you're doing."

"What do you mean?"

"Surprising me." He chuckled. "That's all right. You keep me on my toes."

"How was your day?"

"Busy," he said, "but boring. How was yours?"

"Fun." She told him about the cathedral, the dancing, the interviews, and Kitty-Cat's help.

"Seems Sir Perceval has been leading you along his merry way."

She heard the sarcasm and chuckled. "You'll be glad to hear he and Crow have their juvenile side." She mentioned Ruth's idea about the seven gifts of the Holy Spirit and what a source of pleasure it was for them. She also told him about Crow's four element suggestion.

"Actually, I like both perspectives, and didn't you have an angle about the chalices?"

"Yes, I've got photos from several cathedrals," said Gwen. "I'll see if I can add to the chalice series here."

"Those are three stories you can write while you're waiting for the political scene to develop."

"There's also the Columbus story, and don't forget the Christmas in Barcelona theme."

His tone became serious. "So you think you'll need another four to six weeks to think things over?"

Gwen drew in her breath. "I hadn't looked at it that way."

Gwen spent the next two days writing background articles. Over dinner, she told Ruth, "At least, this way, I'm up-to-date on the churches we've visited for your seven gifts of the Holy Spirit concept and Crow's four element idea."

Her cell phone buzzed, and she answered. "Just a minute, Percy, I'll ask." She muted the phone. "Ruth, would you like to take a walk down La Rambla, looking at the Christmas lights?"

"I can't." Ruth made a sour face. "I have a finance council meeting tonight."

"That's too bad." Gwen took her time, debating whether she wanted to go alone with Percy. Finally, she unmuted. "Is Crow coming?" she asked brightly.

"No, he has something going on," said Percy. "Are you two up for it?"

"Ruth's got a meeting."

"How 'bout you?"

She worked her jaw, deliberating.

"Don't worry." He chuckled. "I'm just asking for your company on a walk, not your hand in marriage."

The tension relieved, a nervous giggle escaped. Then she shrugged. "Sure, why not?"

"I'll pick you up in twenty minutes."

Though the air was crisp, Gwen felt warm in the light jacket and merino wool scarf she had just bought. They bought hot, roasted chestnuts at the Mercado, munching as they meandered along the streets.

"The lights look so delicate, so old-world," she said, looking up at the side street decorations. Fragile snowflakes brightened the sidewalks beneath them. Some lights spelled out *Bon Nadal*. "The lights in the US are bigger, brighter."

"Is bigger better?" His eyes challenged hers.

"Not necessarily," she said slowly as she compared them mentally. Then she smiled. "These have a special charm of their own."

"Glad you approve." Then they turned onto La Rambla. "How about these?"

Animated stars seemed to descend from the stories above. Millions of circular snowflakes twinkled and blinked. Lighted schools of fish seemed to swim down one street. Another area boasted shooting stars. Yet another held gargantuan, lighted ostrich feathers, while the next street sported six-foot-tall bells of light that appeared to ring.

"Ohmigosh, these lights are bigger, more animated than the ones at home." She laughed out loud. "They're amazing!"

They walked to Gaudí's Batlló for its surreal, multi-colored light show. Then they grabbed a cab to the Magical Font. Enormous stars of light hung from every tree. All the trees' branches around the fountain sparkled with miniature bulbs of white, blue, rose, and violet. When the illuminated water danced in rhythm to the music, the fountain came alive with light. A wind gust sprayed them with water droplets, and Gwen was now grateful for her new scarf as the night air grew chill.

Percy asked, "How about a glass of Cava?"

"I wouldn't mind warming up." Her teeth chattering, she added, "My fingers are numb."

"You're shivering." He put her hands between his and rubbed them, warming her with his body heat. "I know a place just around the corner."

Five minutes later, they were sitting in front of a roaring fire.

"This is more like it," she said, unzipping her jacket and then rubbing her hands in front of the fire.

By the time the waiter arrived with the Cava and a bowl of green olives, Gwen had thawed and removed her jacket.

Percy poured and asked, "What shall we toast?"

She chuckled as the bubbles tickled her nose. "To wintery nights and holiday lights."

No sooner had they clinked glasses, than Percy held his up again. "To bubbles and giggles."

"I'll drink to that." As she leaned forward to clink glasses, Gwen felt her new scarf fall to the floor. She leaned over to retrieve it and found Percy had had the same thought. She smiled at the irony until he turned and, hidden by the table, stole a kiss.

She did not kiss him back, but neither did she pull away.

She gasped. *I let him do it! That makes me an accessory!* She was mortified. She sat up straight, feeling her cheeks flush. Wiping her lips with the back of her hand, she jumped to her feet.

"Gwen, this isn't anything to get upset about. It's something that just happened."

Zipping her jacket, she said, "I gotta go." With that, she stomped past him.

"Don't forget your scarf," Percy said, hastily running after her and tossing it around her shoulders as she stalked away.

She hailed a cab and was home in ten minutes. Inside her room, she sat on the bed as Kitty-Cat joined her, rubbing against her, but Gwen was in her own world and barely noticed.

What was I thinking? Am I insane? Here I am wearing Art's engagement ring. What makes him think for a minute I'd be . . . She looked at her left hand. The ring was gone.

No! Did I lose it under the table when he . . . Oh, no. No! She took a deep breath. *Maybe it's what I deserve.* She covered her face with her hands, sobbing, rocking. *What have I done? What have I done?*

I have to find that ring. With that thought spurring her on, she called the restaurant where they had stopped. The hostess could find nothing near her table, so she ransacked her room. First she tore apart her bed. Then she checked every drawer and pocket twice. Finding a flashlight, she looked under the bed. Then she checked every nook and cranny.

From the bedroom, she branched out into the bathroom. *Hope I didn't lose it down the drain. Wonder what a plumber would charge to take the pipes apart? And what about the kitchen sink?*

She decided it was prudent to check everywhere else before calling in a plumber. She checked under every cushion of the sofa and chairs. She checked every kitchen drawer and cupboard.

By the time Ruth got home, Gwen was frantic.

Reacting to her red eyes and tear-stained face, Ruth went white. "What's wrong?"

Too choked up to speak, Gwen held up her bare left hand. She cleared her throat and swallowed. "I've lost Art's ring."

Ruth took a deep breath. "Thank God, that's all."

Gwen could not believe her friend's insensitivity. "What do you mean, 'that's all'?"

Ruth smiled gently. "I thought something had happened to you or Art or Percy. No *thing* is worth worrying about. Only people matter."

Put into that perspective, Gwen saw the futility of worrying about an object. No matter how expensive. No matter how symbolic. She took a deep breath, digesting that, and her real issue became clear.

Thinking aloud, she said, "It's not just the loss of the ring. It's what else happened."

"What do you mean?"

Gwen chewed her lip, knowing she had already said too much, yet reluctant to confess what had happened.

"Gwen, what's wrong? What's happened?"

Struggling against the tears welling up, she blurted it out. "I kissed Percy."

Ruth's eyebrows shot up.

Gwen swallowed and went on. "Just after that, I noticed my ring was gone." She sighed. "This is all my fault. I not only lost Art's engagement ring, I've betrayed his trust."

"First things first," Ruth said. "Let's tear this place upside down until we find your ring. Then you can beat yourself up about Percy."

Gwen nodded as Ruth turned on all the lights and found a second flashlight. "Where have you looked?"

"I've already searched my room, the kitchen, the living room, and the bathroom."

"In that case, start looking in another room, and I'll double-check where you've been."

"Okay."

Ruth had no sooner started searching behind the bedroom furniture than Gwen's cell phone rang. "Want me to get that?"

"Sure."

When Ruth answered, a dubious voice asked, "Gwen, is that you?"

"No, this is Ruth. Gwen's busy looking for her ring." As Gwen walked into the room, Ruth grimaced. "Sorry," she whispered, "it slipped out."

Gwen nodded as she took the cell phone from her. "Hi, Art. Guess you heard what happened."

"I did."

Though he voiced no blame, Gwen sensed his disapproval in his silence.

"I'm sorry." Meant only as an apology for the ring, she surprised herself at the humility in her voice.

"Things happen," he said, his tone indulgent, considerate.

"I'm really sorry." Contrite for more than losing the ring, she began sniffling. "Art, can I call you back when I find it?"

"Gwen, don't cry. You haven't lost anything that can't be replaced."

Oh, yes, I have. "I gotta go." Her words echoing what she had told Percy, her sniffles turned into tears. Hanging up, she felt miserable.

Gwen and Ruth removed every item from every kitchen and bathroom drawer and cabinet. As a last resort, Gwen vacuumed the entire apartment, and then cut open the bag and pawed through the dust, cat hair, and kitty litter. Still, she did not find it.

Then she got an idea.

Using the super-duper-pooper-scooper, Gwen sifted through the kitty litter. Something sparkled among the clay pellets. Lifting it with the scoop, Gwen began to cry.

"Ruth! Ruth! I found it!"

"Where was it?"

Laughing through her tears, Gwen held up the scoop for her to see.

"What happened? Did you drop it when you cleaned the kitty litter?"

Gwen shook her head. "I don't think so."

"Then how would it get in there?"

Gwen removed her ring from the scoop and then sifted through the litter again. Up came a piece of aluminum foil and a paperclip.

"I think Kitty-Cat's a cat burglar."

"What?"

"Haven't a clue why, but I think she's attracted to shiny objects. I've read about this." Studying her ring, she sighed. "When I'm not wearing this, I'm going to have to keep it in a jewelry box from now on."

Kitty-Cat reached out with her paw, trying to bat the ring.

Gwen began laughing. "You little stinker. Do you have any idea what you've put me through?" She caught Ruth's eye. "What you've put *us* through? Just look at this place." Surveying the mess, she looked up. "I'm sorry, Ruth. I'll clean it up. Just let me just call Art to put his mind at ease."

CHAPTER 10:
Basilicas and Cathedrals

"Curiosity is gluttony, and seeing is devouring."
— Victor Hugo

"Art, great news!"

He laughed. "You don't even have to tell me. I can hear it in your voice. Where'd you find it?"

"Would you believe in the kitty litter?"

"Your cat's a critic. Tough crowd, tough crowd."

Gwen chuckled, picturing him pulling at an imaginary tie, a la Rodney Dangerfield.

"Hey," she whispered. "I miss you.'

"I miss you, too."

She sighed. "I'm sorry for more than losing my ring." She chewed her lip, debating how much to divulge.

"Yes?"

"I'm sorry I didn't go to Paris with you. If I had, I'd be with you now instead of feeling guilty on the other end of the phone line."

"Gwen, you know how I feel. I want you to understand how *you* feel. I want you to be sure about us."

"I have a confession to make." She took a deep breath. "I'm almost glad this all happened tonight. It's helped me sort out my feelings."

He gave a rueful snort. "If you feel this bad about losing the ring, it must mean a lot to you."

She shook her head. "The ring's just a symbol. *You* mean a lot to me." *I don't want to lose you.*

❄

Crow emailed them the news:

"Got four tickets for Saturday's concert at Santa Maria del Pi. It starts at nine. Seating's first come, first served, so let's meet early, just inside the doors, at eight thirty. The tickets are in my name. Pick them up at the door."

Gwen and Ruth arrived at eight. They saved four seats near the front, using coats and scarves. Then they took turns exploring the interior architecture while the other guarded the seats.

Gwen was amazed at the wide, open nave. No pillars supported its ribbed, vaulted ceiling. Instead, buttresses supported it, creating a series of small chapels along both sides of the nave.

"It's beautiful," she whispered to Ruth. "But it's austere to the point of being bare."

"That's because left-wing revolutionaries set fire to it in 1936." Ruth's eyes dimmed momentarily and then sparkled with glee. "This is Crow's fire element example."

Gwen grinned. "Duly noted for my article." She turned toward the back. "That round window's huge."

"That's the rose window. Some say it's the largest in the world. Too bad it's dark outside. Its colors are stunning." Ruth's eyes tracked down from the window to the entrance, and she pointed. "There's Crow and Percy now."

Gwen nodded. "I'll go give them their tickets. Back in a sec."

Catching their eyes, she waved, and they started walking toward her.

Percy walked faster, greeting Gwen a few seconds before Crow caught up. He leaned over, whispering in her ear. "Gwen, I want to apologize for the other night. I'm so—"

She shrugged him off and put on a smile. "Hey, Crow." She reached up to give him a hug. "Thank you for the tickets."

"A friend of mine works events at this venue. He says these are the best guitarists in Spain." He grinned. "Hope you like them."

"I'm sure we will." Turning, she motioned them to follow her. "Ruth and I got here early and found good seats. She's holding down the fort now."

"These are great," Crow said as they made their way through the crowd to the front. "Right on, man."

Gwen sat next to Ruth, and Percy grabbed the seat to her left. Ignoring him, Gwen focused straight ahead, her eyes on the chairs and microphones on the altar. Then movement from the choir loft made her glance upwards. There stood her father, waving to her.

Is he following me? Why does his presence annoy me so much? Then it occurred to her. *He seems to siphon off my happiness, feed on my energy.*

Scowling, she again tried to focus on the altar. Within minutes the announcer introduced the guitarists.

"Ladies and gentlemen, the guitar is one of Spain's most significant cultural representatives. Tonight, the Barcelona Jazz Festival and I are pleased to bring you two internationally renowned soloists and one of the most critically acclaimed representatives of the contemporary flamenco guitar."

The three guitarists took their seats in front of the altar and, with a flourish, began strumming a trio. With the incomparable acoustics of the basilica, Gwen was immediately enveloped in sound. Although she liked guitar music, she had never attended a live performance. Nor had she ever experienced music as she did in that basilica. The reverberating composition permeated the fourteenth-century Gothic church, saturating her with sound. Entranced, she felt she had been transported to another time.

When the concert ended ninety minutes later, Gwen felt alive, energized.

"What is this feeling?" she asked over a glass of Manzanilla Pasada.

"You're reacting to the harmonics," said Crow, quietly sipping his sherry.

"I'm not following."

"Within the structure of our physical body, we house our spirit, our soul."

Gwen nodded.

"Our spiritual body generates phonon energetic emissions."

"Huh?" Wrinkling her brow, Gwen glanced from him to Ruth to Percy and back.

"A phonon is sound or vibrational energy," said Percy.

"In other words, our bodies vibrate, create sound," said Crow. "Chi or life force is our body's energy system. It's a network that keeps the spirit flowing through our body and up toward God. This pattern is your spirit's harmonic current of life. All of nature has an energetic harmony. Everything vibrates, man." He picked up his glass. "This looks solid, doesn't it?"

They nodded.

"Even though we can't see it, it's vibrating. Atoms are in constant motion, and that motion creates sound that we sometimes can and sometimes can't hear."

"Hear, hear," said Ruth, grinning, raising her glass. "I'll drink to that."

They clinked glasses. Crow swirled the sherry around his palate, seeming to savor it, before continuing. "Concordant frequencies and harmonious tones—"

"Music?" asked Gwen, struggling to understand.

Crow nodded. "Music lifts the spirit, raises the vibration around us and within us. Your energy literally ascends to God. In exchange, you feel joy or peace in a push/pull, give/take interchange of energy. Compare it to reciprocated love. Music that aligns with that divine harmony deepens the spiritual connection because it's in sync with creative energy." He turned to Gwen. "Does that make sense?"

"Kind of." Squinting, she shook her head. "No, not really."

"Let me try a different approach. Sound created the universe. Sacred tones, sometimes called the 'music of the spheres,' was the source of the spiritual and physical world. 'In the beginning was the Word.'"

"John, chapter one, verse one," murmured Ruth.

Crow nodded, his bushy, straw-colored hair bobbing with his head. "What is word but spoken thought? The frequency and vibration, the *sound* of that first word of creation shaped the world from the thoughts of God. If you look into the field of cymatics—"

"Say what?" Gwen slowly shook her head.

"Cymatics," said Percy. "Basically, it's visible sound, for instance, where vibrations cause sand to scatter and then gather into patterns. Think of waves in a lake. When you toss a rock into the water, it creates a pattern of waves."

She nodded. "Okay."

"All matter is sound and frequency," said Crow. "To take it up a notch, the universe and all within it can be understood in the merging of music and mathematics— the spiritual and physical reflections of the same truth within movement."

"Crow, to use your jargon, that's deep, man." Chuckling, Gwen shook her head. "Too deep for me." She leaned toward him, trying to make her point. "All I said to start this conversation was, I feel alive, energized, after the concert. Why? What causes that?"

"Let me put it this way, the basis of all frequencies is God. Let's call Him the Prime Resonance. To be attuned with God, with that Prime Resonance, is to grow spiritually, so your spirit's literally vibrating in alignment with Him. Music does that."

Gwen blinked. "So, in a word, your answer is *music*? You're saying music is what energizes me, what makes me feel closer to God?"

"Right on, man."

"Where words fail, music speaks," said Ruth. "Music's a path to the sacred. God's beyond our intellect, so using multiple senses helps us get closer. For some of us, that sense is hearing: music."

"You're saying music adds another layer to prayer." Gwen nodded as it began to sink in. "Intensifies it."

"Even the *Bible* mentions psalms and hymns as a means to be filled with the Holy Spirit," said Ruth. "Saint Augustine says, 'When you sing, you pray twice.'"

❄

On the walk home, Gwen confided in Ruth. "I saw my father tonight, waving at me from the choir loft."

"How did it make you feel?"

"Annoyed." Gwen grimaced. "It's as if he drains me, siphons off my energy. He's an emotional vampire." She half smiled at that image.

"Two things come to mind," said Ruth. "I think he's trying to get your attention. He wants you to notice him." She caught Gwen's eye. "He waved, didn't he?"

"True." Gwen nodded slowly. "And the other?"

"We just had this discussion of music." Ruth glanced at her. "Could the fact that he was waving from the choir loft mean anything?"

"I didn't think of that."

"You say your father drains you emotionally, yet earlier you'd said music energized you."

Gwen stopped in her tracks. "Ruth, are you saying my father was showing me a way to restore my energy, recharge my emotional battery?"

Ruth grinned as her eyes lit up. "Yes. Not only that, but I wonder . . ."

"Yes?"

"It sounds to me like he may be asking for your help," Ruth said, starting back down the path.

"What makes you say that?"

"That fact that he drains you emotionally sounds to me like he needs something. Think of a baby in its mother's womb. It takes its physical needs from her. Maybe his soul is taking its spiritual needs from you."

Gwen sucked in her breath. "Now you're sounding like Crow. Far out, man." She felt the hairs stand up on the back of her neck. Shuddering, she rubbed her arms. "You're giving me the willies."

"When did your father pass away?"

"In June, Father's Day."

Ruth nodded slowly, seeming deep in thought. They walked in silence several steps before she spoke. "Are you familiar with the concept of purgatory?"

Gwen made a sour face. "It's been a long time since I studied catechism."

Grinning, Ruth said, "I'll give you the short version."

Thank God. Not in the mood for religious dogma, Gwen stifled a sigh.

"When people die, they don't immediately go to heaven or hell." She caught Gwen's eye. "They go to purgatory."

"Why? I mean, if they've said they're sorry, and their sins are forgiven, shouldn't they go straight to heaven?"

"Think of it this way," said Ruth. "Pretend you broke a lamp at our apartment. You'd say you're sorry, and I'd forgive you, but you'd still have to pay to replace the lamp." Again she caught Gwen's eye. "You see what I'm saying?"

"Purgatory sounds like a kind of halfway house."

"More like a second chance. It's a place where you can pay off your debts, give your soul a clean bill of health before you go on to heaven."

"If you make it to purgatory, you're not going to hell?" At Ruth's nod, Gwen grinned. "So in a long-winded way, you're saying if my father's in purgatory, he's going to heaven?"

"Eventually, yes, but it isn't quite that simple."

Gwen muttered under her breath. "Knew there had to be a catch."

"Souls in purgatory need our prayers."

"Why's that?"

"They can't pray for themselves. They can pray for us, but they can't pray for themselves."

"I get it." Gwen caught Ruth's elbow and looked her in the face. "It's the baby analogy again, where the mother fulfills the baby's physical needs—"

"And we fulfill the spiritual needs of the souls in purgatory." Having made her point, Ruth bobbed her head. "Exactly."

They began walking in silence as Gwen digested the idea. "So you're saying my father's ghost isn't deliberately trying to annoy or drain me. It's just his way of asking for my help."

"He's trying to get your attention so he can ask for your prayers."

Gwen inhaled sharply. "I'll look at him differently the next time I see him."

"Do more than that," said Ruth. "Pray for him."

"But how?"

"When we get home, I'll email you a copy of the Prayer of Saint Gertrude. According to tradition, Jesus promised a thousand souls would be released from purgatory each time the prayer's said."

"Can't hurt." Gwen shrugged.

Gwen wrote down her thoughts before bed. Adding Santa Maria del Pi to the elements article, she listed it under fire. *But how does that fit into the list of the seven gifts of the Holy Spirit?*

She reread that list, naming the churches that seemed to best express the gifts. Understanding from the Cathedral of León, Knowledge from the Cathedral of Compostela, and Piety from the Cathedral of Barcelona. Counsel, Fortitude, Wisdom, and Fear of the Lord are left. *Of these, which best applies to Santa Maria del Pi?*

She reviewed the evening's events, recalling Crow's rant about music and Ruth's discussion of purgatory. *Since I experienced fear of the ghost and joy from the music, it's Fear of the Lord for Santa Maria del Pi.*

Already a routine, Kitty-Cat sat on her lap, dozing, as Gwen typed. All of a sudden, Kitty-Cat's ears perked. Jumping to the floor, she arched her back and hissed.

"What in the world?" Gwen looked in the same direction as the cat.

There stood a wavering light. The word *stood* came into her mind because the light was in the general shape of a person, yet it was a nebulous, shapeless glow that fluctuated, almost seemed to breathe.

Crouching, ready to retreat, Kitty-Cat continued to growl at it.

Gwen also considered running, but the light stood between her and the door. Caught between flight and fight, the hairs on the back of her neck stood on end. This apparition was different from the others. The sensation was not what she would describe as evil, but it made her skin crawl. She swallowed, feeling slightly nauseous.

Finally, she found her voice. "Who are you? What do you want?"

Gradually, the light melded into the shape of a child, a little boy. His eyes wild, he sniffled as his rib cage shook with each sob. Gwen more than sensed his distress. His fear so palpable, she could taste the bile in her mouth. It made her sick. Again, she swallowed.

"Who are you?"

"Mother?" cried a tiny voice.

"Who are you?" she repeated loudly, but she knew.

"Mother, I'm so afraid."

Kitty-Cat began howling in terror.

The boy turned toward the sound. Gradually fading, the light began to lose its structure. With a final flicker, it disappeared.

Depleted, Gwen slumped forward, her fists supporting her head. *Was that my father? Was that the fear he felt when my grandmother deserted him?*

She shuddered. The memory still haunting her, she remembered Ruth's email. Opening it, she read the Prayer of St. Gertrude out loud.

"Eternal Father, I offer Thee the Most Precious Blood of Thy Divine Son, Jesus, in union with the Masses said throughout the world today, for all the Holy Souls in Purgatory, for sinners everywhere, for sinners in the universal church, those in my own home and within my family. Amen."

The nausea left her, and the terror seemed to subside. She said the prayer aloud a second time. Then, exhausted, she turned off the lights and collapsed in bed, falling into a troubled sleep.

In her dream, she spotted her father, looking as he had the last time she had seen him alive. She compared him to the little boy. *Time hadn't been kind to him.* Then it occurred to her. *Her grandmother hadn't been kind to him. His second wife, Mildread, hadn't been kind to him. Admit it. At the end, I wasn't kind to him, either. He didn't have an easy life.*

The next morning, Gwen woke up, recalling an article she had seen about monkeys and maternal deprivation. She grabbed a cup of coffee and searched the web until she found it.

She skimmed it, mumbling as she read. "Pigtail macaque infants . . . severely disturbed after removal from their mothers . . . loud screams . . . distressed . . . deeply depressed . . . hunched over, almost rolled into a ball . . . play virtually ceased."

Gwen despised animal experimentation, but the clinical description seemed to capture the fear she had witnessed the night before. Her heart went out to the frightened little boy that had been her father, as well as to the tortured animals.

When Art called later, he asked about the political story.

"Not a lot's happened since the vote. I interviewed people on the street the day after, capturing public opinion, and there's been speculation in the news, but nothing concrete's happened."

She told him about the previous night's concert. "I've been gradually adding to the two articles on Spain's basilicas, so that's been keeping me busy until the political story heats up."

Then she told him about her father's specter.

"Wow." Art sucked in his breath. "His death must have affected you more than I realized."

She grimaced. "This time I need isn't just to think about us. There are a lot of things I have to work out."

CHAPTER 11:

Stella Maris, Star of the Sea

"As mariners are guided into port by the shining of a star,
so Christians are guided to heaven by Mary."
— Saint Thomas Aquinas

Two weeks later, the four of them met for Mass in the Ribera district. Standing in the plaza in front of Santa Maria del Mar, Crow stomped his foot for emphasis.

"This ground had been a Roman cemetery from the first century until they built the basilica in the fourteenth century." After emitting a low wolf's howl, he joked. "We're not alone."

"Ghost stories aside," said Percy, giving him a sharp look, "it's been an important site since the earliest days of Christianity. The apostle Saint James preached here."

Gwen glimpsed him sideways, scrutinizing him. She had been unable to look him squarely in the eye since he had stolen the kiss. Though she distrusted him, their foursome had bonded into an odd family, where each member contributed to the whole. No matter the personal differences, it was unthinkable to visit a basilica without the other siblings.

"Barcelona's cathedral claims Saint Eulàlia as its own. But for over a thousand years, Eulàlia's bones were buried in a small church on this site."

"Really?" Gwen looked at the building's austere front. "I didn't know that."

"It's unique," said Ruth as they climbed its steps. "It's the only basilica built entirely in the Catalan Gothic style." Pausing by the door, she pointed out two bronze figures of men carrying loads on their backs. "These were the bastaixos, the longshoremen. They and the freed slaves, the Macips de Ribera, carried the building stones from the quarry on Montjuic all the way here."

Percy nodded in agreement. "For more than fifty years, most of the able-bodied men of Barcelona helped build this church."

"So it was a labor of love," Gwen said, "built by the workers, for the workers."

"Even though it's considered a church of the people," he said, pointing out several fire-damaged stones overhead, "it didn't stop anarchists from torching it in the thirties." Gwen's eyes traveled upward toward the blackened stones. The height and depth of the basilica swallowed her. In its immensity, she felt insignificant.

Then the stained glass windows caught her eye as the sun began pouring through the multi-colored panes. In the blink of an eye, it flooded the nave with jewel-tone colors, bathing her in green, blue, and purple hues. The colors made the light visible, nearly tangible. Warming her, the rays washed over her like an April shower.

She suddenly sensed God surrounding her, enveloping her, embracing her. Like a kitten sunning itself, she basked in the nurturing sensation. As skin absorbs vitamins from the sun's rays, her soul absorbed God's love from the light. With a tingling awareness, she closed her eyes to better experience God's healing touch. Time seemed to stand still, though only moments actually passed.

Then she heard Percy's voice breaking through her reverie. "Using the mediaeval foot of thirty-three centimeters, which was the basic unit of measurement in the fourteenth century, the side chapels are each ten feet deep. The side aisles are double that width, and the central aisle is forty feet wide. The total width of the church is a hundred mediaeval feet, which is equivalent to its height."

Panning the interior, Gwen spoke in a hushed voice. "Its size makes me feel so small."

Nodding, Percy gestured toward the side chapels. "Notice how they form a kind of cloister or gallery. Each separate, yet connected to the whole."

She smiled at the image. *Not unlike our dysfunctional crew.*

"See the Jesus Chapel?" asked Ruth, pointing it out. "That's where they placed Mary's statue—Stella Maris, Star of the Sea."

"But wasn't this basilica named Saint Mary of the Sea?" Gwen asked.

"The title Stella Maris emphasized Mary's role as a guiding star for early Christians. Gentiles used to be referred to as 'the sea,' meaning anyone beyond 'the coasts.' Then, over time, she became the patroness of mariners and coastal churches," said Ruth. "This was built when Catalonia's maritime success was at its height. At the time, it was near the seashore."

"Near the shore?" Gwen raised her eyebrow. "This has to be a good half mile from the coastline."

Ruth nodded with a laugh. "The district's name, La Ribera, literally means 'The Shore.' The sea once lapped at its southern edge, but it's since receded, along with Barcelona's seafaring era. Santa Maria del Mar was built for the merchants and seamen."

"You mean it had tourist shops like we see today?"

Ruth shook her head. "In the fourteenth century, this area was the mercantile center of Barcelona."

Gwen tried to mentally picture the neighborhood as it had looked when the basilica was built. "Now it's just one district of a much larger city."

"Think of the streets we took to get here."

Gwen mentally backtracked, reciting the names of the streets. "Carrer Cotoners, Carrer Corders, and Carrer Mirallers."

"Those were named after the guilds," said Ruth. "Carrer Cotoners was the weavers' guild, Carrer Corders was the rope makers', and Carrer Mirallers was the mirror makers'."

Organ music announced Mass was beginning. They filed into a pew as a small group of women began singing.

"Oh, a schola," Ruth said in hushed tones, "and they're singing 'Ave Maris Stella.'" Her eyes lit up. "How appropriate."

"Today we offer Holy Mass in honor of the Blessed Virgin Mary, Stella Maris, Star of the Sea," said the celebrant, "though I wonder if I'm the right person since I've been known to get seasick on a ferry to Mallorca."

Chuckles and grins met him.

"This morning we pray for all seafarers, for those who travel by sea, and those who work at sea. We pray for their safety and their salvation. Even in today's enormous ships with their remarkable technology, travel by sea can be filled with danger."

The lector delivered the first reading. "Or someone else, taking ship to cross the wild waves, loudly invokes a piece of wood frailer than the vessel that bears him. Agreed, the ship is the product of a craving for gain, its building embodies the wisdom of the shipwright; but your providence, Father, is what steers it, you having opened a pathway even through the sea, and a safe way over the waves . . . For blessed is the wood which serves the cause of uprightness."

"In the first reading, the Book of Wisdom's author mocked those who trusted in magic idols, who thought a prayer to a boat's figurehead could protect its passengers from danger. No, only God's providence can keep us safe, just as it was with Noah's Ark, when the hope of the world took refuge on a ship. 'Blessed is the wood which serves the cause of uprightness.' Wisdom is one of the last books of the Old Testament. Saint Ambrose suggested the reference to wood was a foreshadowing of the salvation Jesus won for us on the wood of the cross.

"The point is, every moment of our lives is in God's hands. It's only right to pray for His protection. Before we set off on a trip—whether by sea, air, or land—we should unite ourselves in prayer with Jesus Christ.

"Even if it's an inner journey of the spirit, a pilgrimage, we're all on a voyage. Even now, each of you is sitting in the nave of the church. Nave means ship. The image of a ship sailing across the sea is symbolic to those who see the Church as the Barque of Peter, the Ship of Peter sailing through the storms of history.

"When Francis was elected Pope, I recall a reporter asking someone if he could solve the crisis in the Catholic Church. 'No,' said the person being interviewed. 'He can't. The Church has been in crisis ever since it was in that fishing boat with Jesus on the Sea of Galilee's choppy water.'

"The Church is always in crisis because it's made up of sinners like you and me. It will only drop anchor when we reach the shores of Paradise. That's why we pray for the grace of the Holy Spirit to help us seafarers chart our course to Jesus Christ."

After church, Gwen said, "All this talk about the sea makes me want to set sail."

Percy grinned. "All this talk about the sea makes me hungry for seafood."

"Why not both?" Ruth looked from one to the other. "What about a seafood brunch in Barceloneta, followed by a harbor tour in a gondola?"

"Perfect," Gwen said.

They walked down la Rambla to the Portal de la Pau, passing the *Monument a Colom*. Recalling how they had bumped into each other at the monument, Gwen stole a glance at Percy. Their eyes met, and she looked away, pretending not to have noticed.

Ruth led them into a seaside locale.

"What a charming restaurant." Gwen ran her fingers over the restaurant's multi-color limestone facade and double, arched doors.

"It's been serving seafood in this location for over a hundred years," said Ruth. "But recently they updated the menu with a fusion of marine, Mediterranean, and Catalan cuisine."

"Something for everyone," said Crow, reading the menu on the door.

The weather was balmy, so they sat on the second floor balcony overlooking the street below. A crisp linen tablecloth, delicate wine glasses, and heavy silverware set the mood. Gwen and Ruth sat on one side, with Percy and Crow on the other.

They started with a bottle of local rosado and a bucket of mussels, served with a lightly spiced red sauce.

"Look, you can see the *Monument a Colom* from here." Ruth gestured toward it with her chin.

Percy craned his neck to see and then turned back toward them. "Did you know Gwen and I bumped into each other there on her first day in Barcelona, the day before we met in León?"

"Yeah," said Gwen dryly. "You mentioned it when you met Art." She looked down at her plate as they ate in silence.

"Speaking of the *Monument a Colom*," said Ruth brightly, breaking the hush, "I've always found it interesting that Columbus landed here in Barcelona when he returned from the New World."

"What's odd about that?" Crow looked at her innocently.

"He'd set sail from Cadiz," said Ruth. "You'd think he'd have returned there, but instead he sailed past Cadiz to Barcelona."

"Maybe Barcelona was a safer port than Cadiz." Crow shrugged his shoulders.

"There's the rumor Columbus was a Knight Templar." Percy watched their eyes, as if looking for someone to challenge him.

"Can I get you something else?" asked the waiter.

Gwen looked at the sizzling platter being served to the next table. "What's that they're having?"

"That's Catalonian calamari, crisp-fried in a delicate batter."

Noting the nods of approval, Gwen said, "Let's try that."

"Something to drink?" asked the waiter.

Crow said, "Let's get a bottle of Cava—"

"And sliced bread to dip in herbed oil," added Ruth.

His eyes twinkling, Percy dangled the bait again. "After returning from the New World, Columbus began signing his name as a pyramid of dots and letters, something Knights Templar were known to do."

"There are a lot of theories about that." Ruth shrugged, dismissing it. "I've read he signed in a combination of Latin and Greek, 'Servant I am of the Most Exalted Savior; Christ, Mary, and Joseph; Christ-bearer.'"

Crow shook his head. "I've read he was Jewish."

"Christopher means Christ-bearer." Ruth raised her eyebrow. "Not many Jewish parents I know name their sons after Christ."

"But, if he was a Spanish Jew, maybe Barcelona and Catalonia were a safe haven." Percy's eyes blazed as he heated up for the debate. "And, if he was a Knight Templar, Barcelona was a probable residence for the Knights Templar."

"Not in the late fifteenth century," said Ruth wryly. "The Templars were expelled from Barcelona in the fourteenth century."

"Speaking of expulsion," said Crow. "I've read the Jews were expelled from Spain the exact day Columbus set sail for the New World. Maybe that was his way of escaping."

"You've read a lot of things." Ruth eyed him wearily. "Just not the facts. Columbus was a devout Catholic, not a Jew. Take it from one who knows." She grinned. "In fact, he was a Third Order Franciscan. Next time you look at a painting of Columbus, note the Franciscan habit."

The waiter delivered the crackling-hot calamari and opened the bottle of Cava with a pop.

"A Châteauneuf-du-*pop*," said Gwen, chuckling.

"They're not kidding. That's a delicate batter," said Ruth, savoring as she sampled the calamari. "It's as light as tempura."

Tasting it, Gwen agreed. "Delish." She turned to her adopted siblings. "Keeping with our nautical theme today, we're going for a gondola ride after brunch, right?"

"Either a half-hour gondola ride around the harbor," said Percy, "or a two-hour catamaran tour that leaves the harbor and follows the coast to Port Forum." He looked from one face to the next. "Have we decided?"

Gwen, Ruth, and Crow looked at each other, grinned, and said in unison, "Catamaran tour."

Percy chuckled. "Catamaran, it is."

"Well, then," Gwen said, lifting her champagne flute of Cava, "who knows a nautical toast?"

"May your departures equal your landfalls," said Crow, clinking glasses with each as they toasted.

"There are good ships and wood ships and ships that sail the seas, but the best ships are friendships, and may they always be," said Ruth, toasting each of them.

Percy raised his glass. "To the ship that goes, the wind that blows, and the lass who loves a seaman."

Chuckling, they toasted.

"Here's to being in a boat with a drink on the rocks instead of being *in* the drink with a boat *on* the rocks," said Gwen.

An hour later found them in a catamaran. Despite it being December, a warm breeze embraced them as they headed out of the harbor. Following the Mediterranean coastline, the catamaran's captain pointed out local sites as the city faded into the background: La Sagrada Familia, Montjuïc, Tibidabo, Port Olympic, and Barceloneta Beach.

"Here," the captain said to Gwen. Keeping one hand on the wheel, he stood aside. "Why don't you take the helm?"

"Me?" She looked from him to the wheel and back.

"Sure, just hold it steady."

She swallowed, then stepped closer. Putting one hand on the wheel, she got the feel of it as the captain also steered.

"Ready?" he asked.

"Yup." She put her other hand on the helm as he removed his. *I'm running the ship.* Grinning, she felt the catamaran cut through the water beneath her.

"Why don't you join her?" the captain said to Percy, his camera in hand. "Good photo op."

Looking uncomfortable, Percy tentatively put one hand on the wheel.

"Closer." His eye to the viewfinder, the captain waved him toward Gwen.

Percy took a step closer. His smile looked pasted on.

"She's not going to bite." Grinning, the captain took his eye from the camera to make eye contact with Percy. Waving him over, he added, "Closer, closer." When Percy was practically standing behind her, the captain said, "Perfect."

As he snapped the photo, Gwen felt the blood drain from her cheeks. Her sense of Percy's nearness was acute. She felt his chest muscles pressing against the back of her arm. The hairs on the back of her neck tingled as she felt his breath.

As she caught the subtle scent of lime, she shuddered. He turned toward her, their eyes locking.

The click of the captain's camera made her neck spin towards him.

"Now that's more like it," he said, checking the preview window. He held up his thumb in approval. "The pictures will be ready at the end of the cruise." The captain then turned to Ruth. "Would you like to try your hand?"

Ruth hesitated, seeming unsure until Gwen stepped away.

"Go for it," said Gwen, handing over the wheel. Her eyes rested on her ring. Percy called Crow over, stepping aside to let him take his place.

"Guess the captain thinks we're couples," Percy whispered to Gwen.

She shrugged, uncomfortable in his nearness, even more so now that her body had betrayed her.

"I'm nearly finished with the first edits you gave me. Would you mind if I send you the rest to review?"

Gwen had forgotten about their agreement to collaborate. She opened her mouth but wasn't sure what to say. "Oh . . ."

His eyebrows puckering, he looked wounded. "You haven't forgotten about editing our book about the Holy Grail, have you?"

"No . . . I . . ." She remembered her promise to edit the book. Again, she looked at her ring. *What about that promise? But is it a promise since I've never actually said yes?* She gave a silent sigh. "Sure, you've got my email address. Send it, and I'll add my comments."

Swallowing the lump in her throat, she felt more confused than ever. *I'm wearing Art's ring, so why does Percy's nearness . . . ?*

Fog hovering over the sea took the shape of her father and as quickly dissolved into sea spray.

"What?" From the way Percy was staring at her, Gwen realized he was waiting for an answer.

"You seem a million miles away." He grinned. "I was wondering if we could meet somewhere to go over the edits together."

Shaking her head, she took a step back. "Oh, I don't think that's a good idea."

"I'm nearly finished with the rewrites." His violet-blue eyes searched her face, as if they could peer into her soul. Even without his glasses as a barrier, his eyes were as unfathomable as the Mediterranean. "I think we could wrap this up in two or three hours, if we put our minds to it."

Shaking her head no, she heard herself say, "Okay."

At home, over hot tea, Gwen mentioned the exchange she had had with Percy onboard the catamaran.

"Okay." She sat, chin on hand, looking at Ruth for insight. "What gift of the Holy Spirit, if any, did I receive from Santa Maria del Mar?"

Ruth thought for a moment. "You say you saw your father's ghost again just before you agreed to meet Percy?"

Grimacing, Gwen nodded. "Agreeing to meet him was against my better judgment."

"Why do you phrase it like that?"

"I was shaking my head no, when I literally heard myself agree. If not an out-of-body experience, it was as if someone or something was controlling my response."

Ruth thought for a moment. "Well, the Holy Spirit is the advocate, the Counselor the Father sent in Jesus' name to teach us all things." Ruth appraised Gwen. "What do you think? Could it have been the Holy Spirit you saw in the mist, the One, who put words on your lips?"

Resting her hands on her knees, Gwen raised her shoulders and slowly shook her head. "I don't know."

"Counsel, sometimes called right judgment, is the gift that lets us know the difference between right and wrong, the values taught by Jesus." Again, Ruth studied her. "I won't suggest it's an exact fit, but I believe it captures the events you're describing."

The next evening, Percy knocked on their door at six sharp.

Ruth called out, "I'll get it." Then Gwen heard her say, "Come on in, Percy."

Gwen entered the room just as he handed Ruth a bottle. "It's chilly out there tonight. Thought a sip of port might warm us."

"Thanks, this is great." Glancing at Gwen, she swallowed a smile as she headed toward the kitchen. "Let me get glasses."

"Hi." Gwen felt as awkward as if she was fifteen. "Can I take your jacket?"

"Sure, just let me take the thumb drive from my pocket." Pulling it out, he held it up as he handed her the jacket. "Made a few last-minute changes from the version I emailed you." He grinned. "Mind if we plug this into your computer?"

"Okay." She hung up his jacket before she remembered her manners. "Why don't you sit down at the dining room table while I get my laptop?"

Ruth returned with three wine glasses and the opened bottle of port just as Gwen brought in the laptop. Ruth poured, handed each a tiny glass, and held hers up in a toast.

"'Next to the originator of a good sentence is the first quoter of it,' said Ralph Waldo Emerson." Ruth smiled as she clinked glasses. "To writers, editors, and quoters." Then she glanced at the clock. "Oh my goodness, look at the time."

Gwen blinked. "Are you going somewhere?"

"Didn't I mention it?" Ruth hid a smile as she grabbed her coat from the closet. "I've got a finance council meeting tonight."

"Again?" Gwen stared at her.

Barely hiding a grin, Ruth turned her back as she pulled on her coat. "I'll be back by eight." With a wave, she was gone.

Feeling deserted, Gwen took a deep breath and turned toward Percy. "That was subtle."

He laughed. "Don't worry. We have a clear mission. Finish the edits," he snickered, "by eight."

She placed her laptop on the table and held out her hand. When Percy gave her a blank stare, she added, "The thumb drive, please."

"Oh, sure." Uncapping it, he shrank back and handed it to her.

She swallowed a grin. *Guess I'm not the only one feeling uneasy.*

Gwen made grammatical changes to the manuscript, paragraph by paragraph, with Percy watching over her shoulder, his arms resting on the back of her chair. Kitty-Cat rubbed against him, purring, shamelessly begging to be petted.

Usually nodding in agreement to Gwen's edits, every now and then Percy defended his choice of punctuation.

"No, this is a list within a sentence. These should be semicolons, not commas."

She nodded emphatically. "You're absolutely right. I sit corrected." Grinning, she turned toward him quickly, his lips only inches from her own. Finding herself drawn to/propelled from him, like the black-and-white dog magnets, she started to speak, then stopped. He hovered, teetering, leaning toward, then away from her parted lips. She leaned into him, finally murmuring, "Thanks for clarifying."

She closed her eyes, feeling his breath on her lips.

"Hi, guys," called Ruth, slamming the front door.

They pulled apart, but not soon enough judging from Ruth's muffled giggle. Gwen caught Ruth's amused grin.

Hiding her smile behind her hand, Ruth asked, "How's the editing going?"

Gwen felt the blood drain from her cheeks. Gathering her self-respect about her like slipped bra straps, she sat up straight and glanced at the clock.

"Eight already? We're nearly done," she said in her most businesslike tones. "How was your meeting?"

"Apparently, not as," Ruth looked from one to the other, "dynamic as yours."

Gwen avoided Ruth's smirk. Saving the document, she waited for the hard drive to stop spinning. Then she pulled out the thumb drive and handed it to Percy.

"I think we've covered enough for tonight, don't you?" Before he could answer, Gwen's cell phone rang. She knew from the chime it was Art. "Sorry, have to take this call." Excusing herself, she slipped into the bedroom, closing the door behind her.

She took a deep breath, grounding herself before she answered. "Hey."

"You *are* there." Art's voice sounded pleased. "I was just about to leave a voice mail."

"Yeah," she said, telling the truth while skirting it. "I was just finishing up some editing."

"About Catalonia's independence vote?"

"No, not much development in that story." Gwen shook her head. "The Catalonia High Court of Justice just announced it's opening an investigation of the November ninth vote. The scuttlebutt is they'll investigate Catalonia's president, deputy prime minister, and education minister because of their roles in organizing the vote, but who knows when or even if that'll happen."

"The wait-and-see game. How are your other articles going?"

"Working on the Christmas in Barcelona story." She breathed deeply, congratulating herself for again telling the truth without mentioning any details. "Oh, and I think I'll have the Columbus Day piece ready to send off tomorrow."

"Great." He chuckled. "You're a pro at spinning turns of events into articles."

She chuckled, too, politely, hearing the smile in his voice, but then her eyes narrowed. *Was that an innuendo?*

"Miss you, you know." He paused. A beat later, he added, "Planning on coming home for the holidays?"

"I'm hoping the independence story will develop, plus it's still a few weeks until Christmas. I would really like to cover more of the holiday concerts and events."

"Actually, I was wondering what your personal plans were, not your professional agenda."

"Oh, sure." Her laugh was hollow. "You know me. Nose for news—"

"Gwen, I'm not asking about work. I'm asking if you've thought about us."

She inhaled sharply. Then swallowed. Then cleared her throat. "Yeah."

"But no conclusions?"

Again, she inhaled sharply.

Art's tone was suddenly devoid of humor. Serious, he said, "I don't want to rush you."

"But?"

"I'd like to spend the rest of my life with you, Gwen. Starting with New Year's Eve. I can even juggle my schedule to meet you in Barcelona on December thirty-first, if you like."

She swallowed. "But?"

"But if you're still unsure, if you need more time than that to consider us as a couple." He took a deep breath. "Maybe we're not meant to be."

His tone has the finality of an ultimatum. "Art, I—"

A knock on her bedroom door interrupted her thoughts.

"Gwen, I've got to go," called Percy.

"Who was that?" Art asked, suspicious, his tone lifting on the final syllable.

"Oh," Gwen hesitated, not wanting to lie, but unable to twist the truth cleverly. She crossed her fingers. "Ruth's leaving for a meeting. Can I call you right back?"

Art hesitated. Finally, he said. "Sure. Bye." The phone clicked in her ear.

Gwen covered her face with her hands. Again, an impatient knock on her bedroom door interrupted her thoughts. "Gwen, I've . . . I'd better be going," called Percy.

She opened the door, her left hand resting on the door frame. "Have you got enough edits to keep you busy?" she asked him.

He looked at her, looked at her engagement ring, and grimaced. "Is that what this is, Gwen? Some kind of game? You give me enough to keep me occupied? You throw me a bone?" Shaking his head, he zipped his jacket and walked away, leaving her frozen in surprise.

"Percy?" She rushed to the front door, but he was already gone.

In his place stood her father, his arm raised, waving. *Saying goodbye or good riddance?* In a blink, starting from the ground up, he dissolved into thin air, only his upraised hand visible before he vanished.

Ruth eyed Gwen coldly, then lifted her eyebrow, turned away, and gathered the dirty glasses.

Am I as transparent as the ghost? "Ruth, what's wrong with me?"

"What do you mean?" Never lifting her eyes, Ruth took the glasses into the kitchen.

"You saw Percy leave. Apparently, I'm not very good at deception." Gwen sighed. "That was Art on the phone."

"I figured." Her tone was sour.

"He's ticked off at me. Percy stomped out of here. You're annoyed." *Be honest. Even the ghost seemed to favor Percy.* She put her hand to her forehead. "What's the matter with me?"

Ruth lifted her eyes and repeated, "What do you mean?"

"I . . ." Gwen looked at her engagement ring. "I'm virtually engaged to Art, yet—"

Ruth finished her thought. "You're attracted to Percy."

"What's wrong with me?"

Ruth shrugged. "I've never been in this position, but I remember something my mother used to say."

"What?"

"If you can't decide between two men, neither one's the right one."

"Great," Gwen muttered under her breath, again resting her forehead in her hand.

"On the other hand," said Ruth.

"Yes?" Gwen looked up hopefully.

"You seem to light up around Percy. There's an energy, a synergy about the two of you. Maybe . . . remember the old seventies song, 'Love the One You're With'?"

Gwen's eyes grew wide. "You're not telling me . . . ?"

"I'm just making an observation. I'm certainly not telling you what to do or who to do it with." Her smile fading, Ruth sighed. "That's something only you can decide."

The cat rubbed against Gwen's legs, wanting attention. Picking her up, Gwen said, "Seems you're the only one I haven't ticked off, Miss Kitty-Catalonia." Cuddling the cat to her chest, she turned to Ruth before closing her bedroom door. "I'd better return Art's call."

CHAPTER 12:

Restless Hearts

"Our heart is restless until it rests in you."
— Saint Augustine

Sunday morning, the four gathered at the cathedral. As Gwen met Percy's eyes, she felt her pulse quicken. Then blinking, she looked away. After Mass, the group walked to the Plaça Sant Jaume, where they saw a Christmas nativity scene.

"Oh, look, a crèche." Gwen pointed at the statues of the shepherds, three kings, Mary, Joseph, and the baby Jesus. Live palm and pine trees surrounded it.

As they approached, Percy said, "In Catalan, it's called El Pessebre de Nadal, meaning manger."

"But it's not just a manger scene," said Gwen, standing in front of it, admiring it. "It's a group of scenes. The stable, of course, but also the Archangel Gabriel, announcing to the shepherds, and the Christmas star, guiding the Wise Men."

"The nativity scene stays here until Candlemas, February second, winter's midpoint, halfway between the winter solstice and the spring equinox." Percy turned toward her, adding in a whisper, "Think you'll be here 'til then?"

She glanced at him, read his expression, and then looked away quickly. He seemed to have gotten over being angry at her. That was good for their little group, but she wanted to avoid direct eye contact. She looked around, trying to find something to change the subject. Hidden among the branches of a young pine tree, she saw a stooped figure wearing a red beret. With a cry of disbelief, she asked, "Am I seeing right?"

Ruth and Percy exchanged looks and began chuckling. "That's El Caganer," said Ruth, ducking her chin, trying to hide her grin.

"It looks like an elf with his pants down." Gwen raised her eyebrow. "Oh, my goodness, is that what I think it is?"

"El Caganer's been dropping his pants to . . . uh . . . fertilize the earth since the eighteenth century," said Percy, a mischievous glint in his eye.

"He's a popular figure in Catalonia," said Ruth, grinning, "believed to bring good luck."

"This season, the Independentista Caganer holding the flag of independence is especially trendy." Percy's shoulders seemed straighter as he lifted his head.

"How anyone can look at a pooping figure and take national pride in it is beyond me." Rolling his eyes, Crow shook his head.

"El Caganer's a Catalonian tradition," said Percy. "With him holding the Catalonian flag, it only intensifies his popularity."

"Independence?" Crow gave a derisive laugh. "It's nothing but self-centered nationalism." His brow wrinkled, his head was bent down, as if ready to enter battle.

"Catalonia—" Percy started, but Gwen headed off another political debate quickly.

"Oh, it's chilly." Gwen rubbed her hands together. "What's this hot chocolate and churros I've been hearing about? Is there any place around here that serves them?"

Ruth grinned her support. "Yes, not a block away. This way," she said, leading them through a side alley.

Ten minutes later, they were squeezed together, knee to knee, elbow to elbow, in a tiny booth intended for two. In front of each was a steaming cup of dark chocolate, as thick as pudding. Beside it was a plate of doughnut lengths.

Gwen picked up her cup, about to drink, when Percy said, "No, like this."

He dunked one of the crisp dough wands in the cup, swirled it, and used it like a spoon—eating, not drinking, the thick chocolate.

Gwen tentatively tasted it. As soon as it melted on her tongue, she groaned. "Delicious!" When each doughnut became too soft to dunk again, she ate it, savoring its crunchy texture against the chocolate's velvety smoothness.

Within minutes, Gwen felt warm and full. Sharing a contented sigh, she gave them a wry grin. "I won't think about the calories."

"Let's walk them off," said Ruth. "Where next?"

"Let's go to the Fira de Santa Llúcia Christmas Market on Avenida de la Catedral," said Percy, "just in front of the cathedral."

Five minutes later found them back where they had started that morning. They window-shopped as they slowly made their way through the market's colorful aisles. Stall after stall sold Christmas figurines, including the Caganer, as well as nativity scenes, wreathes, Christmas trees, candies, exotic fruit, and thousands of assorted Christmas handicrafts.

When they came to a display of smiley-faced logs wearing red berets, Gwen pointed at them. "What are those?"

Again, Ruth and Percy exchanged a grin. "That's El Caga Tió," said Ruth, "the Poop Log."

"Similar to El Caganer," said Percy, his eyes with a mischievous glint. "El Caga Tió poops gifts. Children keep them like pets for the month before Christmas, feeding them, covering them with blankets. Then, on Christmas Eve, they sing them a song and beat them with stick until they poop gifts."

Her eyes widening, Gwen stared at them in fascinated horror. "You're kidding?"

"Christmas Eve here isn't like in the States," said Ruth.

"I guess not."

"Christmas Eve is just for small gifts of food," said Ruth. "The big night for exchanging gifts is the night before Epiphany, the Night of the Three Kings or Cavalcada de Reis."

"There's a parade that night," added Percy, "where children deliver their Christmas wish lists to—"

"Santa Claus?" Gwen finished for him.

"No." He shook his head. "They give their letters to the Three Kings."

Gwen began chuckling. "What a topsy-turvy holiday. This is definitely going into my Christmas in Barcelona article."

Ruth and Crow exchanged a glance. "Crow and I have some . . ." Ruth paused, smiling mysteriously, "Christmas shopping to do."

"Oh." Surprised by the sudden announcement, Gwen was unsure what to say.

"Will you be all right getting home on your own?"

"Sure." Gwen shrugged. "Not a problem."

"I'll make sure she gets home safely," said Percy.

"No need." Gwen scowled. "I'm a big girl."

His quick response annoyed her. *What am I, a child?*

"Seriously," said Percy. "I'd like to introduce you to one of Barcelona's special Christmas treats." Glancing at her frown, he quickly added, "Strictly for your article."

"Of course." Grimacing, her eyes narrowing, she gave him a sharp look, but his idea intrigued her. *It is work related.* She shrugged. "Okay."

"Great. See you back home in a couple hours." Ruth splayed her fingers in a wave as she and Crow turned, walked out of the market, and caught a cab.

Gwen followed them with her eyes. "Wonder what they're up to."

"Probably what Ruth said, some Christmas shopping." He shrugged. "Maybe she wants to surprise you with a gift."

"It's plausible." She turned to him. "It's really not necessary for you to see me home. I'm perfectly capable of walking a few blocks unescorted."

"Of course you are." His violet-blue eyes sought hers. "Never meant to suggest otherwise. I just want to show you something and . . ."

"And?"

He took a deep breath. "Have to admit, I have an ulterior motive."

Gwen sighed. "Do you now? Gee, what a surprise."

He shook his head. "It's not what you think."

"How do you know what I'm thinking?" It should be obvious after the other night, but she didn't want to give him the satisfaction.

"I finished the rewrites from the other night. A half-hour's final editing should finish it." His eyes implored hers. "Think we can manage thirty minutes together?"

His expression tugged at her better nature. *Even if he is exasperating, he deserves a half hour.* "Sure."

His face lit up like the marketplace. "Great, but first I promised to show you one of Barcelona's special Christmas treats."

He hailed a cab, and twenty minutes later they got out at Plaça Catalunya. As he led her inside, he said, "This is Pista de hielo en Plaça de Catalunya, the largest ice skating rink in Europe."

"Ohmigosh." She laughed out loud. "I haven't skated since I was a little girl." Then her laughter died down to a nostalgic smile. "With my father."

"Let's rekindle those memories." With a grin, he led her to the skate rental booth.

They strapped on their skates and glided out on the ice. Almost losing her balance, Gwen held out her hand, and he caught her. Their eyes locked as he steadied her. Part of her wanted to pull away, be her usual independent self, and yet part of her enjoyed his nearness. She found herself relaxing in the steady rhythm of his gliding cadence. Her hand in his, they skated around the rink in unison with the organ music.

"Oh, this is fun!" She smiled, enjoying the exercise.

"Glad you like it." Returning her smile, he squeezed her hand.

Suddenly, she saw her father's spirit watching them from the sidelines. Her eyes locked with his, and she began trembling.

"Are you cold?"

"Huh?" Breaking her trance, she turned to Percy. "No, why do you ask?"

"You're shivering."

She looked back, but the ghost was gone. "Now that you mention it, I am a little chilled."

"Then let's get something hot to eat."

Shaking her head, she started to object.

"It's a typical Catalonian Christmas dish called Escudella i carn d'olla." He grinned. "Consider it research for your article."

Swallowing her smile, she deadpanned. "Well, as long as it's research."

Minutes later, they were seated at a candlelit table for two.

"So what is Escudella i carn d'olla, anyway?"

His chin resting on his hand, leaning toward her, he gazed into her eyes. "Escudella means bowl. It's a meat and pasta stew, hot peasant fare that warms you on a chilly December night."

"Sounds wonderful. Actually, it does sound good. All we've eaten today were the chocolate and churros." She rolled her eyes. "Delicious calories, but I'm not sure how nutritious."

With a shrug and a tilt of his head, he put her at ease. "You've skated off the calories."

A smile playing at her lips, she hesitated. In the candlelight, his eyes looked midnight blue, inviting. *Do I tell him?* Taking a deep breath, she took a leap of faith. "I have a confession to make."

He gave her a wry smile, crossed himself, and leaned in sideways, like a priest in a confessional. "Yes?"

"Tonight—actually, quite often lately—I've been seeing the ghost of my father."

Stiffening, he sat up straight. "Really?" He blinked, as if reevaluating her, the situation.

"I know how crazy that sounds." She grimaced. "You're probably wondering what loony bin I escaped from."

"No, tell me about it."

"My father passed away six months ago. Long story short, I came to Spain." Again, she grimaced, correcting herself. "At least, I went on the pilgrimage because of him. Since the first day, I've been seeing his spirit in places." She paused, trying to categorize the times she had seen him.

"What kind of places?"

"Places that resemble or remind me of things in our past."

Squinting, he shook his head. "I'm not following."

"For instance, the first time in León, I stumbled over a stone like one he and I'd found when I was a child."

"What about tonight?"

"My father was the one who taught me how to skate." Suddenly, it occurred to her. With a wry laugh, she looked at him. "Seems like you're usually near when I see him." She nodded slowly as the truth sank in. "You're a common thread between the sightings."

"Why's that?"

"I don't know." She crinkled her brow. "It just is." She watched his reaction. "Do you believe in ghosts?"

With another slight shrug and lift of his eyebrow, he said, "Spirits are Biblical. They're magisterial. They're part of Church teachings. Plus, there are numerous personal accounts throughout the ages. God must allow it for a reason. It's not that I don't believe in them. I've just never seen one."

"This is the only one I've ever seen. Although, I've seen him quite a few times now." She squinted, thinking. "Actually, once he appeared to me in a dream." Narrowing her eyes, she tried to characterize it. "That time, it was more like watching a video or an old, eight-millimeter movie of him as a child, interacting with his mother and grandmother."

"Interesting."

The waiter brought their steaming bowls of Escudella i carn d'olla, interrupting their conversation.

Before they began eating, Percy reached for her hand. "The next time you see this ghost, let me know. Give me a clue." Nodding, she squeezed his hand.

After dinner, they took a short cab ride back to Gwen's apartment. Ruth and Crow were chatting and drinking coffee at the dining room table when they walked in.

"Hi," Ruth called. "Have you eaten?"

"Just finished." Gwen's hand automatically clasped her full stomach. "How 'bout you two?"

"Same here, man." Crow gave Ruth an appreciative smile. "Ruth's a terrific cook."

Gwen and Percy shared a look but said nothing.

"How 'bout a cup of coffee?" Ruth already had the cups out and was pouring.

"Perfect."

"You're going to edit, right?"

"That's all right." Gwen grinned. "It's a laptop. I can balance it on my lap."

Ruth nudged Crow as she gestured toward the sofa with her chin. "Why don't you two take the table? We'll have our coffee in the living room."

Kitty-Cat jumped up on the table, waiting to rub against Gwen and Percy.

"Can you hold Kitty-Cat while I get my laptop?"

Within minutes, Percy and Gwen were collaborating on the manuscript, with the cat alternating between their laps. From the sofa, they heard a muffled giggle.

Gwen turned to see Ruth and Crow separate quickly. *What's up with those two?* she wondered. *Is it my imagination, or are they more than friends?* Swallowing a grin, she exchanged another look with Percy and went back to editing.

Within an hour, Gwen handed him the thumb drive and closed the notebook. "That's it!"

"Great job." Percy held out his hand. Grinning, she shook it. Feeling the warmth of his skin against hers made the blood rise in her cheeks. She pulled away and pretended to fuss with her computer so he wouldn't notice.

"Now what happens?" she asked.

"Tomorrow, I'm emailing it to my publisher. Hopefully, they'll accept it." His eyes caught Gwen's.

Held by his gaze, she smiled. "I'm crossing my fingers." She wanted to reach out and hug him but felt too awkward to do more than stare, her arms dangling at her sides.

Crow's voice boomed from the sofa. "Go on and hug her, man."

Gwen noticed Percy's cheeks flush. Chuckling nervously, they took a step toward each other, stopping at arm's length, and patted each other's shoulders. It felt awkward, but she couldn't face the prospect of actually letting herself fold into his embrace. She might never want to let go.

Crow shook his head. Then taking a thin bag off the coffee table, he strode toward them.

"Almost forgot. Here's your picture from the catamaran."

"Thanks." Percy handed it to Gwen. "You open it."

As she pulled it from its wrapper, Gwen felt the blood drain from her cheeks. "Let me see."

She turned the photo toward him. After Percy glanced at it, he raised his eyes to hers. In their reflection, she saw what she felt. There, on film, was the proof she had denied. Somehow, the photo had captured the frisson between them, the tension, their giddy exhilaration in that moment at the wheel of the boat. His eyes locked with hers in an ah-ha moment.

Gwen felt the buzz before she heard her cell phone ring. She knew from its chime it was Art, but she could not tear her eyes from Percy's. The attraction was magnetic, but on the third ring, she forced herself to break from the hold the intensity of those blue eyes had over her.

"Ruth, have you seen our photo?" Gwen pressed it into her hands as she hurried toward her room. "Excuse me a minute. Have to take this call."

"What took so long?" asked Art.

"Oh, Ruth has a couple friends over for coffee." She crossed her fingers. *It's true.* "So what have you been up to?"

"The usual. Work, more work." His laugh was dry. Then he paused, as if debating whether to mention it. "I did do one thing today that was interesting."

Her mind was racing a million miles an hour. *Should I tell Art? Tell him what? That I took a picture with someone? Why do I feel so guilty? It's a photo, for heaven's sake.*

"Did you hear me?"

"What?" She heard the nearly imperceptible sigh he made when annoyed.

"Are you multitasking?"

"No, sorry, just a little background noise. Could you repeat what you said?"

"*I said*, I did do something interesting today."

"Really? What was that?"

"I downloaded my boarding pass for Barcelona." The smile came through his voice. "It's official. We'll be 'ringing' in New Year's Eve together in Spain." He chuckled. "If you like, we could make it a double ring ceremony."

Not really listening to Art, she heard Percy's voice in the other room, but she could not make out the words. Then, from the dead airspace, she knew Art had asked something and was expecting an answer.

"Sorry, what was the question?"

"Gwen, do you need to charge your cell phone? Is your signal weak?" She could tell from his tone, he was irritated.

"No, no, just white noise." Again, she crossed her fingers. "Sorry, I didn't hear you. It was something about ringing in the New Year?"

He sighed. Then clearly, concisely, syllable by syllable, he repeated. "Would you like to make it a double ring ceremony?"

Blinking, looking toward the door to the living room, she gave a nervous giggle. "Sorry, I'm not following."

His tone exasperated, Art asked, "Do I have to spell it out for you?"

She heard laughter from the living room and turned her head.

When she did not answer, he nearly bellowed, "Gwen, do you or do you not want to get married on New Year's Eve?"

She jerked the phone away from her ear. Then taking a deep breath, she said, "There's no need to shout."

"I'm sorry, Gwen." He groaned. "It's just frustrating to try to set the date for our wedding and…" He ended with a sigh.

"And what?"

"And I get the feeling you're too distracted to listen." He paused. "Gwen, is something bothering you? Is anything wrong?"

"No, no, of course not." Even to her, the answer sounded too quick, too fast. She put her hand to her temple. Licking her lips, she tried again. "You say I seem distracted. The truth is, Ruth has a group of people here, and it's difficult to hear you over their chatter."

That's a bald-faced lie, if I ever told one. She waited, holding her breath, wondering if he believed her.

Finally, his voice dry, he asked, "Is that true?"

Do two people make a group? She nodded. "Yes, that's the truth."

"All right, maybe I'm just a little cantankerous tonight." He attempted a chuckle. "It's been a long week. Would you prefer to call me after your company leaves tonight, or should I call you in the morning?"

Listening to the banter in the next room, she said, "How 'bout a wake-up call?"

"Talked me into it. 'Night, Gwen. I love you."

"Nighty-night, sleep tight."

"Love you."

Cornered. Stifling a sigh, barely moving her lips, she murmured by rote, "Love you," and hung up.

She closed her eyes and breathed deeply. *What am I doing? Why did I just say that?* Silently groaning, she answered her own question. *Because I do love Art. Just not in that way.*

She thought of her father and her grandmother. *What's the wise decision? What's the right decision?*

As she opened the door, she heard Percy's voice. "Gaudí is the finest architect the world's ever seen."

"You're just saying that because he was Catalan, man." Crow's tone was dismissive.

Gwen sighed, grateful for the distraction of another great debate between Crow and Percy.

"Antoni Gaudí was a century ahead of his time." As Percy warmed to his subject, he began gesturing. His index finger tapped the table for emphasis. "Even today, nearly ninety years after his death, his architecture still stands as the touchstone of Catalan Modernism. UNESCO's declared not one, but seven of his works World Heritage Sites."

"He was an inspired man." Pursing her lips, Ruth nodded. "God and nature motivated him. It's so evident in his works, he's earned the nickname 'God's Architect.' They even say he's on the fast track to becoming a saint."

"Oh, man, you've got to be kidding." Crow cocked a skeptical eyebrow.

As if brushing aside all competition, Percy's arm swept across the table. "His work transcended the Modernist movement of the early twentieth century."

"His expression motivates architects, artists, and authors," said Ruth. "Look at Dr. Seuss. Think of the iconic buildings of *How the Grinch Stole Christmas.*"

Crow sniffed sarcastically.

"Gaudí inspired." Ruth nodded vehemently. "Like Gaudí, Dr. Seuss rarely used straight lines in his art."

"The Casa Batlló's a perfect example," said Percy. "Built fifty years before Dr. Seuss published his first book, it's nicknamed the 'Dr. Seuss of masonry.'"

"That building feels so…." Ruth used her hand to reach for the right word, "organic. Walking through it feels like rambling around inside a dragon. Or think of the psychedelic park in the middle of Barcelona that Gaudí and Güell designed," said Ruth.

"Did someone say psychedelic?" Crow's eyes lit up.

Ruth returned his grin with a chuckle. "Picturesque in its natural beauty, Park Güell was a self-sufficient community with every modern convenience."

"Although the garden city movement inspired it—"

"Garden city movement?" Joining in, Gwen crossed to the table. "What's that?"

"It was a movement to build complete communities in natural settings," said Percy. His eyes lit up as she joined them, just like they had in that photo from the catamaran. His eyes sparkling, he stared at her.

She cocked her head as she tried to read him. *You'd think he has no intention of letting what he saw in that photo fade away.*

The look in his eyes only left Gwen with more uncertainty and questions. Crow broke the moment with his own side of the ongoing debate.

"Sustainable development?" Crow laughed. "Man, Gaudí and Park Güell really were ahead of their time. You got my attention with psychedelic, but sustainable development makes a believer out of me."

"Understandably." Percy and Ruth shared a chuckle.

Listening to them, Gwen began making mental notes for another article: "How Gaudí Shaped Barcelona."

"Why don't we visit that park and Casa Batlló?" she suggested.

"Great idea." Percy's eyes smiled at hers. "And Casa Milà."

"And La Sagrada Família," said Ruth, "Gaudí's unfinished basilica."

"Looks like I'll have enough material to write another article, maybe two."

"Whatever it takes to keep you in Spain longer," Percy said, staring at her with open adoration.

His words and expression left no question. *He's definitely interested, but long term or short?* Gwen stifled a sigh.

❄

The next day, Art called. "Good morning, sunshine."

The smile in his voice made her wince. No closer to a decision, she did not know what to say.

Mumbling, "Morning," she stifled a yawn.

"No ongoing party in the other room, I trust." She heard Art's dry laugh.

"No," she yawned again, "but they left late."

"Meaning that I shouldn't have called so early?" His tone was chilly.

"No, of course not, I'm glad you called." *Am I? Really?*

"Gwen, I—" He paused. "I proposed to you months ago, yet you still haven't given me a straight answer. I thought I knew you, but . . . I can't help but wonder. We need to resolve this, or we need to move on."

Stumbling for an answer, she fell back on the tried and true. "Art, I need more time."

"Time's not the issue here. I think the distance between us is due to just that—the distance. Here's what I propose—"

"Art, I—"

"Hear me out." His tone was curt. "I'm flying into Barcelona on New Year's Eve. Get the paperwork for our wedding. If you want, line up a church—"

"It isn't that simple—"

"Actually, it is . . . if that's what you want." Taking a deep breath, he paused. "If not a double-ring ceremony as we ring in the New Year, we can be married a few days after." His tone warmed. "I just want us to meet face-to-face before you make any decision. Gwen, you know how much you mean to me."

She did. Remembering their time together, Gwen caved. She liked him, admired him intensely. She even loved him . . . in a way, just not that way.

No fireworks, yet it's been a stable relationship that's worked. She grimaced. *Is that enough? Am I so hungry for a father, I'd settle for a marriage of companionship, a marriage of convenience?*

"So what do you say?"

She knew the tone—the forced smile, bright tone he used when closing business deals.

"We're not discussing a merger, Art. It's a marriage, a sacred, lifetime commitment we're talking about, not some transaction."

"Don't you think I know that?"

At the sound of his strangled voice, she swallowed the lump in her throat. *I do love him. Why am I so torn?* She felt tears run down her face as she recalled their time together. *I have no history with Percy. How do I even know it's love and not simply physical attraction?*

Nodding, she cleared her throat. "Okay, Art. I . . . I'm not saying I'll marry you, but," she sighed, "I do love you."

"Then you'll take care of the paperwork?" His voice sounded relieved yet somehow triumphant.

She nodded as she swiped at the tears. "I'll get the paperwork started."

"I'll see you New Year's Eve."

CHAPTER 13:

Gaudí

"Nothing is invented, for it's written in nature first."
— Antoni Gaudí

That afternoon, as they approached the entrance to Park Güell, Percy turned toward Crow.

"Besides a garden city, this park was designed to be a symbol of Catalan's nationalism."

"Man." Crow shook his head. "What kind of political propaganda is that?"

"Just look at this staircase." Percy pointed out the features. "All the Catalonian countries are represented here. Gaudí's political identity was closely linked to Catalonian cultural identity."

Gwen snapped pictures of the mosaic salamander between the staircases.

"El drac," said Percy, "the dragon."

Ruth waved them to a path on the right. "There are just as many, if not more, religious symbols here as political. For instance, Monumento al Calvario." She pointed to a chapel. "Gaudí belonged to the Spiritual League of Our Lady of Montserrat, a Catholic Catalan organization."

Nodding, Percy agreed. "Montserrat inspired much of his work."

"God and nature were what inspired Gaudí."

"And that's what surrounds us." Gwen looked up through the palm tree fronds at the flitting green parrots, chuckling at their raucous chirps. "Nature and God."

After stopping for tapas, they walked to Casa Milà.

"There's La Pedrera, the quarry," said Ruth, pointing.

Gwen looked at its bold, undulating stone façade, with twisted wrought-iron decorations on its balconies and windows. "Why do they call Casa Milà the quarry?"

"The facade's made mostly from limestone blocks," said Ruth.

"Now you're seeing Gaudí's blend of function and form," said Percy. "He struck harmony between the structural and ornamental features, between the container and the content." He smiled. "He even designed an underground garage."

"What's so great about having a garage?" Gwen asked.

"Gaudí designed La Pedrera in 1905," said Percy, lifting his eyebrow. "Ford's Model T didn't debut until 1908."

"Oh." Gwen breathed in deeply. "He was a visionary, wasn't he?"

"You'll find religious symbols here too. Words from the rosary are painted on the cornices, and Gaudí's original plans called for a statue of Our Lady," said Ruth, pointing to the figures on the roof. "Because of the anticlerical mood at that time, the owners thought it best not to tweak the agitators' noses."

"Are those statues?"

"They look like statues," Percy shook his head, "but they're actually staircase exits, fans, and chimneys covered with broken bits of marble, Valencia tiles, and glass."

Ruth stifled a giggle. "Locally, they're called espanta bruixes or witch scarers."

"They look scary," said Gwen, "but to me they look more like soldiers than witches."

"Garden of Warriors is what the poet Pere Gimferrer called them," said Percy.

After stopping for a glass of sangría, they walked to Casa Batlló.

"Wow," said Gwen as they approached. "Look at that roof. It's not flat or pitched. Instead, it's so contoured, it looks alive, and those roof tiles look like snake scales."

Chuckling, Percy agreed with a nod. "Some compare it to a dragon's back." He pointed. "Look at the turret and cross just left of center. Some say it represents Saint George's lance plunged into the dragon's back." He turned toward Crow. "Another nod to nationalism since Saint George is the patron saint of Catalonia."

Before Crow could respond, Gwen jumped in. "I see why locals call it the house of bones, but it looks like the dragon's bones are on the outside."

"An exoskeleton." Nodding, Percy agreed. "But wait until you see the inside. That's where you'll see how the dragon's backbone is supported."

They decided to take the audio/visual tour. When it led them to the loft, Gwen looked down a long hallway of arches. "Look at all these."

Percy nodded as he pressed the button. "You're looking at sixty catenary arches that some say create the 'ribcage' for the dragon's spine on the roof."

"What's catenary mean?"

He paused the A/V tour. "See how the arches seem to dip up?"

She tilted her head, holding her headphones in place, as she peered at the oddly shaped arches that also seemed to twist.

"This is like a hanging chain that dips in the middle, only in reverse."

"It dips up." She grinned as it began to make sense. "Got it."

Dusk was settling over the city as the audio/visual tour led them to the roof-top terrace. Chimneys and air shafts were imaginatively disguised as lighted figures, said the tour. Again, Gaudí used trencadís, creating mosaics of embedded, broken bits of ceramic pottery and marble.

"Did you know Gaudí designed these four chimney stacks this way to prevent backdrafts?" asked Percy.

She shook her head. "His architecture wasn't just fluff. He really did marry function with form, didn't he?"

The night air was balmy. Several stars appeared overhead as the lights below began twinkling. Gwen leaned against the railing, watching as the city put on its glittering, evening finery. She lifted her head, breathing in deeply, catching an unfamiliar scent. *It's like I'm inhaling the night's magic.*

As she turned back toward the roof's lit-up figures, her body brushed against Percy's. She opened her eyes wide as a current of electricity shot through her. The pit of her stomach contracted, taking away her breath. She gasped as she found his lips only millimeters from hers. Hovering, they seemed suspended in each other's space, drawing ever closer, yet not touching.

"Isn't this view great?" Crow's voice boomed from behind them.

Again, Gwen gasped as she jumped apart. "Yeah." Blinking, regaining her equilibrium, she said, "Magical." A quick glance at Percy proved she was not the only one affected. His eyes pierced hers with such intensity, she looked away.

After exploring the rooftop terrace, they walked downstairs. Gwen lightly ran her fingers over the shiny surfaces of the walls' Mediterranean-blue tiles. As they descended each floor, the multicolored blues of the tiles gradually lightened from cobalt and indigo to gentian, then to cerulean tones, then to opalescent azures and creams. At each landing, she glanced at the central light well, noticing the gradation of the blue tiles—darkest at the roof, progressively lightening as they descended until they became pastels near the ground floor.

She grasped the wooden railings, feeling their smooth contours flowing beneath her hand like water. Like electricity. Again, she glanced at Percy and felt that tingle run through her. She looked instead at the stairway. Even the sides of the wide, wooden stairs resembled the vertebras of an undulating dragon's backbone. No straight lines anywhere, the wooden molding looked like rippling waves, ebbing and flowing.

She glanced at the round windows, resembling large portholes. Imaginative tiles and mosaics lined the stairwells, while twisted metal balustrades looked like floating seaweed. Whimsical details above the beams resembled octopus tentacles. *I feel I'm swimming in the sea.*

The virtual-reality tour not only included audio, it had Computer Generated Imagery. In real time, it displayed what each room had looked like, furnished as Gaudí had intended. When Gwen took her eyes away from the device, she saw the rooms as they appeared in the twenty-first century. When she looked into the virtual device, aiming it around each room, it revealed Gaudí's twentieth-century tapestries and furnishings. Or skylights became swimming tortoises. Or water ebbed and flowed across the floors. *It's otherworldly.*

In the study, she saw a secluded niche. The alcove's mushroom-shaped entrance led to two parallel-facing seats, separated by a copper fireplace.

"That's a festejador," said Percy, a glint in his blue eyes.

"A what?"

"It's a courting nook for young couples." Pointing to the cushioned benches, he said, "The young couple would sit on one side, while the duenna, the chaperone, would sit across from them, watching, listening."

"Oh!" Cringing, she felt herself blush. "How awkward."

His eyes still twinkling, Percy grinned. "All they could hope was the duenna would doze off by the fire." He shrugged. "It'd be their only way to steal a kiss." Then, his eyes focusing on her lips, his smile relaxed into a thoughtful expression.

Again, she felt herself subtly inclining toward him, leaning into him as she recalled the first time he had stolen a kiss. *My, my, my, haven't things changed?*

"And this is the study," announced a tour guide, leading another group. Instantly, the room ignited with people bustling about, chattering, and peering into their virtual devices.

Shaken from their trance, Gwen and Percy grinned at each other. Percy took her hand in his, gently brushing her palm with his fingers, and led her into the foyer. When the tour finished, they turned in their hardware as they joined Crow and Ruth. Gwen stared at Crow. *What's different? Instead of sixty, he looks sixteen.*

"I've asked Ruth to have dinner with my friends and me tonight," said Crow, stammering, "to introduce them . . . I mean, introduce her to them."

Gwen found it difficult to keep a straight face. Chewing her lip, she avoided looking at Percy, afraid she would burst out laughing. Tongue in cheek, she wagged a finger at Crow.

"I expect Ruth home at a reasonable hour." Swallowing a smirk, she added, "No shenanigans. Remember, we're going to la Sagrada Familia in the morning."

Waving to Crow and Ruth across the street, Percy turned to Gwen. "Looks like we're on our own for dinner."

She checked her cell for the time. "It's so early. I'm not hungry yet. Are you?"

Shaking his head, he thought for a minute. "Do you like Andalusian?"

She lifted her shoulders. "I don't know. I've never had it."

"Then you're in for a treat." Hailing a cab, he said, "Poble Espanyol."

"What's Poble Espanyol?" she asked as they settled inside.

"It's a model Spanish village, with full-sized buildings from all the different regions of Spain. In the Andalusian restaurant, they have typical Andalusian music." His eyes twinkling, he raised his eyebrow, as if baiting her.

She chuckled. "Okay, I'll bite. What's 'typical Andalusian music'?"

"You'll see . . . actually, hear." He grinned.

Within minutes, the taxi dropped them off at the village, where they strolled around, comparing the different kinds of architecture. As soon as they entered the Andalusian restaurant, the host greeted them with a glass of sherry and showed them to their table.

When the waiter handed them menus, he asked, "Would you like the standard meal?"

Gwen looked to Percy for an explanation.

"That's four courses for a set price: soup, salad, entree, and dessert."

The waiter added, "Six options for each of the courses and sangría."

She nodded. "Sounds great. I'll have the flounder."

Percy ordered puntillitas.

"What's that?"

"Baby squid made a la andaluza, dredged in chickpea flour and then deep-fried in olive oil."

Over dinner, she asked, "What was that Ruth had said about Epiphany being Spain's Christmas?"

His eyes crinkled in a smile. "Christmas is for celebrating Christ's birth. Epiphany's party night. Cavalcada de Reis or the Night of the Three Kings is for watching parades and exchanging gifts."

"The Three Kings . . . the Magi . . . you might call their night Christmas Magi-c."

He snickered. "You might."

"What an interesting separation of sacred and secular." Crossing her arms, she chewed her bottom lip as she digested the idea. "I like that. It keeps both Christ and the Mass in Christmas yet allows for the season's material side. No confusion of the two."

As soon as the waiter had cleared the table and refilled the sangría pitcher, a guitarist thrummed a chord. The lights dimmed, and a spotlight highlighted a Flamenco dancer on center stage. As she posed dramatically, the music's tempo picked up. First moving only her hands, she gradually stepped into a lively tap dance, posturing, kicking, and moving in sync with the music.

A man began clapping his hands in time to the beat. Then a singer's voice joined the mix as a second dancer appeared. Gwen more than watched them. Drawn into their world of concentrated sound and movement, she became part of the dance. Their facial expressions and gestures intense, they told a story with their rhythmic bodies and cadenced music. For an hour and a half, they sang, danced, *lived* the music. Watching, Gwen danced vicariously through the performers. She felt one with them. When Percy reached for her hand across the table, she clasped it so tightly at times during the performance, her knuckles turned white.

When the music ended with a flourish, Gwen impulsively jumped to her feet along with the rest of the diners. Her arms raised over her head as she clapped her approval, her praise. Her support only added to the thunderous applause exploding around them.

Then she felt Percy's eyes burning into her. She turned toward him, drawn to him, magnetized. Catching her breath as their eyes locked, her arms gradually lowered from their position. Impulsively, she threw her arms around him as he caught her in his. Tasting each other's lips, they felt their souls embrace as they became one.

Moments later, still quivering in his arms, her blood racing, Gwen opened her eyes. Gradually their lips drew apart as they studied each other. Feeling his heartbeat against her chest, feeling his breath on her lips, she took a deep breath, trying to regain her composure. Faint, giddy, she rested in his arms, grateful for their support.

After a moment, she gently extricated herself from him. To her amazement, the crowd was still applauding. Though it seemed hours had passed in his embrace, only seconds had actually elapsed. She chuckled as she imagined a tabloid headline: *TIME STOOD STILL AS HE SWEPT ME OFF MY FEET.*

"What's so funny?"

Smiling, she shook her head. "Nothing. I'm just happy."

She looked at the stage where the performers had gathered. As they held hands for a final, group bow, one of them suddenly turned toward her and grinned. Her eyes opening wide, she stared. The face was her father's. With a silent gasp, it occurred to her, *He approves.*

She blinked. *Why should I care whether or not he approves? He's made me feel the outcast since I was eight . . . so why* do *I care?*

No cabs were to be found at Poble Espanyol, but the evening was pleasant, so they walked to Plaça de Espanya. Cabs were plentiful there, and within minutes Percy saw her to her door.

As she turned the key to the apartment, she took a deep breath. *Moment of truth. Is Ruth home yet? Do I invite him in for coffee?* Before she could push the door, Ruth opened it.

"Oh, you're home," said Gwen. *Am I relieved or disappointed?*

"Just got in ourselves." Ruth opened the door wide, and Crow waved from the sofa. "Coffee's almost ready, and we picked up some saffron cake at the bakery. Hungry?"

Gwen looked at Percy. "Sure," he said.

＊

After Percy and Crow left, Gwen helped Ruth put away the dishes.

"Am I detecting a romantic interest in Crow?" Gwen tried to hide her smirk.

Ruth turned away to stack the plates, but not before Gwen saw her blush. "Jim and I are just friends."

"Jim?" Gwen opened her eyes wide. "Right. Seems like the pilgrimage's paid off for you."

"What do you mean?" Ruth turned back to her, and Gwen gave her a mischievous grin.

"As I recall, when we met, you said you'd reached a point where you needed to decide what to do with your life. You said you were looking for two things from the pilgrimage. You wanted to find the spiritual in the ordinary, and you wanted something to confirm your faith."

"That's right. I did, didn't I?" She gazed into space.

After a moment, Gwen asked, "Have you?"

"Have I what?"

"Have you found the spiritual in the ordinary or found anything to confirm your faith?"

Ruth frowned, thinking. "I hadn't analyzed it, but now that you bring it up, yes, I believe I have." She bobbed her head in a firm nod.

"How?"

"All four of us have made progress on our spiritual journeys." She met Gwen's eyes. "You've lost some of your anger toward your father and Father. As a result, there's less distance between you and God. You're closer to Him."

Furrowing her brow, Gwen said, "Hadn't looked at it that way."

"Jim had been searching for God in all the wrong places, but I believe he's finally found Him. Percy seems to have found his stride. He's confident in his beliefs."

Gwen laughed out loud. "Passionate in his beliefs."

Wearing a gentle smile, Ruth glanced at her. "Through you three, I've experienced God vicariously. Through your eyes, I've experienced the spiritual in the ordinary."

"For instance?"

"For one thing, that rock you found and left at the Iron Cross. Its importance to you was obvious."

"That's right." *Never was the 'Our Father' so significant.* Swallowing the sudden lump in her throat, she looked at Ruth. "What else?"

"For another thing, the miles we hiked with blisters and sore feet, each in our own way drawing nearer to God. Think of the dinners and discussions we've shared. Think of the family we've become. Ordinary things, but, oh, so meaningful."

Gwen digested that, recalling the little things, the camaraderie over tapas and their fireside conversations, where they had shared their dreams and fears. Each person had magnified the experience of the others. It was their combined insignificant events that had grown into close friendships.

"With God at the core, the compounded trivials become the significant."

"Okay, I see how you've . . . *we've* experienced the spiritual in the ordinary, but you also said you wanted something to confirm your faith. Have you found that?"

"We still haven't gotten to Montserrat, where I'm going to research the Ark of the Covenant, but every basilica, cathedral, chapel, and church we've visited has reaffirmed my faith. Every prayer, every blessing has brought me closer to God. Each step of our pilgrimage has bolstered my belief, confirmed my faith." Sighing, she nodded slowly. "Just hadn't thought of it before."

"Has this helped you decide what to do with your life?"

Ruth grinned mischievously.

"Let me guess." Gwen swallowed a smile. "Do you see Crow fitting into the rest of your life?"

"Jim," she corrected.

Later in bed, Gwen lay awake, thinking of Percy. *Was it the music? The sangría? Why was I so attracted to him?*

"Me-ow-ow." Kitty-Cat jumped up on the bed.

"What do you think?"

"Me-ow-ow." Kitty-Cat began purring as Gwen scratched her neck. In the dim glow of the nightlight, she saw Art's engagement ring.

What do I do about Art? And Percy? New Year's Eve is only two weeks away. I can't dismiss the attraction. She caught her breath. *I feel fireworks with Percy, but this is nothing but a passing fancy, not a lifetime commitment.*

Suddenly, there was a crash of thunder. And then another. Kitty-Cat moved closer. In the flickering flash of the lightning, Gwen thought she saw a man in her room. She yelped.

Bright lightning followed another peal of thunder. And another. Kitty-Cat arched her back and began hissing as Gwen recognized her father's silhouette.

"Why are you here?" she asked in a hoarse whisper. "You never cared about me, not past the age of eight. Why are you here now, harassing me?"

Another peal of thunder followed by bright lightning outlined his form, but the figure made no sound, no movement. He just stood, silently watching her, as if letting nature speak for him.

"What do you want?"

Kitty-Cat began a low growl.

Gwen heard the pitter-patter of raindrops beginning to strike the window. Another crash of lightning struck just outside the building. She saw the light as she heard the sound.

With a loud growl, Kitty-Cat leaped off the bed, pouncing at the figure.

Along with the thunder, rain, and growling, Gwen also mentally heard what sounded like a sigh: "Fffffrgvvvvv."

What? Again, she heard a sigh, but this time she made out a word. "Forgive."

Once more lightning struck just outside the window, but in its flash she saw the figure had vanished.

Kitty-Cat jumped back on the bed, curling up beside her. Now all Gwen heard was the cat purring and the rain splattering against the window.

Did I imagine hearing anything else? Her mind replayed the sound. *Forgive.* She lay awake, unable to sleep.

Then, in what seemed the next moment, she woke, blinking at the light. Kitty-Cat was still curled up beside her, but the sun was shining brightly. *Guess I dozed off.*

She recalled having seen her father. *Maybe I dreamed it. No, I can still hear that eerie sigh. Forgive.*

Suddenly, she understood, as if her mind had worked it out while she slept. She and her father were simply the last two links of a chain reaching back to her grandmother.

Or further. Who knows how many generations are connected? The sins of the father are *inherited. Family violence and abuse are passed down from generation to generation. Maybe dysfunction's also taught. Poor choices affect not only those involved, but their children and their children's children.*

I have to break the cycle. But how?

Ruth's words came to mind. "Pray for him. Your father needs healing as much as you." *Forgive.*

Internalizing the advice, she said a quick prayer. Then her eyes fell on the clock. *Yikes! Time to get dressed.* Moving gingerly, trying not to disturb Kitty-Cat, Gwen crawled out of bed.

CHAPTER 14:

La Sagrada Familia

"The straight line belongs to men, the curved one to God."
— Antoni Gaudí

Gwen and Ruth met the men at the entrance to la Sagrada Familia's crypt.

Disappointed that they came in through a side entrance that led downstairs, Gwen said, "I thought we'd see the basilica."

"We will." Crow held up four tickets. "After Mass."

"How did you get those?"

Crow shrugged. "Friends."

"You've got a lot of friends." Ruth's eyes crinkled at the sides in a private smile. He gave her a sly smile in return.

Gwen scrutinized him, realizing Crow had gradually changed over the previous weeks. *Odd I hadn't noticed. And what had Ruth called him? Jim?*

Gone was his bandanna. Gone were the bushy gray-blond strands of hair peeking out the sides. His hair was pulled back neatly into a ponytail. Though he still wore jeans, his jacket was a well-cut, supple leather. Even his facial expression and demeanor had changed.

She blinked at the transformation. "Crow, you look more like James Rutherford the Third than Jimmy Black Crow. What happened to you?"

He glanced at Ruth and then turned to Gwen with a grin. "She did."

Gwen wanted to ask more, but the organ began a fugue, signaling them to take their seats.

The second reading was from First Thessalonians. "Always be joyful. Pray constantly. And for all things give thanks. This is the will of God for you in Christ Jesus. Do not stifle the Spirit or despise the gift of prophecy with contempt; test everything and hold on to what is good."

Gwen mulled it over. *Pray, give thanks, and test everything. Isn't that what I'm doing? Trying to make heads or tails out of what's happened in my life, what's happening?* She glanced at Percy, and he turned toward her with a smile. Then he raised his eyebrow, silently asking, *What?*

Nothing, she mouthed with a shake of her head, but she reached for his hand.

"Today's the third Sunday of Advent," said the celebrant. "With Christmas nearly here and so many decisions to make, what better time than now to ask for advice? Do I get an artificial or a real tree? Do I want a white Christmas? Have I left anything off my wish list?"

Chuckles and grins met him.

"What better time to ask God for wisdom? In this chaotic season, we need all the help we can get. How can we make the right decisions, make the right choices? Turn to the book of Proverbs. Most proverbs come from Solomon. You remember him? God let Solomon choose anything he wanted, and what did he request? Wisdom.

"Wisdom's an elusive quality only a few seem to possess, yet, depending on the translation, the word occurs forty-one to forty-six times throughout the book of Proverbs.

"We're talking about heavenly wisdom, which teaches us the skills for godly living. Why's it so important? Here's what Proverbs says. Wisdom's 'more precious than rubies, and nothing you desire can compare with her.' Or it's 'better to get wisdom than gold, to choose understanding rather than silver.'

"For the Lord gives wisdom, and from his mouth comes knowledge and understanding. But where do we find it? Like love, we often look for wisdom in all the wrong places. My favorite restaurant's a Chinese buffet. Not only do I like Chinese food, but each meal comes with a small dose of wisdom. Fortune cookies."

The assembly chuckled.

"Obviously, you can't find heavenly wisdom in fortune cookies, but where can you find it? Since you're searching for heavenly wisdom, go straight to the heavens. Ask God, who gives generously to all.

"He gives us wisdom in two ways. The first way's through His Word. The Bible's not just a collection of stories. It's our manual to godly living. It's a blueprint, where God reveals his plans to us.

"The second way God gives us wisdom is through other people. We know God uses us and others to accomplish His plans. It makes sense that God would also use other people to voice His wisdom. Surround yourself with people you trust, so they can advise you. A word of wisdom often helps you make the wise choice, the right decision."

The wise choice, the right decision. Gwen glanced at Percy sideways.

"Wisdom also serves as a defense. God's a shield to those who take refuge in him. Think how much heartache we could avoid if we'd accept God's heavenly wisdom. Though it's true we learn from past mistakes, think of the negativity we could have escaped if we'd only listened to God in the first place.

"Heavenly wisdom protects us from making wrong choices. It guards us from taking the wrong paths. It guides us daily.

"Finally, consider this. Your search for wisdom is really a search for God since He's the source of all wisdom, all good. During this Advent season, make Christmas an *advent*ure. Like the Magi, the Three Wise Men, seek wisdom. Seek God."

Wisdom. Gwen sighed as she said a silent prayer. *Please give me the gift of wisdom. I could sure use it.*

For the recessional hymn, they sang 'O Come, O Come, Emmanuel," where the lyrics of the second verse jumped out at her.

> *O come, thou Wisdom from on high, who orderest all things mightily;*
> *to us the path of knowledge show, and teach us in her ways to go.*

As Mass let out, Crow handed them each a ticket as he took them aside. "This tour will let us skip the lines." He led them to the Nativity façade and pointed above the door. "Interesting that the priest was just talking about the Magi. This is where we're meeting our tour guide."

Within minutes, the guide joined them, introducing herself as Núria.

"Núria," repeated Gwen. "What a lovely name. What's it mean?"

"It's Catalan, meaning the wisdom of God."

Gwen grinned at the irony. *Here we are, standing beneath the Magi, talking to the wisdom of God.* "Can you tell us about the Magi carving?"

"Of course." The woman smiled as she pointed out the details. "The Nativity façade represents hope. As you can see, Gaudí's plan includes carvings of nearly a hundred plant and animal species, which, as well as three doors, are dedicated to faith, hope, and charity. All the names of Christ's ancestors are engraved on the column above the central door. The serpent and apple are engraved at the base, and the baby Jesus is carved on the door. The Annunciation is carved above it. The Magi, as well as the signs of the zodiac as they appeared in the heavens at Christ's birth, are also visible in this façade."

"The signs of the zodiac?" Crow moved closer for a better view.

She nodded. "The rest of the façade includes different episodes of Jesus' childhood and the mysteries, such as the Holy Trinity and the Immaculate Conception. Notice how the towers of the Nativity façade begin in a square shape. Then, partway up, they become round. They completed this façade in 1926."

Núria then took them to the other side of the basilica. "This is the Passion façade," she said, "opposite of the Nativity's. Notice its coarser, more angular lines. They represent Jesus' pain and sacrifice. The crucified Christ is carved over the middle door. Around Him, you'll find those figures present at his anguish. The holy women and good thief are on one side, while the evil thief and soldiers that mocked Him are on the other. See the cryptogram?"

"Cryptogram?" Crow craned his neck for a better look. "Where?"

"There, just behind the *Kiss of Judas* statue," Núria said, pointing. "Normally, in squares of four, where the numbers run sequentially from one to sixteen, the magic constant is thirty-four."

Gwen squinted. "The magic what?"

"The magic constant is the sum of the numbers in a single line, row, or diagonal, but this square does not contain the numbers twelve or sixteen. Instead, ten and fourteen are included twice, making a magic constant of thirty-three, the age of Jesus Christ at His crucifixion."

Mentally, Gwen added up a diagonal row. Then she added a column. When each equaled thirty-three, she smiled to herself.

"Three Latin words appear on this façade—*Veritas, Vida,* and *Via*—since Jesus is the Truth, the Life, and the Way. Although this façade's plans were begun in 1892, its construction was not finished until 1978."

"So there'll be two main entrances?" asked Gwen.

"Actually, there'll be a third. Construction began in 2002 on what will be the main façade, the Celestial Glory of Jesus. It'll symbolize the path to God: death, judgment, and glory." Núria swept her hand across a city block of buildings. "To complete it, this entire block across the Carrer de Mallorca will have to be demolished. A huge staircase will then be built, leading over an underground passage representing hell, purgatory, and death, while seven large columns dedicated to the seven gifts of the Holy Spirit will support the façade."

As Núria led them toward the basilica's entrance, Gwen caught Ruth's eye. "The seven gifts of the Holy Spirit," she whispered. "Wisdom."

Ruth's eyes lit up as she nodded. "I do believe you've stumbled upon another gift. After this morning's homily and then meeting Núria, la Sagrada Familia had to offer you the gift of wisdom." With a warm smile, she squeezed Gwen's hand. "'Joyful is the person who finds wisdom, the one who gains understanding.' Proverbs three, thirteen."

Before Gwen could respond, they entered the basilica. Awestruck, she felt like dropping to her knees. The sight was overwhelming. Immense columns shot up into the sky, branching out like granite trees to create a massive stone canopy.

Barely able to comprehend its enormity, Gwen's eyes slowly roamed the interior, listening as the guide described it. "La Sagrada Familia is one hundred and seventy meters high."

"That's over five hundred and fifty feet tall, nearly two football fields high," whispered Percy.

Open-mouthed as she looked above her, Gwen nodded. Gothic yet modern, the soaring dimensions of the architecture were awe-inspiring.

"To give you a point of reference, Barcelona's cathedral is only fifty-three meters high, less than one-third the height of la Sagrada. The central nave vaulting you see above you was enclosed at the turn of this century." Núria pointed out the features. "The principal construction since then has been on the transept vaults and apse."

Gwen reached out to touch the rose-tinged pillar beside her. Silky to the touch, it had twelve indented sides, smoothly flowing into each other. Though cold, it felt alive, almost as if it were breathing.

"Several kinds of stone were used in this basilica. The one you're touching is Iranian porphyry," said Núria. "This sturdy stone is used for the load-bearing pillars that support the intersections of the transept and nave. The dark-gray columns are granite basalt, and the light-gray to cream-colored pillars are local Montjuïc stone that contains minerals, such as muscovite and tourmaline."

Gwen's ears perked. *Muscovite was the stone I picked up in León, the same kind my father and I found.* The thought brought a smile to her lips.

"Wasn't Montjuïc stone used to build Santa Maria del Mar?" asked Crow.

The guide nodded. "It's been the primary building material for most of Barcelona." Núria gestured to the surrounding loft. "This choir loft can hold twelve hundred vocalists. In addition, the basilica can accommodate eight thousand worshipers."

Again, Gwen's eyes scanned the immense interior. Suddenly, the morning sun shone through the windows, and the basilica erupted in color. From one end to the other, blue and green light flooded in through the eight-story windows.

Caught in a kaleidoscope of color, Gwen recalled Percy's earlier description of la Sagrada Familia. "The hues are so intense, so saturated." She looked at him, standing in the light, his violet-blue eyes sparkling, his body reflecting the light. On impulse, she put her arm around his waist and shared in the dappled, blue-green light swirling about them. Percy was quick to respond with an arm around her shoulders.

La Sagrada Familia definitely represents the element wind.

"As you see, the eastern side captures the morning light," Núria said. "Starting at this end, the yellow-green colors are more prominent. As each window progresses toward the back of the basilica, the yellow-green tones blend into the green-blue tones, which meld with the bluer-green tones, until, at the end, the colors are various shades of blue. As the sun moves across the heavens, it lights up the other side of the basilica. If you think this is amazing, wait until you see the afternoon colors. As with nature, Gaudí used these colors to symbolize the procession of time. Greens and blues for morning, spring, and youth. Yellows, oranges, and reds for afternoon, autumn, and old age."

"When the sun pours in the western windows," said Percy, "it looks as if the air's on fire."

Her arm still around his waist, Gwen looked up into his eyes. Happy chills ran up her spine.

"By the time we finish our tour, the sun should be shining in through the western windows," said Núria. "Before we take the elevator to the tower, does anyone suffer from claustrophobia, vertigo, or fear of heights?"

"No," said Gwen. "Why?"

"We'll take the elevator up, but going down, we have a choice. We can either take the elevator or walk down the narrow, spiral staircase. Keep in mind, there are three hundred and fifty steep steps," said Núria. "Since there's very little headroom, you'll have to watch your heads, gentlemen." She looked at each of them. "Take the elevator or walk down?"

"Walk," they all said, looking at each other.

"By the time we reach the bottom, you'll have a good idea how Frodo felt in *Lord of the Rings*."

They rode the elevator up and saw the spectacular view from the rooftop. Then they walked down the spiral stairs, checking the shifting views from each level of windows.

By the time they arrived on the ground floor, the sun had crossed the sky. The light flooding in through the western windows infused the nave with an aura of yellow, orange, and red light. As the sunlight filtered through the countless pieces of leaded glass, the air had a dappled effect, moving as if enveloped in a firestorm.

"Ohmigosh, it does look like it's on fire." Gwen gazed in amazement. An optical illusion that tricked her mind, she almost heard flames crackling.

Then she saw her father in the midst of the flames. She gasped and as quickly covered her mouth.

"Is anything wrong?" asked Percy, watching her closely.

Shaking her head, she said, "No, just want to check something." Drawn to the image, she dodged the crowds, never taking her eyes from her father.

As she approached him, the light shifted, and the image began fading like a rainbow, becoming fainter, dissolving in the multicolored light until it finally disappeared.

What was that?

"Gwen?" Percy's voice came from behind her.

Flinching, she turned toward him, her jaw slack.

He put his hands on her shoulders, looking into her eyes. "Gwen, are you all right?"

She nodded, still too overcome to speak. Blinking, she took a deep breath. "I just saw my father."

"It's not the first time, right?"

"This was different. This time . . ." She took another deep breath and exhaled quickly. "This time he was enveloped in flames."

Raising his eyebrow, Percy studied her.

"You think I'm crazy, don't you?"

He grunted uneasily as he looked at the glowing reddish light around them. "Maybe, in this fiery light, what you saw was an optical illusion. I'm not saying you didn't see something. I'm just suggesting it might not have been what it seemed. Like heat mirages, maybe it was just the play of light that caused your brain to think you saw your father and flames."

Slowly shaking her head, Gwen said. "If I hadn't been seeing his ghost for the past few weeks, I'd say that was a plausible explanation, but . . ."

"But?"

"I know what I saw. There's no question about it. What concerns me is . . ." She grimaced as she looked up into his eyes. "What does it mean? What's he trying to tell me?"

That night at home, Gwen shared the story with Ruth. "What do you think he's trying to tell me?"

Hunching her shoulders, Ruth shook her head. "I don't know. You say he's never appeared to you this way before?"

"Once before I saw him surrounded by smoke, but never by fire." She rolled her eyes. "A logical explanation is he's in hell."

"Why do you say that?" Ruth scrutinized her.

"Well, smoke, fire, and . . ." She debated whether to share her other reasons. "Twice Kitty-Cat's hissed at his ghost, and then the other night, when he appeared in the lightning, she pounced at him." Gwen grimaced. "That doesn't sound like a benign ghost to me."

"Another possibility is he's in purgatory. Next time he appears, here's what you do. Say, 'In the name of the Father, the Son, and the Holy Ghost, how can I help you?'"

Gwen inhaled quickly through her nose. "That'd take a certain amount of chutzpah."

"Chutzpah." Grinning, Ruth said, "Maybe, but it'll accomplish two things. One, by calling on the Father, Son, and Holy Ghost, you'll ensure this spirit's benevolent. If it's evil, it'll leave."

Gwen digested that. "And the second thing?"

"It still sounds to me like your father's ghost is trying to communicate with you. He wants something from you. If he's in purgatory, prayers and Masses said for him would help." She narrowed her eyes. "Have you prayed for him?"

Gwen nodded slowly. "A little, but if anything, his appearances have become more frequent, have gotten bolder." She looked up. "You don't think this is a dybbuk, do you?"

Ruth sighed. "I don't think it's a malevolent spirit, so pray for him. Ask him what he wants from you. Ask how you can help. That's the only advice I can give you."

Gwen rubbed her forehead. "There's another possibility." Trying to swallow a grin, she said, "Maybe I'm just a meshuggana shiksa."

Ruth laughed out loud. "Yes, you are, my crazy friend, but I also believe there's a good reason God's letting you see this apparition. We just don't know what it is yet."

Gwen's smile disappeared. "There's something else."

"What?" Ruth looked serious.

"I need to make a decision about Art."

"Yes."

"I'm still on the fence," she glanced at her ring, "but I just can't commit to him."

Ruth tilted her head, listening. "Why?"

"It probably sounds silly, but I've been having a recurring dream."

"Nothing silly about it." Ruth smiled. "'All that we see or seem is but a dream within a dream.'"

"I dreamt . . . actually, I keep dreaming variations of the same theme." Gwen grimaced. "Basically, it was late afternoon, February fourteenth, and I'd forgotten to buy Art a Valentine's Day card."

"How did you feel in the dream?"

"Guilty, since I knew he'd have found the perfect card for me, and I wouldn't have gotten him anything."

Wearing a wry grin, Ruth shook her head. "Again, I'm no psychologist, but that sure sounds like your subconscious is trying to tell you something."

"I agree, but what?"

"Was Percy in this dream?"

"Sometimes, sometimes not." Gwen sighed. "Like I say," she glanced at her ring, "I just need to make a decision."

"It isn't fair to keep Art in suspense." When Gwen did not respond, Ruth asked, "How much of this uncertainty has to do with Percy?"

Lips pressed tightly together, Gwen shrugged. "I don't know."

"Have you talked to Art or Percy about it?"

"Thought about it, but . . ." Again, Gwen shrugged.

"Over-analysis creates paralysis. Don't let the fear of what could happen make nothing happen. Tell Art how you feel. See what he says, and go from there."

Alone in her room, Gwen rehearsed what she would tell Art when she called him. *I've given this a lot of thought. I respect you too much to keep you waiting any longer. Though I truly love you, I'm just not sure about marrying you, and it's not fair to keep you in limbo. Maybe the best thing to do is call off our engagement.*

The phone rang, interrupting her thoughts.

"Art, I was just about to call you."

"Were you? Glad we're on the same wavelength." The smile came through his voice. "Then you must know how much I miss you. Have you gotten the paperwork for our wedding?"

She drew in a long breath. "About that."

"Yes?"

"Art . . . I've given this a lot of thought. I respect you too much to keep you waiting any longer." She sighed.

"What are you trying to say, Gwen?"

"I . . . I truly love you, but . . ." Glancing at her ring, she made a fist. "I'm just not sure—"

"Before you say anything you'll regret, listen to me."

Rolling her eyes, she groaned. *I can't do this. I can't hurt him, especially not over the phone.* Fist to her head, she massaged her temple.

"Art, it's not fair to keep you in limbo. Maybe the best thing to do—"

"Gwen, you're not listening. I changed my ticket. I'm here."

She swallowed. *What?* "You're in Barcelona?" She heard a knock at the front door.

"I'm right outside your apartment."

Phone still in hand, Gwen cracked the door and peeked with one eye. Her face hidden from him, she closed her eyes as her heart sank. *Trapped.* Then, putting on a bright smile, she swung the door wide open.

"Art, it's good to see you."

"And you." He grabbed her in a bear hug, pressing her against his chest. "I've missed you, babe."

Babe. The name resonated in her mind. From the corner of her eye, Gwen saw Ruth, watching. Pulling away from his grip, she stepped back, putting away her cell phone, and gesturing toward Art with her hand. "Ruth, you remember Art, don't you?"

"Sure, I do." Hand extended, Ruth greeted him. "Welcome back to Spain, Art."

He shook hands warmly, taking her hand in both of his. "Good to see you again."

"Look," said Ruth, starting for the coat closet. "I . . . uh . . . I have to make a trip to the store. I'll be back in an hour or so. Bye." Her coat half on, half trailing, she closed the door behind her.

Blinking, Gwen looked from the shut door to Art. *Trapped.*

"That was considerate," he said.

She gave a halfhearted laugh. "Wasn't it, though?"

"Aren't you going to invite me to sit down?"

"Of course." She threw up her hands. "Where are my manners?" She rushed toward the kitchen and busied herself opening and closing cupboards.

"Gwen—"

"I'm sure we have a bottle of wine here somewhere."

"Gwen—"

"Make yourself comfortable," she called, popping her head in the doorway. "I'll just be a second."

A few minutes later, she returned with a bottle of Cava and two glasses. "Here we go." She handed him the bottle with a flourish. "Would you do the honors?"

Wrinkling his forehead, Art quietly said, "Sure." He glanced at her from the corner of his eye. "You don't have to stand over me." He gave a wry chuckle. "Sit down. Relax."

She gave another lukewarm chuckle. 'Of course, what's wrong with me?" She sat across from him in an easy chair.

Blinking, he studied her. "Gwen, is anything wrong? If I didn't know better, I'd swear you're not glad to see me."

"Oh, no, not at all." She pressed her fingers to her forehead and took a deep breath. "I'm . . . I'm just surprised to see you. That's all." She gave a nervous giggle.

"In that case," he patted the seat beside him on the sofa. "Come join me."

She looked at his honest, open expression and cringed. *What's wrong with me? This guy loves me, and I'm treating him like an old boyfriend at my wedding.* She forced a smile and joined him.

He peered at her, blinked, as if reading her, and then opened the bottle. He poured and then handed her a glass. Raising his glass, he looked her in the eye. "To our marriage." He watched, eyes narrowing, as she hesitated.

Finally, with a sigh, she shook her head and put down her glass. "Art . . ."

Setting down his glass, he turned to her. "What's wrong?"

"It's me. I'm not ready to get married."

Silence.

Gwen saw Kitty-Cat in the other room, but the cat made no move to join them. More silence.

"Art, say something."

He opened his mouth to speak, but the motion turned into a sigh. Finally, he shrugged. "What's there to say?"

"I'm sorry." Shaking her head, she looked at her ring. "I'd never have accepted this if I'd had any idea it would turn out this way." Her shoulders sagging, she slowly pulled off her ring. The significance of the action made her lips tremble. She swallowed. "Art, I'm just so very sorry. I had no idea you'd show up on my doorstep like this. I was going to tell you before you flew out here, save you the trip."

Tilting his head, he chuckled. "Thought I'd surprise you."

She returned a sad smile. "You did." When he made no move toward her ring, she reached for his hand, put the ring in his palm, and closed his fingers over it. For a moment, she held his hand in hers. Then she thought better of it and let go.

"Now what?" He looked sadly into her eyes.

Gwen grimaced, sighed, and shook her head. "I think it would be wise to give you two weeks' notice since you're the editor in chief of Trails n' Treks Publications." She gestured toward her laptop. "Two of the articles are done. Just need to polish a third, and I'll give you an update regarding the Catalonian independence piece." She shrugged. "There hasn't been as much news for that movement as we'd expected. It seems to have fizzled out."

He looked at her with wounded eyes.

She quickly inhaled. *Bad choice of words.* Pursing her lips, she looked away.

She heard him sigh. Then she heard the tinkle of glasses being picked up. As she turned back to him, his eyes met hers. He held out a glass to her, and her hand shook as she accepted it.

He held up his glass. "To your happiness, Gwen."

Her bottom lip trembling, she felt tears well up. She tried to take a deep breath, but it came out a sob. As she blinked, a tear escaped down her cheek. When she did not raise her glass to toast, he touched his to hers, drained his glass, and stood up.

Suddenly, the consequences of her actions occurred to her. "Where will you go?"

"I've booked a hotel nearby." He grimaced. "The honeymoon suite."

Raising her hand to her forehead, she hung her head. "Art, I never meant to hurt you. I am so sorry."

He gave her a wry smile. "Take care of yourself, Gwen." With that, he turned and walked out.

Only as the door closed behind him did she realize the finality. *It's over.*

❄

An hour later, jingling her keys, making a racket, Ruth unlocked the door. "I'm home," she called loudly before entering and slamming the door.

"Hi," Gwen called from the sofa, Kitty-Cat on her lap.

"Where's Art?"

Gwen held up her naked left hand. "Gone."

❄

In bed, Gwen stroked her bare finger as she recited her litany of independence. *No ring, no fiancé, no husband, no father, no one.* Instead of taking pride in her self-reliance as she once had, she felt vulnerable. Icy fingers of fear gripped her chest.

What have I done? Thrown away my chance at happiness? Maybe my only chance? She thumped her forehead with her fingertips.

I'll call Art. Tell him I was wrong. Tell him I changed my mind. Again. Tell him I love him. Her shoulders sagging, she took a deep breath to brace herself.

I can't lie, so what can I do?

"Pray."

Snapping to attention, she sat up, searching the darkness. An automatic reflex, she knew before she looked that no one was there. She had heard it with her inner ear. *Pray.*

176

Dear God, at Compostela I asked for help to work out my issues with men. I believe the relationship with my father, the first man in my life, has affected all other interactions with men. Help me right that relationship with him, with You. Help me resolve these issues.

Suddenly, a thought struck her. *Maybe you've already begun helping me. Maybe it wasn't my idea to break off the engagement. You were the inspiration. You kept me from making the same mistake my father and, before him, his mother made.* She took a deep, cleansing breath.

Thanks for not letting me marry the wrong man for the wrong reasons. Help me recognize the right man, and please always give me the strength to do what You ask of me. Amen.

CHAPTER 15:

Montserrat

"It's not the years, honey, it's the mileage."
— Indiana Jones, *Raiders of the Lost Ark*

The next morning, Gwen eemailed two articles, promises to complete a third article and provide an update on the independence movement, and a letter of resignation to Trails n' Treks Publications.

"That's that." Symbolically brushing her hands, she turned to Ruth. "Now what?"

"God closes one door—"

"Yeah, but I'm the one that slammed and bolted it." Gwen grimaced.

"Then He opens a window. The Holy Spirit was guiding you, inspiring you. You did what you had to do." Ruth sat down across from her at the breakfast table, folded her hands, and looked Gwen in the eye. "Before I leave for work, there's something I have to discuss with you."

Ruth's no-nonsense expression did little to put Gwen at ease. "What's wrong?" She took a deep breath, expecting bad news. *Is the cat a problem? Is she worried about my not having rent money?*

A shy smile crossed Ruth's face and as quickly vanished. "Not wrong, but something's happened."

Gwen searched Ruth's face for clues. "What?"

"I was waiting for the right time to bring this up, but with last night's turn of events." She sighed. "I guess now's as good a time as any."

Gwen's eyes opened wider as she imagined the worst. "What is it? Are you ill? Are you in some kind of trouble?"

Ruth laughed. "Whatever gave you that idea?"

"You look so solemn, I'm not sure what to think." She took a deep breath, grounding herself. "What's happened?"

"I'm going to be moving in February."

"Oh." Gwen felt her cheeks flush as she guessed the reason for Ruth's talk. "I guess you'll need me to move out as soon as possible."

"That's not it. At least not any time in the immediate future." Ruth shook her head as she grimaced. "I hate to mention this now, when you've just broken up with Art and quit your job." She paused, apparently gathering her thoughts.

"Oh, for heaven's sake, Ruth, just spit it out. The suspense is killing me."

"Jim's asked me to marry him."

"What?" Stunned, her jaw slack, Gwen felt the wind had been knocked out of her.

Ruth's eyes pleaded. "Say something."

Remembering her manners, Gwen finally mumbled, "Sure . . . congrats." Then joy began replacing the shock. With a squeal, she jumped up and hugged Ruth. "Congratulations! When's the big day?"

"February second."

Squinting, Gwen stared at her friend in disbelief. "How long have you known?"

Ruth grinned. "A couple days."

"A couple days? And you didn't tell me? How could you keep something like that to yourself?"

Ruth shrugged sheepishly. "I was hoping something would work out with Art . . . or Percy."

Gwen gave a sarcastic laugh. "Something has worked out with Art, just not what I thought it'd be." As she looked at Ruth, her grimace morphed into a grin. "But this is fabulous news. Tell me all about it. Don't leave out a detail."

"I will," Ruth chuckled, "when I get home tonight. Promise." She looked at her watch and groaned. "But I've got to get to work. Have a meeting today with the Madrid headquarters of Child and Family Welfare." She pulled on her coat, waved, and said, "See you later."

"Everything," Gwen called after her, chuckling. "I want to hear every single detail tonight." Grinning at Ruth's good fortune, Gwen sat down again at the table.

What suddenly struck her was the silence. Except for the ticking of the clock, she heard nothing. Not a sound. Gradually, her smile faded as it occurred to her how very alone she was.

"Me-ow-ow." Kitty-Cat jumped on her lap and began purring.

Petting her, hugging her, Gwen whispered, "It's just you and me, Kitty-Cat. You and me, and wherever I go, I'm taking you with me."

Her cell phone rang a few hours later.

"Gwen," said Percy's voice, "are you busy today?"

Not really. "Finishing up an article, but nothing that can't wait. What's up?"

"Want to go to Montserrat? There's something I'd like to investigate."

"I thought Ruth and Crow were going with us." Gwen felt shy about traveling with Percy. *Why? Art's not in the picture, anymore.*

"Crow's busy, and Ruth's working, isn't she? Besides, Saturday's when we'll take the full tour. This is just research."

Why not? Butterflies in her stomach at the prospect of not only meeting alone with him, but meeting him as a free woman, she whispered breathlessly, "Sure."

An hour later, they were boarding the train at Plaça de Espanya.

As the train jerked to a start, Percy turned to her.

"I ran across a detail I hadn't seen before," he said. "Something Eschenbach wrote that ties Montserrat to the Holy Grail."

Her eyes narrowed as she searched his face. "Who's Eschenbach again?"

"Wolfram von Eschenbach was the medieval German poet who wrote *Parzival* in the thirteenth century," said Percy. "That was the first mention of the Holy Grail and the Arthurian knight Perceval."

She grinned. "Perceval."

"Yes, I come by this quest honestly since my mother named me after him." He pursed his lips, as if hiding his grin. "I read something last night by the Catalan historian Jeroni Pujades. He might have the missing link tying the Grail to Montserrat. A ruby."

"A ruby?" She lifted her eyebrow.

Percy nodded. "It's a stretch, but Pujades compared Montserrat to Mount Tabor in Galilee. Using the flowery writing style popular in his time, he compared Montserrat, encircled by mountains, to a jewel, encircled by a golden ring. The same way the ring's setting enhances the central jewel, the mountains surrounding Montserrat highlight its 'jewel,' its sacred image."

"I thought you said ruby, not jewel, and now you're saying sacred image." Frowning, she shook her head. "I'm not seeing a connection."

"I'm getting to that. Eschenbach described a ruby in the hilt of Perceval's sword, the Holy Grail. Pujades compared that jewel to the 'jewel' of Montserrat, a euphemism for the Black Madonna."

Gwen took a deep breath. "Yeah, that's a stretch all right."

"But it's a clue, a piece of the puzzle I hadn't found before," said Percy. "This is a paper trail, not a treasure hunt. It's documentary evidence to support my theory. It doesn't mean I'm going to physically find the Grail."

Glancing out the train's window, watching the terrain fly by, she smirked before turning back to meet his eyes. "Or that you're Indiana Jones."

"Exactly." His violet-blue eyes sparkled. As the train began slowing, he looked out the window. "This is our stop, the Aeri de Monserrat."

They crammed into the packed cable car and huddled close to the windows, watching the spectacular views as they climbed through the air. At one particularly large jolt, Gwen reached out, steadying herself by placing her left hand on Percy's arm.

He looked from her bare left hand to her eyes. In the close confines of the cable car, he said nothing, but his eyes spoke volumes.

Gwen removed her hand and turned to stare out the cable car's window. Her heart rate increasing along with the altitude, she felt too giddy to meet his eyes.

When they reached the mountaintop, they silently exited and began following the signs toward the complex. As soon as they were out of earshot of the other passengers, he turned to her.

"In your rush this morning, did you forget to put on your engagement ring?" She took a deep breath. "I didn't have it to put on."

She started to walk on, but he caught her hand. "What are you saying?"

"Last night I returned it to Art."

Her hand still in his, he drew her to him. "Gwen, I—" Hearing footsteps behind them, they flinched and drew apart. They walked on, hand in hand, until they found a more secluded path. Again, he turned toward her. Placing his hands on her shoulders, he gazed into her eyes. "You're no longer . . . spoken for?"

As she shook her head slowly, Percy drew her to him in a warm embrace. Sternum to sternum, even through heavy coats, Gwen could feel the rise and fall of his breath.

"Well then," he said, "we'll have to conduct more 'research' while we're here."

She leaned into him in a kiss, but a tour group rounded the corner, breaking the spell. She smiled. "Come on. This obviously isn't the time or place for privacy. Let's follow your paper trail. Where to?"

"For starters, the library. Let's research first. Then let's hear the boys' choir, have lunch, and visit the cave."

She looked at her Trans Montserrat Ticket schedule. "That should get us back in time to catch the last cable car of the day to meet our train."

The library was located near the main complex's museum. Shelf after shelf, row after row of books meticulously filled the oak-paneled rooms.

"This library was created in the eleventh century. In the twelfth century, Montserrat established its own scriptorium."

"Scriptorium?" Gwen squinted, trying to remember its meaning. "Was that where they copied bibles and other manuscripts?"

He nodded. "The monastery even had its own printing press at the end of the fifteenth century. It was a thriving cultural center until Napoleon destroyed it in 1811. Unfortunately, most of the books were lost."

"What a shame." Gwen looked at the records of human development surrounding her. "Who knows what information's gone forever?"

"Despite that, it's still got a collection of philosophy, theology, and bible studies, which is why I want to follow up my research about Eschenbach and Pujades here." He watched her reaction. "It shouldn't take me more than an hour. Would you want to explore the museum?"

"Actually," she said, scanning the library, "there's something I want to research too. This might be just the place to find the information I need."

Gwen found the section on purgatory, reading what the scholars and doctors of the church had to say. The time flew by.

"Hope I haven't kept you waiting," said Percy over an hour later.

"Nope." She shook her head. "Seems like I just sat down, but I did find some valuable information, just what I needed. How about you? Did your research here help support your theory?"

He shrugged. "Not directly, but every clue leads me closer to the truth."

She smiled, thinking of her own findings. "I know just what you mean."

"If we hurry, we can hear the Escolania."

"The what?"

"The boys' choir. It's one of the oldest choirs in Europe."

As they walked into the immense basilica, Gwen's eyes swept the walls, ceiling, and altar—covered in ornate artwork, tile, carved alabaster, and gold leaf. Hardly an inch was bare.

They found seats just as the choir boys began filing in. Then Percy drew her attention to a niche in the balcony overlooking the altar.

"That's the Black Madonna," he whispered.

From where they sat, it appeared as if the statue was floating in midair, but Gwen could see people walking in front of it, touching it.

After the introduction and welcome, the boys began singing.

"First they'll sing the 'Salve' and then the 'Virolai,'" whispered Percy.

"What's the 'Virolai'?"

"It's the chant to honor Our Lady of Montserrat. Sometimes it's called 'Rosa d'abril' or Rose of April, its opening words."

After the "Salve," she listened for the first words of the "Virolai." Her ears perked at "Rosa d'abril."

Percy watched her, raising his eyebrows. Smiling, she nodded. She had heard. Then she looked at him more closely. Tears were forming in his eyes. *Why?* Silently, she took his hand in hers.

After Mass, they walked to the cafeteria for lunch.

"What moved you when the boys were singing?" she asked as they enjoyed their meal.

Glancing down at his plate, he seemed to gather his thoughts. Then he raised his eyes to hers.

"During the Franco regime, despite the ban on speaking Catalan, the monastery resisted. The boys sang the 'Virolai' in its native tongue. As a result, many hundreds were persecuted here, including over twenty monks. The 'Virolai' is a symbol of Catalan independence."

"Independence is important to you, isn't it?"

He nodded, his eyes shining. "But to you, too."

"Why do you say that?" Gwen blinked. "I'm not the one who's patriotic."

"There's more than one kind of independence." Watching her, he raised his eyebrow, as if asking her to agree. 'Recently, something's become even more important to me than independence." He reached across the table for her hand. "You."

Meeting his deep-blue eyes, she squeezed his hand. *How right this feels. No nagging questions, just a sense of well-being.*

Caressing her ring finger, he looked from her bare hand to her eyes. "Could I ask what happened?"

Shrugging, she looked down at her plate, not wanting to go into detail. "I just wasn't ready to get married."

"There's that streak of independence again." The corners of his eyes crinkling, he grinned. "Married to Art, or to anyone?"

She looked up through her lashes into his eyes. Squirming in her seat, she found it difficult not to return his grin. "No one else has asked me."

Nodding, his hand still holding hers, he raised his eyebrow. "Is that—"

"Are you finished?" asked the busboy, starting to clear the table. "Can I take your plates?"

They looked up at him, glanced at each other, and burst out laughing.

"Sure," said Percy, recovering his composure. "Thanks."

Gwen checked the train schedule until the busboy left. "It's probably just as well he interrupted. If we want to see the cave and catch the last train back to Barcelona, we'd better get going."

After they zipped their jackets, Percy playfully put his arm around her shoulders, hugging her to him. "That's what I like, a woman with an agenda."

As they left the cafeteria, an icy gust of wind took Gwen's breath away, reminding her they were in the Pyrenees. Glad for the warmth of his arm, Gwen huddled closer as they walked to the Santa Cova funicular.

The train to the cave plunged straight downhill. Standing in the front car during their steep descent, Gwen captured panoramic pictures of the mountain range's magnificent views. She watched as their train danced a do-si-do with a second train, the two counterbalancing each other on the tracks. Then she glanced behind them, noting they were the only passengers. At the end of the track, they found the path to the cave.

"Must be too late in the day for anyone else to venture here," said Percy.

"Or too cold." Gwen pulled her hood over her head, fastening her collar to keep out the wind. She stuck her hands in the coat's pockets and was surprised to feel the chestnut and rolling paper. *Guess I haven't worn this coat since our pilgrimage.*

The path hugged the mountainside, but there was no shelter from the howling wind. By the time they reached the chapel, she was freezing.

As they walked inside, Gwen immediately felt protected. Not only shielded from the elements, she sensed a tranquility she had never experienced before. Candles burning in prayer provided warmth, soft lighting, and a general aura of peace.

"Are you familiar with Santa Cova?" Though they were alone, Percy's voice was hushed.

She shook her head.

"This is the actual cave where they found the Black Madonna, the statue I pointed out in the basilica."

As her eyes scanned the small chapel built around the grotto, she nodded. "I sense a certain serenity here, a holiness. Thousands, possibly millions of prayers have been said here." She took a deep breath. "It's as if each of those prayers etched itself on this cave, infused it with a living spirituality."

Something compelled her to walk to the back of the cave, near the altar. Standing tiptoe on the chapel floor, keeping outside the consecrated space, she stretched across the railing as far as she could reach until her right hand connected with the cave's stone. Instantly, she sensed a joining, a bonding. It was electric.

"Oh, wow." She jumped back, breaking the link.

"What?"

She snickered at herself. "Oh, nothing. My hand must be so cold, it's just tingling."

She waited until Percy turned away to continue exploring the chapel. Then, standing tiptoe, overextending, she again strained to reach the grotto's wall. This time, she felt a vibration or subtle throbbing in her hand, almost like a faint pulse. Gradually, it became stronger until she could not only feel it, she could see her hand shaking.

Unable to maintain that overstretched position any longer, she slumped, hanging onto the railing for support.

What was that?

Then, catching her breath, she leaned back against the wall, composing herself. Across the chapel from her, the glow of the votive candle rack caught her eye. Hypnotized, she watched as the candlelight intensified until the tiny, individual flames merged into one roiling inferno. Her father's ghost blazed among its flames. Recalling Ruth's advice, she mentally repeated, *In the name of the Father, the Son, and the Holy Ghost, how can I help you?*

Gwen heard with her inner ear, "Have a Mass said for me."

Here, in this chapel? The ghost nodded. *Why?*

"It will release me."

From where?

"Purgatory."

The heat of the flames was overwhelming, and she slumped against the wall.

"Are you all right?" Percy asked.

"What?" Blinking, she took her eyes off the fire to look at Percy.

"Are you all right?"

She nodded, but as she put her hand to her forehead, she realized she was perspiring.

"A moment ago you were freezing. Now you're burning up. What happened?"

Wiping her brow with one hand, she pointed at the apparition with the other.

Percy looked where she pointed, squinted, and then looked back at her. "What are you pointing at, the votive candles?"

Shaking her head, she wracked her brain to think of a way Percy could witness the vision before her. Suddenly, she recalled the story Ruth had told her of the little girl, who had thrown a tissue into her vision's flames. Reaching into her pocket, she felt the rolling paper. Balling it up in her fingers, she threw the tiny wad into the fire, where it flashed into flame and immediately burned out.

"Did you see that?"

"See what?"

"My father's ghost, surrounded by flames." Sighing in frustration, she searched her other pockets until her hand connected with the chestnut.

"Now, watch!"

She threw the raw nut into the flames, where it hissed, blackened, and then shot out as it popped from its shell. Immediately, the conflagration sputtered out. As quickly as the vision had appeared, it vanished. All that remained were the flickering votive candles and the steaming chestnut.

She grabbed at Percy's arm. "Did you see that?"

"I saw the chestnut catch fire." He raised his eyebrow. "Why did you throw it into the votive candles?"

"I didn't. I threw it at . . ." Dumbfounded, she stared at him. "Didn't you see that?"

"Like I said, I saw the chestnut catch fire from a votive candle."

Her shoulders slumped. "You don't believe me."

Stifling a sigh, he said, "I don't doubt you saw something. I'm just not convinced what you saw was your father's ghost in flames."

She described the incident and apparition in detail, hoping to persuade him.

"The difference this time was my father gave me specific instructions. He wants a Mass said for him in this chapel."

"Gwen, there wasn't time for all that to happen." Percy raised his eyebrows. "This vision, or whatever you experienced, occurred in a matter of seconds. One moment, you said your hand was cold, tingling. The next moment, I found you slumped against the wall, sweltering."

"Really?" She blinked. "That's all the time it took?" At his nod, she reviewed the series of events. "Between the sensations of the pulsating wall, the blazing candlelight, the conversation with the ghost, and the return to the flickering candlelight, at least five or ten minutes had to have passed."

His eyes unsmiling, he shook his head. "It was literally instantaneous."

She checked her watch. "You're right." Then she pulled the timetable out of her purse. "Actually, that's a good thing." Calculating, she made a wry face. "According to this schedule, we've only got a few minutes before we have to start back for the funicular so we get back to the monastery in time to catch the last cable car back down the mountain so we're at the station in time to catch the train to Barcelona."

His eyes crinkled at the corners. "But there's time for a quick prayer before we go."

Three connections and three hours later, they were back at Plaça de Espanya.

"I'm starving after the hike and the cold," said Gwen. "Could you go for some tapas?"

"Definitely."

Still bundled in their winter coats and hoodies, they decided to dine al fresco in an outdoor café. Dusk was just settling over the city as the lights began twinkling. The waiter lit the table's candle, slipped the glass cover over it, and brought a heat lamp, making the atmosphere warm and intimate. Chatting, they sipped Rioja wine as they waited for the tapas.

"I can't convince you that I saw my father at the cave?" Gwen was not angry, just annoyed at Percy's stubbornness.

"Let's not start this conversation again. Please?" Crinkling at the corners, his eyes pleaded as he grinned.

"Okay, but it's so frustrating. You don't accept what I say as the truth." She grimaced. "It's as if you don't trust me to recognize fantasy from reality." Shaking her head, she sighed. *He reminds me of my father.* "It's like a chauvinistic pat on the head."

The waiter interrupted as he brought tiny plates and a mixed platter of tapas. "Can I get you anything else?"

"This is great, thanks," Percy said.

Glancing over his shoulder, Gwen noticed a small face hiding in the shadows, spying on them.

"Don't look now, but we're being watched."

"Okay, I won't look, so describe our spy to me." He gave her an amused grin before he popped an olive into his mouth.

"Why do I feel you're humoring me lately?" Rolling her eyes, she tried to see more of the little person. "He's partially hidden by the hedge, but it's a small boy."

Percy nibbled a piece of cheese as he deadpanned. "Oh, so *this* vision's three-dimensional?"

"That isn't funny." She glanced back at the boy, straining to see him in the gloom outside the café's candlelit piazza. "Now he seems to be talking to someone." She made a wry face. "And he's pointing at us." Suddenly, her eyes widened.

"What?" Percy turned in his seat to see what had caught her attention. "Okay, I see a kid talking to himself."

In a hushed voice, she shook her head. "He's not talking to himself."

Percy looked again. "Fine, he's walking toward us, talking to himself."

Gwen's eyes opened wider as the boy cautiously approached them and then hesitated as he argued with her father's ghost. Never taking her eyes off them, Gwen called the boy over. "It's all right. We won't hurt you."

Percy frowned. "What are you doing?"

She watched as the boy talked animatedly with her father's ghost.

"It's okay," she said. "Come on over. Would you like some tapas?" When he heard the word tapas, the boy tentatively approached. "Here, sit down and join us."

As she pulled out a chair for him and patted it, he looked up at the ghost for reassurance. Her father smiled and nodded.

"Why are you encouraging the boy?" Shaking his head, Percy whispered, "I don't think inviting him over's such a good idea."

"Yes, it is." Raising a triumphant eyebrow, she grinned gleefully. "My father's the one talking to him."

The boy bashfully joined them as he pointed at her father. "He told me it's all right."

Percy's eyes flew open.

"Of course it is." Smiling, Gwen looked from the boy to her father to Percy. She placed several tapas on a plate and handed it to him. "Go ahead, eat." As Gwen watched the boy tear into his food, she studied his features. Dark haired, his skin was pale, and he was wearing some kind of uniform.

He inhaled the tapas. Then, looking up at her with big eyes, he asked, "Could I have some more?"

"Sure." Gwen blinked as she stared from the boy's face to her father's. The resemblance was uncanny. Then, remembering her hostess role, she pushed the tapas platter closer to him. "Take as many as you like. Eat up." Still looking at the boy, she asked, "What's your name?"

"Cristóbal Perez."

Gwen's eyes widened. "Doesn't Cristóbal mean Christopher?"

The boy nodded, his mouth full.

She studied the boy, then she looked at her father. For the first time, she saw him grin. *Those eyes.* Squinting in the candlelight, she gazed at the boy. "What color are your eyes?"

"Avellana."

"Hazel," said Percy. "Why?"

"My father's middle name was Christopher, and he has . . . had the same hazel-colored eyes." She exchanged a look with Percy.

"Are you trying to tell me—?"

She nodded and then turned to the boy. "How old are you?"

"Eight," he said, covering his full mouth with his tiny hand.

"Eight," she repeated. As he helped himself to another tapa, she asked, "How long has it been since you ate?"

"Since breakfast."

Scowling, she glanced at Percy and then turned back to the boy. "That's a long time between meals. Is anything wrong?"

"I've been waiting for my mother. She was supposed to meet me when my train arrived at noon."

"Your train?"

Cristóbal nodded. "I came home for Christmas."

"From where?"

"From my school in Valencia."

Percy studied the insignia on boy's light jacket. "You go to a boarding school in Valencia?"

Nodding again, Cristóbal pointed to the nearby hotel's main entrance. "My mother said to meet her there."

"So you've been waiting," Gwen checked her watch, "about seven hours?" She shot Percy another worried look. "And you're all by yourself?"

Cristóbal looked at her father. "I was until this man came and waited with me." He smiled at the ghost.

As the boy bit into the tapa, her father said, "His mother isn't coming."

Hearing with her inner thoughts, she silently asked, *Why?*

Grimacing, her father shook his head slowly and disintegrated like smoke in a breeze.

Gwen scratched her chin, wondering what to do with the boy. "Do you have any other relatives in Barcelona?"

His mouth full, Cristóbal shook his head.

"What about your father? Any aunts or uncles?"

His eyes tearing up, he gulped and then shook his head.

Gwen looked to Percy for help.

He gave her a sympathetic nod and then asked the boy. "Is it okay if we call you Chris?"

The boy's eyes lit up. "That's what my mother calls me."

"Good. What about school? Is it—?"

"It's closed for the holidays."

Percy took a deep breath. "Is there anyone we can call in Valencia?"

His hazel eyes brimmed with tears as he shook his head.

Percy turned to her. "Now what?"

"What's the name of your school," she asked.

When he told them, Percy checked with information and got a number. A moment later, he was dialing. Then sighing, he hung up.

"What's wrong?"

"A recorded message says the school will be closed until after Christmas break."

"What are we going to do with him?" she whispered.

"We can't just leave him here."

"No. Just a minute. I've got an idea." Gwen dialed Ruth. "Don't you work for Family Services?"

"I work for Child and Family Welfare, if that's what you mean." Gwen heard the apprehension in Ruth's voice. "Why?"

Gwen walked a few steps away for privacy and then told Ruth the story.

"Let me make a few phone calls," said Ruth. "Not sure who I'll get at this hour, but I'll try to find him a place to stay."

"What'll we do in the interim?"

"Bring him home," said Ruth. "At least he'll be safe here until we can find the proper authorities. See if you can find out his mother's name and make a few inquiries with the police . . . and hospitals."

Gwen's shoulders slumped. "Oh, no, you don't think—?"

"I don't know what to think, but we'll need that information to register him in the system."

Gwen sighed. "Okay, thanks, Ruth. We'll find out what we can, and then I guess we'll bring him home." *What are we getting ourselves into?*

When she got back to the table, she saw Chris and Percy were eating churros and hot chocolate.

"Have one." Percy handed her a churro.

Dipping it in the hot pudding, she used it like a spoon. Then she whispered to Percy, "Ruth's checking with her contacts at Child and Family Welfare, but she wants us to call the police and hospitals." Turning to Chris, she asked, "What's your mother's name?"

"Montse Perez."

Percy wrote it down and then, with a grave look at her, stepped away to start calling the authorities.

Gwen tried to learn what she could. "Do you have any brothers or sisters?"

He shook his head.

"What about your friends at school. Who's your best friend?"

Chris said in a monotone, "Pedro, but he moved away last month."

"So now who do you play with?"

Shrugging again, Chris grimaced.

"I see." She sighed. "How about a grandmother or grandfather? Is there anyone you know that you could stay with until we find your mother?"

Looking down, he shook his head.

She noticed his light jacket. *Too light for this weather.* "Do you have a suitcase or backpack?"

"No," he mumbled. Each time he shook his head, his frail shoulders drooped a little more. His head hung lower, and his eyes were beginning to well up with tears.

She wracked her brain. *How do I help him? How do I cheer him up?* "Here, why don't you take my last churro? I'm full."

When she saw his eyes light up, she breathed a sigh. Then she pushed her cup of hot chocolate closer to him. "Enjoy."

Finally, Percy returned to the table. His lips pressed into a tight line, he shook his head slowly.

Silently, she mimed, *What?*

He leaned close to whisper. "They have a woman by that name in the morgue."

"What?" Gwen covered her mouth with her hand. Then, to keep Chris from seeing her reaction, she stood up and stepped away, holding back her tears until she was out of sight, out of ear shot.

Eight years old and possibly motherless. She cried for Chris. She cried for the little boy that had been her father, Clark Christopher. *Is that why you brought him to me? Am I supposed to help him? Help you?* She rolled her eyes. *Where's my father ever been when I've needed him?*

With those thoughts, he appeared as a blur of light above a neon sign.

Why? Why did you bring Chris to me?

"Help him," he said in her mind. "Be kind to him."

Like you were kind to me when you abandoned me?

"As kind as I knew how. Chris needs you. When you help him, you help me."

How?

"I was allowed to visit you and Chris for a reason, but we both need your help. Be kind to him, and have a Mass said for me. Those two things will release me."

With that, he was gone. She stared blindly at the neon sign for several moments, thinking. Then she turned and watched Percy entertain Chris. It took several minutes to compose herself. Sniffling her last, she brushed her tears away and took a deep breath.

Returning to the table, she handed Chris her cell. "Is there anyone you want to call?"

His eyes lit up. He dialed a number and spoke at the first sound. "Mother?"

Gwen could hear the recording from where she stood. She exchanged a forlorn look with Percy.

Hanging up, Chris handed her the phone. "The number's out of order."

"Isn't there anyone else you'd like to call?"

He shook his head no.

"Are you still hungry?" Percy asked.

It brought a half smile to Chris's face, but again, he shook his head.

"We know you promised to wait here for your mother, but it's getting cold," said Gwen. She said a silent prayer the next step would work. Using her most persuasive tones, she asked, "How'd you like to come home with me . . . just for tonight?"

Chris fearfully looked back at the hotel next door and shook his head. "I have to wait here for my mother."

She glanced at Percy and tried again. "Your mother wouldn't want you to catch cold."

Looking down, he shook his head.

She thought a moment and added, "How 'bout we come back here first thing tomorrow morning?"

Percy gave her a dark look, but Chris seemed to like the logic. "Okay."

With Chris between them, they each took a hand and caught a cab. Ten minutes later, they walked into Ruth's apartment.

"Well, who's this?" she asked.

"This is our new friend, Chris Perez," said Gwen, carefully choosing her words. "He's going to stay with us until tomorrow—"

"When we go back to wait for my mother," he finished.

Kitty-Cat peeked out from Gwen's bedroom. "Me-ow-ow."

"A kitty!" He looked up at Percy and Gwen. "Can I play with her?"

"Sure," said Gwen. "We'll be right over here at the table."

When he was out of earshot, Ruth asked, "What's the story?"

"We'd better sit down," said Percy. After they got settled, he shared what the police had told him. "There's a woman by that name in the morgue, but to be sure it's his mother . . ."

"He'll have to identify her." Ruth grimaced. "Apparently, he isn't aware of any of this."

Percy shook his head.

"Did you have any luck getting the paperwork?" asked Gwen.

"Lucky for you, I did." Ruth gave them stern looks. "Technically, you've just kidnapped him."

"No!"

"How else would you describe it?"

"We couldn't just leave him on the street." Gwen glanced at Percy and, taking a deep breath, met Ruth's eyes. "Now what?"

"Normally, a child welfare officer would take him into custody, but this being so close to Christmas," she raised an eyebrow, "and me pulling a few strings, he can stay with us a day or two until we can make other arrangements."

"Look," said Gwen, lowering her voice, "we don't know for a fact that the woman in the morgue is his mother. Let's call the hospitals and police station again in the morning to see if there's a second woman of that name."

"But if she's the only one . . ."

"We promised him we'd wait by the hotel tomorrow morning," said Gwen. "For his sake, let's try everything, no matter how slim the odds, before that little guy has to grow up way too soon."

"There was one more thing," said Percy. "The police said the woman had a distinguishing birthmark on her neck."

Gwen listened to Chris playing with Kitty-Cat. "Let's ask him in the morning."

CHAPTER 16:
Cristobal

"I shall not leave you orphans; I shall come to you."
John 14:18

As the first rays of sunlight peeked through the shutters, Gwen opened her eyes. She looked around, wondering where she was. Then she recalled giving Chris her bed while she slept on the sofa, near the front door.

"Just in case he decides to go looking for his mother," she had told Ruth.

She got up, cracked the door to her room, and saw Chris fast asleep, Kitty-Cat curled up in his arm. Then she looked at her bare left hand resting on the door and sighed.

Haven't had time to think about Art or anything else. She looked back at the boy and recalled the dream she'd had of her father at that age. His pain in that dream was still vivid. *My grandmother abandoned my father when he was eight. If the woman in the morgue is Chris's mother, she'll have orphaned him at eight. Poor little guy. What does today have in store for him?*

An hour later, Percy rang the doorbell. His expression was somber. His arms hung slack at his sides, his shoulders drooped.

"Bad news?"

His lips pressed tightly together, he slowly nodded. "I called the hospitals and police station again this morning. No other Montse Perez."

"Montse. What an unusual name."

"It's a common Catalan nickname for girls."

"Really? What's it mean?"

"Virgin of Montserrat." He made a sour face.

"What?"

"It's not right to speak ill of the dead, but apparently Montse didn't live up to her name."

She squinted. "What do you mean?"

"She had a police record. Drugs, soliciting . . ."

Gwen raised her eyebrow. "That would help explain the boarding school, lack of relatives, and disconnected phone."

"Oh, just remembered." Percy held up a shopping bag. "I bought a change of clothes for Chris. Hope they fit."

"Thanks, that was really thoughtful." Taking the bag from him, she gave him a wan smile.

"It's the least I could do." He sighed. "This is going to be a tough day for him."

"I just wish we could be sure it's his mother before putting him through the trauma of going to a morgue."

"Me, too." His eyes narrowed. "They said the body had a distinguishing birthmark on her neck. I'm wondering if Chris might have a similar birthmark." He shrugged. "It's a long shot, but if he does . . ."

"I've got an idea." Gwen handed back the clothes. "After he's dressed, pretend to see if the shirt fits, but check his neck for birthmarks."

He nodded and then tapped at Chris's bedroom door.

"Hey, buddy, got some clothes for you in this bag. Try them on, and then let's see how they fit."

A few minutes later, Chris joined them in the living room.

"Looking good, buddy," said Percy, "even if they're a little big. Come closer and let me have a look." Percy lifted the shoulder seams of the shirt, allowing a clear view of his neck. "Is that a birthmark?"

The boy's eyes lit up. "Yes, it's exactly like my mother's."

Gwen's eyes met Percy's. She knew what she had to do.

"Chris, I'm afraid there's been an accident," she said gently.

"No!" The boy burst into tears. "He told me my mother had been hurt, but I thought it was a nightmare."

"Who?"

"The man who waited with me by the hotel last night. I thought I'd dreamed it, but he told me she'd been hurt." Tears running down his face, he looked up at Gwen with his sad, hazel eyes.

She grabbed a chair to steady herself. *Those eyes. They're like my father's.* "Did he . . ." She cleared her voice. "Did he say anything else?"

He nodded. "He said not to be afraid, that you'd take care of me."

Getting down on her knees, she threw her arms around Chris, hugging him. She felt his little body sobbing against her as she looked up at Percy through wet eyelashes.

The police let them view Montse Perez's body over closed-circuit television.

"Identification isn't as traumatic over a monitor," said the officer. "It's not as real. It's like watching a movie, not gazing at a dead loved one."

When Chris saw his mother, he whispered, "She looks like she's sleeping."

The camera panned in on her birthmark.

"Is this your mother?" asked the officer.

"No, sir." His eyes brimming, he said, "My mother's in heaven now."

Percy took him for a walk as Gwen made arrangements for the body's cremation.

"How did it happen," she asked the officer.

"Hit and run. She was struck while crossing Plaça de Espanya."

"When was that?"

"Yesterday morning."

"What time?"

He checked the records. "Time of death was eleven thirty-five am."

Gwen exhaled. *So she was on her way to meet Chris.* "How sad."

She made a call, then met Chris and Percy outside where she noticed a florist shop.

"Let's get some flowers for your mother. Do you think she'd like that?"

Nodding, he looked at her. "But where would we put them?"

"Didn't we promise you we'd go back to the hotel this morning?"

He nodded again.

"We're keeping that promise."

A few minutes later, the taxi let them out at the hotel, where they found a tiny garden between the hotel and the café next door. Gwen recognized the shrubbery. *It's where I first saw Chris.* In the garden's center was a tree surrounded by bristly, red flowers. "Callistemon," read the sign.

"They look like bottlebrushes," said Chris. Then he gazed up at the tree. "Do you think my mother would like us to leave her flowers here?"

She nodded. "I think she'd like that a lot."

They spent the afternoon walking around the hillside parks of Montjuïc. When they came to one garden, Chris dashed over to a patch of red flowers.

"Look, here are more of those bottlebrushes."

In another park, he discovered a series of musical cushions. Each, when stepped on, sounded a different note. By quickly jumping from one to another, he played "Twinkle, Twinkle, Little Star." He found a pair of parabolic reflectors six feet apart. Percy whispered into one, and he listened at the other.

His face lit up. "I can hear you!"

They took the Transbordador cable car to the top of Montjuïc to visit the seventeenth-century castle. Chris scrambled over the artillery and cannons, amusing himself with imaginary games. Then, after climbing the trails and descending the stairs, they finished up in the cactus section of Jardins del Mirador.

"What are those spiny trees?" Chris asked.

"Saguaro cactus," said Gwen. "Big, aren't they?"

Chris agreed, then, his shoulders sagging, he became silent.

"Are you getting tired? Ready to go back to the apartment?"

Deflated, he seemed to shrink in size. "I forgot," he whispered.

"Forgot what?"

He gestured to the gardens. "While we were here, I forgot . . . everything."

I almost did, too. "Back to reality. I guess it has to come sooner or later." Gwen looked at Percy over his head and sighed. *What now?*

⁂

After dinner, Chris fell asleep, and Percy carried him into Gwen's bed. They tucked him in and shut the door. Then she poured two glasses of wine.

Staring into Percy's violet-blue eyes, she voiced her earlier question. "Now what do we do?"

He took a deep breath. "I don't know." Glancing toward her room, he said, "That poor kid's already been through more than I have."

Nodding, Gwen thought of her father. Because of Chris, she began to understand him, empathize with him. Then her mind returned to the issue at hand.

"Incidentally, I called Montserrat this morning. They'll say a Mass at the chapel the day after tomorrow for my father and Chris's mother."

His eyes caught hers. "That's a nice gesture. I think they'll both like that."

"Both?" Her eyebrow shot up. "Chris and who?"

"Your father." He gave her a crooked grin. "You've made a believer out of me."

"How'd that happen?"

"You were convincing, but when Chris saw him, too." He snickered. "How could there be any doubt in my mind?"

"You sure took your time about accepting it."

"Did you say the day after tomorrow? That's Christmas Eve."

She nodded. "Which brings us back to where this conversation began. What do we do?"

"About Chris in general or about Chris at Christmas?" He blinked.

"Yes." She gave him a wry grin. "Those questions and a dozen more. There are so many aspects to this dilemma, but let's start with the first. Should we take him to Montserrat with us?"

"Why not?"

She drew in a long breath. "Chris can see my father. Frankly, some of the visions I've had are frightening, especially for a child. He's appeared to me in lightning, sea mist, neon light, a monk's cowl, smoke, and fire." Shaking her head, she said, "I never know what to expect. It might be another traumatic experience for him."

"On the other hand," said Percy, "it's a formal farewell to his mother. Maybe we shouldn't deprive him of that. I say take him with us. All in favor?"

"Aye." She chuckled. "Okay, long term, what do we do with Chris?"

"You said we." His eyes caught hers. "You said what do we do?"

"Figure of speech." She shrugged it off.

His violet-blue eyes glinting merrily, he said, "That's what they call a Freudian bra."

She giggled. "You mean slip."

"Slip, bra," he grinned. "The point is, your subconscious was making a statement."

"I wasn't stating anything. I was asking a question."

He shook his head. "You were stating the obvious. We're a *we*." He took her hand in his. "We're in this together."

The next day, Gwen went through her bureau and closet, consolidating her things and making room for Chris' few possessions. When she found her backpack still unpacked, she snickered. *Had other things on my mind, I guess.* She glanced at her bare left hand as she went through each pocket, pulling out small, forgotten treasures. *I'd forgotten about the shell and the penny.*

She looked at the penny, remembering. *That's the elusive 1943 copper cent my parents and I'd tried to find for my penny collection.* Opening up her laptop, she researched it. *If it's a 1943 plain, it's worth . . . Wow.*

She found Ruth and Crow sitting at the table. Holding up the penny, she asked, "Do you guys know anything about numismatics?"

Ruth looked up. "I know a little, but my uncle's a coin dealer. He can answer any questions I can't."

"What can you tell me about a 1943 copper cent?"

"Off the top of my head, I can tell you it's rare, but a lot depends on its condition and mint mark."

Squinting, she shook her head. "It's been years since I collected pennies. What's a mint mark again?"

"That's the little letter appearing under the year. D means it was minted in Denver, S in San Francisco, and P or no mint mark means it was minted in Philadelphia."

Reading it, she said, "This one was minted in Denver."

Ruth's ears perked. "It's got a D mint mark?"

She nodded.

"Can I see that?"

"Sure." She handed it to her.

Ruth squinted at it, turned it over, and examined it in the sunlit window. "Before I say anything else, let me call my uncle."

Five minutes later, she returned, her eyes wide.

"What?"

"Gwen, you'd better sit down."

She pulled a chair up to the table. "What'd he say?"

"Everything depends upon the penny's condition."

Gwen nodded. "Right."

"Obviously, it's been in circulation. It's not in perfect condition, but to my poor eyes it looks pretty good."

"So what did he say?"

"He said to warn you there are lots of fakes out there, where people file down 1948 pennies to look like 1943 pennies. And if it's copper-plated steel instead of solid copper, it's not worth a plug nickel." Ruth grinned at her joke.

"All right, already, what did he say it was worth?"

"If it's authentic, if it's solid copper, if it's in perfect condition, at auction, it's worth . . ." She grinned devilishly. "Drum roll, please. It's worth up to one and three-quarter . . . million dollars."

"What?"

"Before you get your hopes up, like I say, this coin's been circulated. It's not in mint condition, and it could be a fake," said Ruth, passing the penny to Crow. "Don't count your chickens before they're hatched."

Chuckling, Gwen shook her head. "You and your maxims, but I get the point."

"My uncle wants to see it," said Ruth, "appraise it, certify it if it's genuine, and offer it for auction."

"Heady stuff." Gwen took a deep breath, grounding herself. She told Crow the story of finding it in the Compostela cathedral. "I'd *just* asked for a sign, when I noticed this penny rolling toward me."

"That's one heck of a sign, man." Crow handed it to Gwen. "And makes for one helluva story." He winked.

Gwen glanced at Chris playing in the living room with Kitty-Cat. "Maybe this 'penny from heaven' will help pay some of these unexpected expenses."

"Well," said Ruth's uncle, putting down his jeweler's eyepiece. "Christmas has come early for you."

Gwen exchanged a gleeful grin with Ruth and Crow. "Really?"

"Keep in mind, Uncle Ari, she's a friend of mine." Ruth raised her eyebrow in warning.

He sighed. "It's flawed. It's been circulated, but it's genuine. If you're interested, I'll offer it at next week's auction. For a small fee, of course." He grinned at Ruth.

"Of course." Gwen chuckled.

"Business is business," said Ruth.

"Ruth told us the most to expect at auction is just under two million dollars." Gwen's eyes drilled into Ari's. "Can you give us a more realistic expectation?"

Shaking his head, he laughed. "All I can say is, it will be *nothing* like her estimate. As I've mentioned, the coin's flawed, and it's been in circulation for years, so the base value's *substantially* lower. Then from that *greatly reduced* selling price, you'll need to deduct my fees and pay taxes. I don't want to give you any false hopes." He glanced at Ruth. "At least not any additional false hopes. We'll find out what the market will bear next week." A hint of a smile crossed his face. "But I doubt you'll be disappointed."

When Percy and Chris returned from Christmas shopping, Gwen met them at the door.

"Oh, Gwen," said Chris, bubbling over with a secret, "guess what Percy—"

Percy hushed him with a finger to his lips. "It's a surprise."

His hazel eyes flashing, he asked, "Then can I tell Ruth and Crow?"

Percy shook his head no. "If you tell them, it won't be a surprise."

Gwen watched the two of them, grinning at their newfound camaraderie. Glad for the moments they could keep his mind off his mother, she recalled all too clearly his muffled sobs at night. She turned to Chris. "If it'll make you feel any better, I'll tell *you* a secret."

"What?" His hazel eyes danced.

She told them about Ari and the penny. "And after the auction, we'll go to Tibidabo to celebrate, and you can ride the big Ferris wheel."

His small face erupted in a smile. "Oh, I can't wait for the auction!"

She laughed. "You mean you can't wait for the auction to be over."

Saturday dawned sunny and mild. As the five of them caught the first train to Montserrat, they were all in a holiday mood, except for Gwen.

Concerned about Chris, she wondered what his reaction would be at the Mass. She frowned. *Will he see my father?*

On the cable car ride up the mountain, Crow started chuckling. "Chris's eyes are as big as saucers. Flying saucers, that is."

"That reminds me. What time's the Mass?" asked Ruth.

"Not until one this afternoon," said Gwen. "Why?"

"You and Percy inspired us." Ruth glanced at Crow. "Jim and I are going to do some research—"

"About references to UFOs in ancient literature and artwork," said Crow.

"As well as legends and traditions about the Ark of the Covenant being hidden here," Ruth added.

Gwen checked her timetable. "Okay, we'll show you where the funicular station's located. Let's meet there at noon. That'll give us plenty of time to catch the train and walk to the Santa Cova chapel."

After directing Ruth and Crow first to the funicular and then to the library, the three of them set off for the basilica. They lined up at the Angel Door to view *La Moreneta,* along with the hundreds of other pilgrims.

"Look at all the designs of angel musicians." Gwen pointed them out to Chris as she ran her fingers lightly over the door. Then, following the long line before them, they slowly climbed the many flights of steps and walked past numerous stained glass windows. Finally, they approached the carved onyx threshold. Though it, she could view the Shrine of the Black Virgin and Child. As Gwen lightly ran her fingers over the smooth onyx doorway, she sensed the electricity in the hallowed atmosphere. *Millions of pilgrims just like us have passed through this portal.*

Then she saw the holy water font made from an immense, natural shell, outlined with silver. *The shell!* Suddenly, she knew the journey she had started in León, her pilgrimage to Compostela, was nearing its end. She thought of their *Wizard of Oz* analogy and inwardly chuckled.

Leaning over, she barely whispered in Percy's ear. "Montserrat is Oz."

Squinting, he shook his head.

"Montserrat is Oz," she repeated in a slightly louder whisper.

His eyes twinkling, he nodded. "Okay, then," he whispered, his lips so close to her ear, his breath tickled. "Who's the Wizard?"

Because of his tone, his cadence, Gwen grinned and murmured what it sounded like. "Who's your daddy?"

As she uttered those words, it suddenly occurred to her. All the emotional distance, all those years of separation were tied to those three words. *Who's your daddy?* From the age of eight, her father and her Father had been intertwined throughout her life.

She glanced down at Chris, imagining her father at that age. She felt an attachment to the boy that reached back two generations. *Maybe, on some level, I could give Chris what my father lacked, somehow filling that hollowness in his soul, in my soul.*

She felt Percy's eyes on her and realized he was waiting for her answer. *Who's the Wizard? Easy.* She smiled as the answer came to her.

Leaning over, she gestured toward the heavens with her chin and barely whispered, "The Father."

His eyes met hers in a private smile just as they passed through the carved onyx portals and stood before the Black Madonna. Gwen caught her breath.

"La Moreneta," said Chris, his hazel eyes growing round.

Enthroned in silver, gilded in gold leaf, her blackened hands held the Christ child and an orb. Her serene face had blackened over the centuries, yet it gazed tranquilly, filling Gwen with a deep sense of peace.

She nodded to herself. *Yes, Montserrat's the final destination of my pilgrimage.*

The entire statue was encased in glass, all but a small portion of the orb and the Virgin's hand.

Chris stretched to touch it, but his little arm could not reach. Percy lifted him so he could pay tribute. With one hand, he touched the orb. The other he held up to the baby Jesus and waved. Percy set him down and did the same.

Following their example, Gwen raised one hand, as if answering the Baby's wave. With the other, she lightly traced her fingers over the wooden orb and the hand holding it. Smoothed by a million caresses, the wood's grain felt as glossy as silk. When she touched the Virgin of Montserrat's hand, Gwen felt a tingling as she physically connected with what she had only sensed previously: the hallowed atmosphere's electricity. She stood rooted, gripped in its timeless current.

In that link with the statue's hand, it was as if the Madonna passed a certain strength of character to her, a fortitude. With a woman's intuition, Gwen recognized the resilience of the Virgin's love for her Son. She felt the pain of her own grandmother when she had to give up her son, Gwen's father. For a fraction of an instant, she felt the pain of Chris's mother, Montse, named after the Virgin of Montserrat, when she realized she would never hold him again. As the current loosened its grip, she looked at Chris. Having connected with his mother, with her father's mother, with their holy mother, Gwen knew what she had to do.

Shaking, Gwen flinched as the current let go its hold. She gasped.

"Are you all right?" whispered Percy.

Too choked up to whisper, she nodded. Swallowing the lump in her throat, she brushed off her tears and stumbled away from the Black Madonna, allowing the next pilgrim to experience her.

Overcome, Gwen fought her tears as they made their way along the luminous Cami de l'Ave Maria, the Path of the Hail Mary. Thousands of votive candles, rows upon rows of votive candles, each representing a prayer, lit the passageway. Reflecting candlelight on the smooth stone walls and tiled tribute to Our Lady lent a dreamy quality to the corridor, a transition from one world to the next, from the ethereal to the real.

"Gwen," asked Chris, "can I light a candle for my mother?"

"Of course," she said, clearing her throat, blinking back her tears.

They left donations for their candles at the self-service counter. Then, as they lit them, each placed their candle in a rack and said a silent prayer.

Gwen knelt, asking the Madonna to intercede. *Please, pray that I can fulfil what my father's life lacked, that his soul can be released. Please, pray that I can help Chris.*

As she crossed herself and stood up, her eyes fell on the boy. His lips moving silently, his eyes tightly shut, tears trickled down his small cheeks. She glanced at Percy. Wearing a tender smile, he was also watching the boy. Then he turned, and their eyes met. Her eyelashes fluttered in a shy smile as she looked away, embarrassed he had caught her witnessing his vulnerable underside. Leaving the corridor, they walked into the courtyard.

"Santa Cova, where we're headed next," Percy told Chris, "is the place they discovered the Virgin of Montserrat."

"Really?" Chris looked up at him with reddened eyes. "My mother was named after her."

In that millisecond, Gwen saw the child that had appeared in her dream, the abandoned boy who had become her father. She took a deep breath. *I can't let Chris become emotionally crippled the way my grandmother stunted my father's spiritual growth.*

She recalled the only time her grandmother had ever babysat her. Other than teaching her how to make a row of crochet stiches to keep her occupied for the hour, the woman had completely ignored her. When her mother had picked her up, Gwen had said, "Grandma doesn't like me."

"Not just you." Her mother had given her a wry grin. "She doesn't like children, period."

Had that experience of abandoning my father hardened her? Had I, his child, been too vivid a reminder of the wrong she'd committed when my father was as vulnerable as Chris?

"Montse is a beautiful name," said Percy, putting his hand on the boy's shoulder. "Did you know, tradition has it that Saint Luke carved the Virgin's statue with Saint Joseph's carpentry tools?"

His eyes widening, Chris shook his head. "No."

Lowering his voice, Percy leaned toward Gwen. "Critics contest it. Carbon dating suggests it was carved in the twelfth century."

She gave him a sharp look. "Shouldn't you tell him the truth?"

He shrugged. "Who but God knows the whole story?" Then he looked at Chris. "As the legend goes, Saint Etereo brought it to Spain. Then, when Saracen infidels invaded, Christians defended the Virgin's statue for three years. In 718, just before they were defeated, they hid it in a cave. Though the location was forgotten for nearly two hundred years, people did not forget the holy statue. In 890, shepherd boys saw flashing lights and heard singing coming from the mountains of Montserrat. Finally, they rediscovered the statue of Our Lady in Santa Cova."

"And that's where we're going next?"

"That's exactly where we're going next, to hear Mass said for your mother."

❄

After meeting Crow and Ruth, they caught the funicular and raced downhill to the Santa Cova station. They paced themselves along the windy mountain path to match Chris's short stride and finally arrived at the chapel.

The moment they entered, Gwen felt the heightened energy of the atmosphere. Similar to the sensation she had experienced while touching the Black Madonna, she had felt the same grip of electricity during the previous visit, when she had connected with the cave's walls. She breathed in deeply. *We're on consecrated ground.*

She glanced at the rack of votive candles, recalling the last time she had seen it, when her father's image had appeared. Then she peered at Chris, watching closely for any sign he could see her father. Not detecting any indication, she breathed a sigh of relief.

They took their seats in the front row of pews just as Mass began. Sitting between Gwen and Percy, Chris gripped their hands tightly.

As the priest began the homily, he asked, "What happens to us when we die?"

Chris drew in his breath as Gwen and Percy shared a worried look over his head.

"First, we believe we'll be judged," said the priest. "Following that, not two, but three choices." Glancing at each face, he looked at the small congregation. "Hell, heaven, or purgatory awaits us. Hell is for those who've rejected God, heaven is for those who die as saints, and purgatory is for the rest of us sinners."

He smiled, and the congregation chuckled.

"Purgatory, my friends, isn't a punishment. It's a second chance. Though we'd all like to go directly to heaven, not stop at 'Go,' let's be honest. Not all of us die as saints. Though our sins are forgiven, purgatory's a kind of 'clean room,' where we go to be decontaminated."

Again, he glanced at each person. "Only perfected love can meet God face-to-face because God is a pure being of light and beauty. Despite us being grimy, imperfect souls, God loves us and wants us with Him."

He leaned over the pulpit. "Here's the twist, my friends. It isn't God that *makes* us go to purgatory. It's we who *choose* to go. We want to freshen up, detoxify, purify ourselves from the grime of our crimes. Think of purgatory as a kind of spiritual spa, a place where we can cleanse ourselves and find healing, so we can meet God looking our heavenly best."

Reading from the Prayers of the Faithful, the priest said, "Today we pray for all the souls in purgatory, but we especially pray for Clark Christopher Alton and Montse Perez."

The congregation responded, "Lord, hear our prayer."

Gwen glanced at Chris when he sniffled. After she saw him straighten his back and square his shoulders, she turned back to the pulpit.

Instantly, she saw a blaze of blue-white light in the candlelit cave's chapel. Squinting at the abrupt light level change, straining to see the silvery-bright image at the light's core, Gwen blinked, trying to adjust her eyes.

As quickly as it appeared, the intense light's dazzling image began to fade. Only in its waning could she open her eyes wide enough to make out the brilliantly lit image of her father, smiling. Then, like a candle blown out, the image disappeared.

"For the repose of their souls," said the priest, "we pray to the Lord."

"Lord, hear our prayer," said Gwen along with the congregation.

Glancing around, she realized that no one else noticed the burst of light, not even Chris. Taking a deep breath, inhaling the sacred atmosphere, Gwen sighed. *My father's at peace.* She put her arm around Chris and hugged him to her. When he looked up, Gwen saw her father's hazel eyes.

After their Christmas Eve dinner, the five of them gathered around the Christmas tree.

"What's this?" Ruth pulled something out from under the tree and handed it to Chris.

"Caga Tió!" His eyes sparkling, he reached out for the log that had two legs, a red hat, and a smiley face. "Caga Tió!"

Chuckling, Crow asked, "Is there anything else under there?"

Chris climbed underneath and, grinning ear to ear, brought out a package of chestnuts.

While he was beneath the tree, Percy stashed two small gifts under the branches. "Look again. Isn't there anything else?"

Chris grinned at him mischievously and then searched under the other side of the tree. This time, he brought out a sack of nougat and a small box.

"Who's the nougat for?" asked Percy.

"Me!" Smiling, Chris popped a piece into his mouth.

"Who's the box for?" asked Percy, his eyes twinkling.

Chris shared a private smile with him as he dutifully read the gift tag. "It's for Kitty-Cat."

Lifting her head, Gwen spoke to the cat on her lap. "It's for you."

"Me-ow-ow," said Kitty-Cat.

"Why don't you give it to Gwen. Let her open the gift for Kitty-Cat," said Percy.

"Sure!" Again, Chris shared a private smile with him as he brought the box to her.

"Thanks." Gwen read the gift tag. "From Percy." She smiled at him and then opened the box. "Look, Kitty-Cat, it's a collar." Then she silently read a note hidden beneath it.

"Read it again, *out loud.*" Percy swallowed a grin as he and Chris exchanged smiles.

"Merry me-ow-ow." Gwen scratched behind the cat's ears. "Aw, Kitty-Cat, that's exactly how you sound: me-ow-ow."

"Read it again," Percy said.

Gwen gave him a puzzled stare, but read. "Merry me—"

"Stop right there." His smile became serious as his violet-blue eyes homed in on hers. "Marry me, Gwen?"

She wasn't sure whether to laugh or cry. Her shoulders shaking, it was a combination of chuckles and tears. Then, sniffling, she reached over to hug Percy.

"Yes!" Reaching her arm behind his neck, she pulled him to her in a lingering kiss.

When they finally parted, Percy gave Chris a wink. "In that case, there's one more gift under the tree."

On cue, Chris retrieved and handed him a velvet box. Percy opened it, slipped the diamond ring on her left hand, and hesitated. "Your grandfather promised your grandmother their marriage would be a journey. Like them, we're two pilgrims. We've already walked the Camino de Compostela together. Now we'll walk, hand in hand, along our journey of life."

He remembered my family's story.

Gwen reached out and pulled him to her in a hug. Then she held up her left hand, admiring the ring, and hugged him again. "Both the sentiment and the ring are beautiful. I love you, Percy Gowan."

The five of them attended Midnight Mass at la Sagrada Familia's crypt. As Gwen raised her eyes to the towering columns that seemed to rise to heaven, she got an idea. She leaned closer to Percy, whispering in his ear.

"How would you like to have our wedding here?"

CHAPTER 17:

The Three Kings

"I never made one of my discoveries
through the process of rational thinking."
— Albert Einstein

The day after Christmas, Ruth called Gwen from the headquarters of Child and Family Welfare.

"Good news. I called in a few favors and expedited Chris's paperwork. Can you and Percy come in to the office to sign a few hundred pages?"

Gwen recognized the smile in her voice. "I hope you're exaggerating."

"Only a little."

That afternoon, after they signed the paperwork, Ruth said, "Congratulations! You're now officially Chris's foster parents." She turned to Gwen. "But the Hague Adoption Convention governs adoption between the U.S. Government and Spain, which means first the U.S. has to find you eligible. Then Spain. It's basically double the paperwork."

"That's if we plan to live in the U.S.," said Gwen, exchanging a glance with Percy. At his nod, she turned back to Ruth. "What if we stay here? Adoptive parents have to be legal Spanish residents, right? Percy's a Spanish citizen, but what about me?"

Ruth grinned. "Residency in Spain's automatically granted when you marry a Spanish national."

"That takes care of that." Grinning at Percy, Gwen went through the motions of brushing off her hands.

When the phone rang that evening, Gwen knew from the chime it was Art. For an instant, she considered letting the call go to voice mail, but on second thought, she picked up.

"Hello, Art."

"Gwen, it's good to hear your voice."

"Yours, too." A smile tugged at the corner of her lips. *No matter what, I always liked him, respected him.*

"About this resignation letter of yours."

Her forehead puckered. "Yes?"

"The magazine doesn't want to accept it." He took a deep breath. "I wonder if we could talk about it."

She groaned internally as she chose her next words. "I thought it would be better if I bowed out. I don't want any hard feelings, any awkward encounters."

"You're too good a photojournalist for us to let personal feelings interfere. The publications team wants to keep you on staff, and I'd like to meet with you to discuss it."

Squinting, she took a deep breath. "I'm not sure that would be wise."

"Besides, it seems the Catalan independence movement's heating up. We might even keep you on location as a foreign correspondent."

Covering her gasp, she pressed her fingers to her lips. "Art, that would be awfully generous."

"It'd be sound business practice." He hesitated as a smile came through his voice. "Why don't we meet over a glass of Cava?"

Something's up. Gwen felt a constriction in her chest and it occurred to her she had been holding her breath. Unable to breathe easily, she forced herself to fill her lungs. *Take it slow. Let's be professional about this.* Swallowing, she chose an intellectual meeting of the minds: the news.

"You're absolutely right about Barcelona's political scene. Catalonia's Supreme Court has accepted all criminal complaints filed against the president, vice president, and minister of education for authorizing and coorganizing the vote."

"Things could get ugly."

"It's extremely controversial. Catalans are outraged at what they call the Spanish Government's abuse of power."

"What's Madrid have to say?"

"Rather than negotiate, it's imposed a recentralization of power as it's attacked the Catalan culture and language."

"In other words, Madrid's reversed decades of progress."

"Another issue, the center-right, pro-Catalan and center-left, pro-independence presidents can't decide on the next step in the independence movement."

"So there's infighting, as well."

"As a result, the movement's stymied."

Again, his tone flipped from business to persuasive. "Looks like an opportunity to stay in Spain a while. Why don't we meet to discuss it?"

She gave a nervous laugh. "I really don't think that would be a good idea."

"Come on, just one glass of Cava. For old time's sake. What do you say?"

She breathed uneasily. "Thanks, but—"

"But what? Are you so smitten with Sir Perceval you're willing to turn down the opportunity to be *Trails n' Treks Magazine's* foreign correspondent?"

"I just don't think it would be fair to you—"

"Fair to me?" he bellowed. "What do you call fair? Do you call stringing me along all those weeks fair? Do you call running around with Sir Perceval behind my back fair? Do you call breaking up with me after I flew nearly four thousand miles to marry you fair? How do you think I felt going back to that honeymoon suite alone? Please enlighten me. I'd like to hear your definition of fair."

She swallowed the lump in her throat, knowing he spoke the truth. "Art, I never meant to hurt you. What happened between Percy and me . . . just happened. It wasn't anything I planned." In a small voice she added, "When you gave me the ring, you said to wear it until we made . . . a more permanent commitment. Technically, we weren't engaged."

"*Technically,* two can play that game." She heard the sneer in his voice.

As the pause lengthened, she took the bait. "What do you mean?"

"'Something' just happened between Suzanne and me, too."

"Suzanne? My cube mate?" Blinking, she tried but could not recall any exchange between them. "I'm not following."

"Do I have to spell it out for you? Suzanne covered for you on more than news articles. While you were catting around Spain, I wasn't alone, pining for you, either." He snickered. "Forget becoming foreign correspondent. I accept your letter of resignation." With that, he hung up.

The dead phone still in her hand, Gwen raised her eyebrows. *To think he actually made me feel guilty while he . . .* Sniffing, she shook her head. "Thank you, God," she whispered, "for showing me You've been my guide all along."

As Gwen finished up the "Four Elements and Seven Gifts" article, Ruth's uncle Ari called.

"The auction's over, and a bid was accepted."

She crossed her fingers. "How much did the 1943 penny bring in?"

"After fees and taxes, your net will be just over three hundred and eighty thousand euros."

"In dollars, that's about . . ."

"At today's rate, that translates to over four hundred and twenty-five thousand dollars."

Gwen whistled. "Not a bad return on a penny." *Thanks, Dad.* As soon as she hung up, she dialed Percy. "Looks like we'll be celebrating with Chris at Tibidabo."

They began their trek up Mount Tibidabo in an old-fashioned trolley car. At the halfway mark, they transferred to the funicular, zipping straight to the top.

"This park opened in 1901," said Percy, "so don't expect any white-knuckle rides."

When they reached the summit, Gwen looked out across Barcelona to the sea. "What a magnificent panorama." She turned to Percy with a grin. "The rides may not be white-knuckle, but the view's breathtaking."

"Look! There's the Ferris wheel," said Chris, pulling her in the opposite direction.

"Okay, that's where we said we'd celebrate." Chuckling, she glanced back at Percy as Chris tugged her toward the ride.

They climbed into one of the covered gondolas, and Chris squealed as it catapulted them another sixty-five feet into the air.

"See that?" Percy drew Chris close as he pointed out the site. "That's la Sagrada Familia."

With the "Four Elements and Seven Gifts" article fresh in her mind, Gwen recalled how Percy had designated wind as la Sagrada Familia's element because of the stained glass windows' play of light and kaleidoscope of colors.

In her mind's eye, she again saw how the sunshine had infused the nave with a fiery glow. As the sunlight had filtered through the leaded glass, the air had taken on a dappled-reddish color, like a firestorm moving in a heat mirage. It was in the midst of those flames the Father had let her see her father.

Thanks to the gift of Wisdom, I now know he was asking for my help. She smiled inwardly, recalling how even their guide's name, Núria, meant wisdom of God. *La Sagrada Familia was definitely the basilica of wind and wisdom.* She glanced at Percy. *And that's where we're getting married.*

As the Ferris wheel descended and then started its next revolution, Chris watched expectantly, his eyes huge in anticipation. When they climbed higher, Percy pointed out the cathedral's spires to him.

Gwen recalled labeling the cathedral the earth element because its immense columns rooted heaven to earth. She remembered a man watching her there until she realized he was her father. *Piety was the gift there.*

Again, the Ferris wheel descended and started another revolution. This time, Percy drew Chris' attention to Santa Maria del Pi's bell tower.

Their foursome had dubbed it the fire element since radicals had set it on fire during the revolution. *Because I experienced fear of the ghost and joy from the music, the gift from Santa Maria del Pi was Fear of the Lord: fire and fear.*

She thought of the two gifts she had gained along the pilgrimage. *At the cathedral in León, I was given the gift of Understanding, and in Compostela, the gift of Knowledge, along with the penny.*

Once more, the Ferris wheel descended and started its next revolution. She scanned the cityscape but could not find what she wanted.

"Do you see Santa Maria del Mar?"

"No." Using his hand, Percy blocked the sun from his eyes. "It's hidden among the Ribera's narrow streets, but it's in that general direction." He pointed northeast of Santa Maria del Pi.

Because Santa Maria del Mar was the Star of the Sea, their group had labeled it the water element. Looking over Chris's head at Percy, she grinned, recalling how something outside herself had made her agree to their first date. At the time, Ruth had thought it was the gift of Counsel, possibly the Holy Spirit that had personally given her that gift.

"Where's Montserrat?" Chris twisted his neck and turned in his seat to look behind them.

"Back in that direction," said Percy, pointing over his left shoulder, "but it's too far away to see."

Gwen shivered as she recalled touching the Virgin of Montserrat's hand, where she had received the seventh gift, Fortitude. She smiled to herself as the memory evoked the gifts' blessings.

Once I was reunited with my heavenly Father, I could be my father's heart and hands. With prayers and my love for Chris, he was released to heaven.

She glanced at Percy. *I met the love of my life. Once we're married, we'll adopt Chris, making us a real family, along with our extended family, Ruth and Crow.*

How different life would be if I hadn't begun this pilgrimage, if I hadn't taken that first step.

She reached for the crucifix around her neck, lightly fingering the tiny scallop shells at its four points. *This is all I have of my mother's, but it's what began the pilgrimage and led me here.*

CHAPTER 18:

Castles

"Do not worry if you have built your castles in the air.
They are where they should be. Now put the foundations under them."
— Henry David Thoreau

On Epiphany Eve, the five of them stood near Port Vell, watching the fireworks as they waited for the Three Wise Men's arrival by boat. They looked on as Barcelona's mayor greeted the kings, giving them the key to the city and free reign to enter all the houses. Then, after the kings reminded the children to be good, they kicked off their Cabalgata de Reyes, Cavalcade of the Kings, parade.

His eyes wide, Chris watched the camels and massive floats pass by. As he listened to the live music, Percy lifted him onto his shoulders. From his vantage point, he waved his arms, dancing along with the passing groups, and caught the candies the kings tossed from the floats.

Ruth asked Chris, "Did you remember to write your letter to the kings?"

He nodded. "Gwen mailed it to the royal pages last week." Then he turned toward Gwen. "They'll give it to the kings, won't they?"

Suppressing a smile, she nodded sincerely.

"And have you been a good boy?" asked Crow, looking like King Caspar with his bushy, blond ponytail. Winking, he added, "They won't deliver your presents tomorrow if you've been naughty."

"Oh, no." Concern clouded the boy's hazel eyes.

"Don't worry," said Percy, throwing Crow a sharp look. "You've been on your best behavior. Tonight, just remember to put out water for the kings' camels and turrónes and Cava for the kings. You'll be fine."

Gwen watched the celebration from the advantage of being an outsider looking in. She remembered the Thanksgiving parades of her youth, when Santa had come to town. She also recalled learning the facts about Santa at all too tender an age.

What impressed her here was everyone's effort to keep the childhood magic alive, from the mayor's active role to the newscasters' reporting on the kings' progress through Barcelona. She glanced at Chris.

This is about celebrating childhood and reciprocating the joy kids bring us. Through Chris, maybe I can give my father the childhood he was denied.

When they got home, they helped Chris put out a bowl of water for the camels and a bottle of Cava, three glasses, and a plate of chocolate turrónes for the three kings.

"Now, you've got to go to sleep," said Percy as Gwen readied Chris for bed, "or the kings won't stop here."

After they closed the door, Ruth found a fourth glass, and they opened the Cava.

"To the magic of childhood," said Gwen, toasting the others.

They clinked glasses as Percy said, "To the child within each of us."

Toasting, Gwen gave a satisfied sigh. "To experiencing childhood . . . vicariously."

"To the inner elf," said Crow, smirking.

"Age may not protect you from love," said Ruth, returning his mischievous smile, "but love can protect you from aging."

The next morning, Three Kings Day, Percy arrived early with a circular coffee cake studded with glazed fruit. A golden, cardboard crown rose from its center.

"This isn't just a coffee cake," he said, pretending indignation. "This is tortell de reis." Grinning, he kissed her, then added, "Kings' cake. Is Chris up yet?"

Watching him, love welled up inside her, but she shook her head, smirking. "He got up at two, four, and five this morning. Luckily, I kept guard on the sofa, assuring him the kings hadn't come yet."

He kissed her again. "How much sleep did you get?"

She gave him a wry grin. "Not much, but it's okay. I'm enjoying being a child because of him. Through him."

He laughed. "I think we all are."

"Happy Dia de Reis," said Ruth, noticing and whisking away the fourth wine glass from Chris's gifts for the three kings and camels. She glanced at Percy's cake. "Oh, that tortell de reis looks lovely. Coffee's on its way."

Gwen answered the knock at the door. "Come on in, Crow. Coffee's on, and Percy's brought a kings' cake."

"Is Chris up yet?" Crow asked.

Noticing his armload of gifts, she gave him a warm smile and hug. "Not yet, so you've still got time to hide these under the tree."

Standing back a moment, she looked at their group and swallowed the lump in her throat. *What a strange 'family' we make. Wouldn't have it any other way.*

Five minutes later, Chris and Kitty-Cat joined them. Sleep in his eyes, hair matted, mouth an astonished oval, and eyes round, Chris said, "The three kings came!"

The following day, Gwen scanned the quaint café. With its black-and-white marble tiled floors, it looked like a big checkerboard. The dark wood chairs and white marble tabletops adding to the board-game effect, the scene reminded her of Sunday's homily.

Comparing the universe to a chess game, the priest had said, "God's the supreme chess player. We can't always understand His 'moves,' but don't make the mistake of thinking we're insignificant pawns in some careless game." Paraphrasing Matthew, he had said, "Look at the birds in the sky. God takes care of them. Don't you think God takes even better care of us? The next time God 'pushes' you in a different direction, follow His lead. Trust His 'moves.'"

As she fingered her crucifix, she wondered how much her free will had entered into God's divine plan to lead her here. Then, sipping the white brew from her tall, narrow glass, she looked up at Percy.

"What do you call this drink again?"

"Horchata. It's made from pressed chufas, tiger nuts." His violet-blue eyes sought hers. "Like it?"

She nodded. "It's something like almond milk, but tangier." She picked up a long doughnut. "And what are these ladyfinger things?"

"Fartons," he mumbled from behind his hand, his mouth full.

"Delish." Gwen nibbled the powdered sugar dusted sponge cake. Then she brushed off her hands and looked Percy in the eye. "Okay, let's discuss logistics. We have la Sagrada Família's crypt reserved for our wedding, but where will we hold our reception? You haven't liked any place I've found."

His eyes sparkled. "Actually, that's why I asked you on this day-trip."

"That's another thing." Squinting, she tilted back her head as she appraised him. "I didn't know you owned a car."

"Why wouldn't I?"

"I thought, living in the city, you didn't need one." She shrugged. "Everyone walks or takes a cab, bus, or train."

His eyes twinkling merrily, he grinned. "There are lots of things you don't know about me."

"You're being so evasive." Smiling, she leaned over the tiny table to kiss him. "First this surprise trip." Scrutinizing him, she sized him up. "Then this mystique of yours. What are you up to?"

"I like to keep you guessing." He leaned toward her in another kiss. "Drink up, and I'll show you."

Ten minutes later, they were back on the road. She twisted to see out the window.

"Is that Montserrat in the distance?"

"Yup, we're only a few miles away."

"Is that where we're going?"

He turned to her and, beaming, silently shook his head.

"Oh, you're infuriating." Chuckling, she turned from him to the view. "At least the scenery's gorgeous." Blinking, squinting, she pointed to a round tower in the distance. "Is that what I think it is, a turret from a castle?"

He shrugged. "I don't know. Is it?"

"You're exasperating." She rolled her eyes. As they drove closer, she nodded. "That's definitely a tower. Wow!" She turned to him, grinning. "I've never seen a castle before."

A few minutes later, they turned off the main highway onto a long drive. As they approached, the castle loomed larger and larger.

"Ohmigosh. Look at that ridged, saw-toothed tower."

"Crenellated tower," he corrected.

"What?"

"The ridges at the top are called crenels."

"Didn't know there was a word for that. Leave it to the English Lit professor to know the technical term." She sighed as she gazed at the ancient architecture. Ivy covered the first floor's stone walls. Manicured trees and shrubbery surrounded it. An immense, double staircase led up to the front entrance, and a pool reflected the castle, doubling its splendor. "Isn't it beautiful? It looks like something right out of a storybook."

He gave her a lopsided grin. "Want to go in?"

"Oh, I don't think . . ." Then it dawned on her. "This is one of those places you can rent, isn't it?" Her smile drooped. "But I seriously doubt it's anything we can afford."

He shrugged. "It's free to window-shop."

As he reached for the door, Gwen lightly placed a restraining hand on his arm. "Have we got an appointment? I mean, I don't want to be caught trespassing in a place like this." She gave him a nervous giggle. "They might call the hounds on us."

He laughed. "Come on. It's all right. I promise."

As she stepped out, a gray-haired man hurried down the steps toward them.

"He doesn't *look* angry." She took a deep breath, but held back.

Percy laughed as he took her hand and gently pulled her along to meet the man.

"Percy, good to see you." The man reached out to hug him.

He let go Gwen's hand long enough to hug him back. Then he said, "Gwen, I'd like you to meet my half brother, Gerardo."

Her jaw slack, she glanced up at Percy, then turned to the gentleman. "Gerard . . . Gerardo, it's a pleasure to meet you."

As she held out her hand to shake, he bent, brushing his lips against her fingertips.

Raising her eyebrows, she turned to Percy. "Got to say, that's a first."

"I've heard so much about you, Gwen. Now, I can see why my brother's in love with you."

Scratching her ear, she tried to gather her thoughts as she gazed at Gerardo and the castle. *Somehow, Percy's connected to all this? How?*

"You're flattering me, Gerardo, but I'm afraid you have the advantage." She gave Percy a sharp look, then turned back to his brother. "You knew about me, but this is the first I've heard about a brother, who lives . . ." Then it occurred to her. "Of course, I've got it. You're the property manager or wedding planner or something." Relaxing, she laughed at herself. "For a minute, I thought you actually *lived* here."

"I do." Not blinking, he nodded.

"You're Percy's brother, and you live here?" She glanced at the castle. "Okay, would someone care to explain what this is all about before I make a fool of myself . . . again?"

Grinning, Percy said, "I just wanted to surprise you with the family business. You're right, we rent the facility out by the day or week." His tone teasing, he added, "Gerardo only lives here because his mother's related to the duchess of Medinaceli, as well as the marchioness of San Vicente del Barco."

"Who happens to hold over one hundred and fifty hereditary titles of nobility, as well as the title grandee sixteen times over, but who's *count*ing." Eyes twinkling, Gerardo chuckled as he emphasized the syllable.

"Officially, he's Marqués Gerardo Martínez."

She looked at the two skeptically and then turned to Percy. "If you're bothers, why isn't your surname Martínez?"

We're half brothers, different mothers." Percy grinned at Gerardo. "When my parents divorced, my mother had my family name legally changed to hers, Gowan."

Her eyes opening wide, she asked, "By any chance, do you have a title?"

He nodded. "I'm Marqués Perceval Gowan, but it doesn't mean anything because Spanish nobility is irrelevant these days." Putting his arm around her shoulders, he hugged her to him. "It's simply a hollow label, nothing more."

"But since you're joining our family," said Gerardo, "we'd consider it an honor if you'd hold your reception here. Our wedding gift to you."

"Ohmigosh!" Looking from Gerardo to Percy to the castle, Gwen shook her head. "This really is going to be a fairy tale wedding."

❄

The moment they were alone in the car, driving home, Gwen turned to him. "You're a marqués, and you never told me?"

"Would it have mattered?" He glanced at her.

"No. But I fell in love with an English Literature professor not . . ."

"Forget the title. It's meaningless." Keeping his eyes on traffic, Percy glanced at her quickly. "In fact, no one at the university knows anything about it. In Barcelona, I'm just Doc Gowan."

She looked into the distance without seeing. "So would that make me a marquess or something?"

"It's marquesa, but it's just a courtesy title, nothing more." Grinning, he shook his head. "It doesn't mean a thing."

"Maybe not to anyone else." Snickering, she sat up straight. "But it sure means something to a Jersey girl, born on the wrong side of the tracks." *If my parents could only see me now.*

"I just want you to be happy. If holding our wedding reception at Graymar sounds like a good idea, let's do it."

"Graymar?" Arching her eyebrow, she stared at him skeptically. "It's even got a *name?*"

Two weeks later, Gwen answered the polite knock at the dressing-room door. "Who is it?"

"Elspeth."

Ruth glanced at Gwen. "Who?"

"Percy's mother," Gwen mimed more than whispered. Then she cracked the door and looked in both directions before opening it wide. "Elspeth, come on in. I just didn't want Percy to see me before the wedding."

Elspeth hugged Gwen. "You look lovely."

"If so, it's all because of your dress." Gwen smoothed its satin bodice. "Thank you, again, for letting me borrow it."

"Nonsense, it's yours. I'm just so glad to finally have a daughter. Save it for when *your* daughter marries."

Gwen caught a glimpse of herself in the full-length, triple mirrors, appreciating the backless, vintage-lace sheath gown with its eight-foot train that gathered just beneath the derriere. *When my daughter marries. What a concept.* Then she saw Ruth's reflection in the mirror.

"Elspeth, you remember my maid of honor, Ruth, don't you?"

"Yes, we met at the rehearsal dinner," said Elspeth, giving Ruth a warm hug. "I understand your wedding day's fast approaching, too."

Ruth nodded. "In two weeks." She turned to Gwen. "At least, if the matron of honor and best man are back from their honeymoon by then."

Elspeth laughed. "We wouldn't want to rush that."

"We'll only be gone a week, and it'll fly by all too quickly." Then she heard the music start. Eyes widening, she said, "Ohmigosh, this is it."

Elspeth hugged Gwen again. At the door, she said, "Next time I see you, you'll be Mrs. Percy Lancelot Gowan."

Gwen blinked as it dawned on her. *Gwen Gowan. Gwendolyn Gowan. Mrs. Percy Gowan.*

"That's right. No more Gwen Alton. My father's name dies out. The end of an era."

"The beginning of a new era," said Elspeth, smiling as she closed the door behind her.

Gwen looked through the peephole into the basilica above.

"Do you remember when we toured here, Ruth?"

"Sure do. With the sun beaming through the stained glass windows, the air seemed on fire that afternoon."

Gwen thought of her father, recalling how he had appeared in the glow's virtual flames. *A sign.* "But the light's coming in through the morning windows today, blue and cool." She turned to Ruth. "You know, I haven't seen my father's ghost since his Mass at Montserrat."

"Is that good or bad?"

Her forehead creasing, she tried to put her thoughts into words. "I'm grateful he's been delivered from purgatory, but I wish I could see him one last time. Today, especially."

She breathed shallowly, remembering all the band competitions and photo exhibitions he had missed, even her high school graduation, and always with the same words. "You don't mind, do you?" *He had always had something more important to attend. Something had always taken precedence over her. Now, he was gone.*

"I'm sure he's here in spirit."

A shudder passed through her. "It's not the same thing."

The pipe organ's volume increased. "This is our cue." Ruth straightened Gwen's train and trailing veil for the last time. "Are you ready?"

"Wow." Gwen took a deep breath, grounding herself. She nodded and opened the door. There stood Chris with the rings. She bent down, giving him a quick hug. "Take these to Percy. After this ceremony, we'll be a real family," she whispered. When he started down the aisle, she stood up, then waited until Ruth was a few steps in front of her before following at a sedate pace.

Walking alone, she again thought of her father, wishing he could be there to give her away. Instead of thinking of the past, she focused on Percy, so handsome in his white tux, watching her, waiting for her at the altar, and her heart swelled. *Wish my father could have met him. Or had he?*

Suddenly, the morning light burst through the windows, illuminating the central aisle as Gwen marched toward Percy in sync with the music. Sensing something graze her arm, she shivered and turned to her left. There was her father, his arm lightly brushing against hers, as he walked her down the aisle.

This time, there were no flames, just a dazzling, bluish-white display of light engulfing the chapel. She gasped and would have stumbled except for his steadying arm on hers. Tears welled up and then silently brimmed over as she cast her father a grateful smile and kept marching forward. *He's here for my wedding.*

At the altar, he kissed the tears on her cheek, his lips leaving behind a tingling tickle. As her fingers lightly stroked the spot, Gwen saw Percy's eyes widen as he looked from her cheek to the apparition. Later, he confided, for that one brief moment, "I saw your father." She turned back in time to watch her father's spirit fade into the morning light. Then, turning toward Percy, she smiled, embracing the unwritten story that lay before them.

The End

Reading Group Guide for
Christmas in Catalonia

Why is the title, *Christmas in Catalonia*, significant? Why do/don't you like it? What would you have named *Christmas in Catalonia*? Is the title a clue to the theme(s)?

Did you enjoy *Christmas in Catalonia*? Why/why not?

What do you think *Christmas in Catalonia* is essentially about? What's the main idea/theme?

What other themes or subplots did *Christmas in Catalonia* explore? Were they effectively explored? Were they plausible? Were the plot/subplots animated by using clichés or were they lifelike?

Were any symbols used to reinforce the main ideas?

Did the main plot pull you in, engage you immediately, or did it take a chapter or two for you to 'get into it'?

Was *Christmas in Catalonia* a 'page-turner,' where you couldn't put it down, or did you take your time as you read it?

What emotions did *Christmas in Catalonia* elicit as you read it? Did you feel engrossed, distracted, entertained, disturbed, or a combination of emotions?

What did you think of the structure and style of the writing? Was it one continuous story or was it a series of vignettes within a story's framework?

What about the timeline? Was it chronological, or did flashbacks move from the present to the past and back again? Did that choice of timeline help/hinder the storyline?

Was there a single point of view, or did it shift between several characters? Why would Bartell have chosen this structure?

Did the plot's complications surprise you? Or could you predict the twists/turns?

What scene was the most pivotal for *Christmas in Catalonia*? How do you think *Christmas in Catalonia* would have changed had that scene not taken place?

What scene resounded most with you personally, either positively or negatively? Why?

Did any passage(s) seem insightful, even powerful?

Did you find the dialog humorous? Did it make you laugh? Was the dialog thought-provoking or poignant? Did it make you cry? Was there a particular passage that stated *Christmas in Catalonia's* theme?

Did any of the characters' dialog 'speak' to you or provide any insight?

Have you ever experienced anything that was comparable to what occurred in *Christmas in Catalonia*? How did you respond to it? How were you changed by it? Did you grow from the experience? Since it didn't kill you, how did it make you stronger?

What caught you off guard? What shocked, surprised, or startled you about *Christmas in Catalonia*?

Did you notice any cultural, traditional, gender, sexual, ethnic, or socioeconomic factors at play in *Christmas in Catalonia*? If you did, how did it/they affect the characters?

How realistic were the characterizations?

Did any of the characters remind you of yourself or someone you know? How so?

Did the characters' actions seem plausible? Why/why not?

What motivated the characters' actions in *Christmas in Catalonia?* What did the secondary characters want from the main character, and what did the main character want with them?

What were the dynamics between the characters? How did that affect their interactions?

How did the way the characters envisioned themselves differ from the way others saw them? How did you see the various characters?

How did the 'roles' of the various characters influence their interactions?

Who was your favorite character? Why? Would you want to meet any of the characters? Which one(s)?

If you had a least favorite character you loved to hate, who was it and why?

Was there a scene(s) or moment(s) where you disagreed with the choice(s) of any of the characters? What would you have done differently?

If one of the characters made a decision with moral connotations, would you have made the same choice? Why/why not?

Were the characters' actions justified? Did you admire or disapprove of their actions? Why?

Gwen had moments where she struggled with her faith. When was the last time your faith faltered? What helped you get through that time?

What previous influence(s) in the characters' lives triggered their actions/reactions in *Christmas in Catalonia?*

Did *Christmas in Catalonia* end the way you had anticipated? Was the ending appropriate? Was it satisfying? If so, why? If not, why and what would you change?

Did the ending tie up any loose threads? If so, how?

Did the characters develop or mature by the end of the book? If so, how? If not, what would have helped them grow? Did you relate to any one (or more) of the characters?

Have you changed/reconsidered any views or broadened your perspective after reading *Christmas in Catalonia?*

What do you think will happen next to the main characters? If you had a crystal ball, would you foresee a sequel to *Christmas in Catalonia?*

Have you read any books that share similarities with this one? How does *Christmas in Catalonia* hold up to them?

What did you take away from *Christmas in Catalonia?* Have you learned anything new or been exposed to different ideas about people or a certain part of the world?

Did your opinion of *Christmas in Catalonia* change as you read it? How? If you could ask Bartell a question, what would you ask?

Would you recommend *Christmas in Catalonia* to a friend?

RECIPES FOR

Christmas in Catalonia

"God forgives the sin of gluttony."
— Catalan Proverb

Caldo Galego White Bean Soup

Ingredients

2 tablespoons olive oil
1 medium yellow onion, sliced
4 oz. Chorizo (or other sausage), sliced
10 cups chicken or vegetable stock
1 half-pound ham hock
2 medium potatoes, peeled and cubed
1 turnip, coarsely chopped
2 (15.5 oz.) cans cannellini beans
4 cups turnip greens, collard greens, or green cabbage, chopped

Directions

Using a large saucepot, sauté the onions and chorizo in the oil until golden brown, about 10 minutes.

Add the stock and ham hock. Bring to boil. Add the potatoes and turnips. Reduce heat and simmer, stirring occasionally, for thirty minutes. Skim off and discard any foam.

Add the cannellini beans (including the liquid) and the greens. Simmer until the greens are tender, about 20 minutes.

Remove ham hock. Trim the ham from the bone, discarding the bone. Stir the ham into soup and serve. Ten servings.

Catalonian Tortilla (Potato Omelet)

Ingredients

4 tablespoons olive oil, divided
6 large potatoes, peeled and finely sliced
2 medium yellow onions, peeled and julienned
Salt, to taste
6 large eggs, beaten
1 baguette, sliced, optional

Directions

Using half the oil in a large skillet, sauté the potatoes over medium heat until soft and golden. Remove the potatoes and set aside.

Using the rest of the oil, sauté the onions over medium heat until golden brown.

Add the potatoes to the onions. Salt to taste. Gradually add the eggs, lightly stirring until the egg mixture is nearly set. Remove from the heat and invert the mixture over a large platter. Slide the inverted mixture back into the skillet and cook the other side of the tortilla for 4-5 minutes or until golden brown and the eggs are set.

To serve as an appetizer, cut the tortilla into 8 wedges. Top each bread slice with a potato-omelet wedge. Eight appetizer servings.

To serve as an entrée, cut the tortilla into 4 wedges and serve with bread, if desired. Four entrée servings.

About Karen Hulene Bartell

Author of *Sacred Gift, Sacred Choices, Sovereignty of the Dragons, Untimely Partners,* and *Belize Navidad,* Karen is a best-selling author, motivational keynote speaker, IT technical editor, wife, and all-around pilgrim of life. She writes multicultural, offbeat love stories steeped in the supernatural that lift the spirit. Born to rolling-stone parents who moved annually, Bartell found her earliest playmates as fictional friends in books. Paperbacks became her portable pals. Ghost stories kept her up at night—reading feverishly. The paranormal was her passion. Wanderlust inherent, she enjoyed traveling, although loathed changing schools. Novels offered an imaginative escape. An only child, she began writing her first novel at the age of nine, learning the joy of creating her own happy endings. Professor emeritus of the University of Texas at Austin, Dr. Bartell resides in the Hill Country with her husband Peter and her *mews*—five rescued cats.

Visit Karen at:

WEBSITE: KarenHuleneBartell.com
FACEBOOK: KarenHuleneBartell
TWITTER: KarenHuleneBart
AMAZON AUTHOR'S PAGE: Karen Hulene Bartell
GOODREADS AUTHOR PAGE: Karen Hulene Bartell

SPECIAL BONUS!

HERE ARE TWO FREE SAMPLES OF KAREN'S NOVELS,
SACRED CHOICES AND *SACRED GIFT*, AVAILABLE
AT PEN-L.COM, ONLINE, AND IN BOOKSTORES.

EXCERPT FROM *SACRED GIFT*

Everyone has a gift, but some never open their packages.

Develyn's black-outlined eyes opened wide. Then she looked down, hiding what- ever slid through her mind. "I had a grandmother."

Angela smiled politely, thinking she was joking. "You mean your mother was older when she had you?" Nodding her head, she snickered. "I can relate."

"No, I mean I never knew my mother, never had a mother. My grandparents raised me." She sipped from her straw.

"Why's that?"

She grimaced. "My grandparents only gave me a sketchy summary, no details. Basically, they said she died giving birth to me." She grunted. "It was like this for-bidden topic. Every time I brought it up, my grandmother got teary-eyed and left the room."

"Did your grandfather ever talk to you about it?"

Develyn scoffed. "He'd just shake his head, sigh, and mumble things like, 'maybe when you're older.'"

Angela raised her eyebrows. "And I thought I had it rough."

"Why?"

Angela sighed, and then licked her lips. "I knew I was adopted. It was an open adoption, for heaven's sake. I grew up with two . . . three…mothers, but recently my birth mother told me she almost aborted me." . . . "No." Stopping, Develyn grabbed Angela by the shoulder and turned her so they faced. "You're serious?"

"Yeah." Angela grimaced. "Talk about wondering if you were wanted—"

Her eyes big, Develyn said, "I'm a survivor."

"A survivor of what?" Angela snickered, again thinking she was joking. "The Titanic?"

"No," she started slowly, keeping her eyes on her cup. "Abortion."

"What do you mean?"

She looked Angela in the eye. "My mother tried to abort me. The abortion failed. She died, and I survived."

Angela's jaw dropped. "Ohmigosh." She blinked. "Are you sure? I mean, how could you know—"

Develyn's lip curled. "My darling cousin told me one day, laid it right between my eyes in no uncertain terms." She caught Angela's eye.

Grimacing, Angela shook her head slowly. "Sorry."

Develyn tried to shrug it off. "To quote the tee-shirts, it is what it is." She looked away.

In step, they turned and walked in silence, each sipping her coke, each lost in her thoughts. People passed them. Tour boats floated by.

Finally, Angela asked, "Have you ever . . . communicated with your mother?"

"Like in séances or Ouija boards?" Develyn held up her hands, shaking them as if she were scared, then abruptly dropped them and made a sour face. "What do you think?"

Angela heard the sarcasm. It was hard to misinterpret. She raised her eyebrows and was ready to back off. Then shoulders slumping, she groaned. Taking Develyn by the elbow, she stopped her.

"Look, whether you want to believe me or not, there's someone here who'd like to speak to you."

Develyn's left eyebrow and lip curled. "Yeah, right." She started off, but Angela again caught her elbow.

"I'm serious."

"And I'm Cleopatra." Develyn smirked.

"Fine, you don't want to listen, that's your business." Angela sighed. "I tried. I'm done," she said to the night.

"Who are you talking to?"

"Nobody." She sullenly sipped her coke. Then she threw back her head and groaned. "Okay, but this is the last try."

"Who the hell are you talking to?" asked Develyn.

"Ginny." Angela grimaced. "She's asking if the name Ginny means anything to you." When she was met with silence, she peered at Develyn. "Does it?"

Develyn's eyes reminded Angela of an owl's. "You're not kidding, are you?"

"Who's Ginny?"

Develyn shook her head. "Ginny only to her family, Virginia was her name."

"All right, who is she?"

"My mother."

FIND *SACRED GIFT* AT YOUR FAVORITE BOOKSELLER OR AT
www.Pen-L.com/SacredGift.html

EXCERPT FROM *SACRED CHOICES*

The woman shrugged as the air emitted a crackling or frying sound that seemed to run up and down the musical scales.

"It . . . it almost sounds like singing." Ceren looked around, wondering who would be singing at a time like this. Following the contours of the angel's wing, her eyes were drawn upward. At the wing's crest, violet-blue tufts of flame flashed and arced to the crown of the angel's head and gradually dropped, tracing along the blade of its sword.

"What is that?" Ceren stepped back, partially to get a better view, and partly to move away.

The high-pitched, musical hissing crackled louder as the short, tufted flames followed the sword's edge down through the serpent's stony profile. Then the violet-blue tufts leapt to the angel's leg, and began a slow descent along its periphery, gradually creeping closer. Frozen now with fascination, Ceren stood riveted, unable to recoil or retreat. Only her eyes moved as they tracked the flames' descent. Nearer and nearer they edged toward the statue's feet until the violet flames blazed inches from her and the old woman.

Bound in wonder, Ceren watched the impossible happen. The flames jumped from the statue's toe tips to the old woman's metal armband, seeming to shoot out from her jewelry's serpentine head and tail. Ceren blinked. The armband seemed to wriggle around the old woman's withered bicep as the flames inched down her arm to her fingertips. Her nails began glowing violet-blue like tiny jets of flame.

The old woman looked at her fingers, looked at Ceren, and then cackled as if she had thought of something amusing. Never taking her eyes from Ceren's, she reached over, and touched Ceren's hand, igniting her fingertips.

"Passing the torch," she hissed against the wind.

Ceren watched in horror and fascination. Her fingertips sparked and flickered with violet-blue flames. Other than a slight shock when the old woman had touched her, she felt nothing. No pain, it wasn't consuming her. It wasn't fire, at least as she knew it. She watched the tiny hairs rise on her arms and shuddered as the hair rose on the back of her neck.

Tickled, laughing with relief, she said, "It's static electricity on steroids."

Again she felt a drop of rain, but this time it gave off a mild shock as it touched her. It reminded her of the time she had visited a farm as a child. She had held onto the electric fence, almost enjoying the tingling sensation of the slowly pulsating, electric current.

Another drop and then another sprinkled them, each drop generating milder and milder shocks, diminishing the flames' intensity, until their fingertip flames went out. Ceren checked her hands, but the flames had left no trace, other than their memory. She looked at the sky and watched the squall line move on, leaving only cirrus clouds in its wake. As quickly as the storm had blown up, it blew away, leaving the air refreshed.

Ceren breathed deeply. The peculiar experience left her feeling like a child who had gone out to play in the rain. She felt cleansed, carefree, cheered, until she remembered her appointment.

Again, she checked her watch. Thanks to the traffic and crowds, it had taken longer than expected to reach the chapel. It would take at least as long to return. She sighed, hating to leave Tepeyac, loathing her next destination.

She turned to say goodbye to the old woman, but she was gone. Ceren looked in all directions, checked the chapel's courtyard, but, except for a couple standing on the steps, she was alone.

FIND *SACRED CHOICES* AT YOUR FAVORITE BOOKSELLER OR AT
www.Pen-L.com/SacredChoices.html

AND DON'T MISS *BELIZE NAVIDAD* BY
KAREN HULENE BARTELL

FIND MORE AT
www.Pen-L.com/BelizeNavidad.html

www.ingramcontent.com/pod-product-compliance
Lightning Source LLC
Chambersburg PA
CBHW052032260626
47163CB00006B/190